THE LOOM FIXER

THE LOOM FIXER

JOHN BARLOW

PALMETTO
PUBLISHING
Charleston, SC
www.PalmettoPublishing.com

The Loom Fixer

Copyright © 2022 by John Barlow

All rights reserved.

No portion of this book may be reproduced, stored in a retrieval system, or transmitted in any form by any means–electronic, mechanical, photocopy, recording, or other–except for brief quotations in printed reviews, without prior permission of the author.

First Edition

Paperback ISBN: 978-1-68515-856-9

Lucinda sat before the mirror on her dressing table. She had just come from her shift at the mill, and there were small clumps of cotton lint clinging to her hair and clothes. She picked at them disgustedly, dropping them randomly on the floor. She admired her reflection. *Still young looking; won't be much longer if I'm still working in the mill. Why should I have to? Wade left me with the boys and just took off. Having a good time wherever he is. It's not fair. Why do men always get to have fun? I deserve fun too before I lose my looks. I can leave. Tony will be home soon, and he can take care of himself. Mitch is no trouble. Grandma can take care of him. When I get settled, I'll send for them.* If she was going to leave, she needed to go now before Grandpa got home, so she raked her makeup and toiletries off the dresser into a cardboard suitcase with a few clothes that she took from her closet. She left a note on the kitchen table and went out the back door and through the neighbors' backyards, dodging clotheslines and shooing off curious dogs until she got to the embankment that led down to the street that further led to town and the bus station. She remembered the first time she and the boys had climbed the embankment.

The day they decided to leave, they tried to pack their things in one beat-up suitcase. It wasn't big enough, so Lucinda put what was left into an old seabag she had got from some cousin who had been in the navy.

"Why do we have to go?" Mitch, the younger boy, whined. "I like it here."

Lucinda was busy packing, so Tony shushed his little brother. "Dad's gone. We ain't got enough money to stay here anymore."

"This is best, Mitch. Maybe it won't be for long," Lucinda said.

"Where are we going?"

"We're going to Grandma and Grandpa's in Maple Grove. You remember them, don't you?" Lucinda asked.

If his brother didn't remember, Tony did. He remembered from earlier visits. Grandpa was a wizened little man, always dressed in overalls and wearing a brown fedora stained with sweat and lint from the mill, with brown teeth and a mouth browned in one corner from dipping snuff. Grandma, except for being smaller, looked like Grandpa, but she was quiet and kind and loved the boys.

They caught a bus from Dillon to Maple Grove. Tony and Mitch sat side by side, swapping the window seat from time to time. Mitch fell asleep, and Tony watched the South Carolina countryside go by, towns with many churches and small business areas, looking deserted in the sultry afternoon. Then he fell asleep, too, and was wakened by Lucinda. "We're here. Let's go." They were on a street in a downtown in front of a bus station that was empty except for one or two people dozing, waiting for a later bus. Lucinda looked up and down the street, then she went inside the bus station and asked how to get to Pine Street.

"That's in the Holler," the ticket agent said and gave her directions.

"Is there a bus that runs to it?" she asked.

"No, ma'am. You drive or walk."

"How far is it?"

"I reckon about two miles or so."

So they set off walking along the dusty right of way. It was hot. Tony had to carry the seabag, and Lucinda carried the suitcase. Mitch walked behind them, and they had to stop from time to time to let him catch up. When they came to a place where the road was surrounded on both sides by a high red dirt embankment, Lucinda said they didn't have much further to go. Then they came to where people had climbed the embankment, and Lucinda told the boys to start climbing, that Grandma and Grandpa's was just past the top. Tony was in front dragging the seabag, and Mitch was behind him. Lucinda came last pushing them along. They got to the top, and Mitch fell down in the weeds and rested, sweating and panting.

"There it is," Lucinda said, pointing at a house in a long row of similar white-frame houses along a street lined with cars parked on the curb and chinaberry trees in every other yard. "It's downhill from here, Mitch. Get up and let's get there."

They walked down the street with Tony dragging the seabag and Mitch stumbling behind him. When they got to the house, Lucinda knocked on the screen door. A dim figure appeared behind the screen. The sound of a television came from within.

"Oh my," said Grandma as she came out on the porch. "Look who's here." She hugged the boys and Lucinda. Then there was another figure at the screen. An ill-tempered-looking little man, Grandpa came out and stood with his hands on his hips. He watched the small group hugging one another for a moment, then he said, "You come back here after that sorry asshole left you."

"Hush," Grandma said. "Don't talk like that in front of the boys."

"I told you not to marry him, and it's worked out just like I told you it would." He spat brown tobacco juice into the yard. "I heard he's got married again down in South Carolina."

"Hush," Grandma said again.

He made to go back inside but turned back to them. "Don't think you can stay here without working and paying your way. I ain't feeding two kids and you for a long time." The screen slammed as he disappeared.

"Come on." Grandma said, "Here, Tony, let me carry that bag. I'll show you where you're staying. You must be hungry and thirsty."

And so they moved in with Grandpa unhappy and Lucinda hoping it would be a short visit. The boys and their mother shared a bedroom in the small house. The boys slept in one bed, and Lucinda had a bed. The room was one of two bedrooms off the main room where Grandpa watched television most of the time. Grandma's kitchen was in the back.

Their only heat came from a brown oil furnace in one corner of the main room. In the winter it kept the immediate area around it stifling hot, but the other rooms were frigid. The year before, the mill had installed indoor plumbing, so there was a bath between the two bedrooms. The old privy was still behind the house with the path that led to it now overgrown with weeds.

Their stay became much longer than Lucinda or Grandpa wanted. Grandpa harped after her from the first day about finding a job. "They're hiring on the first shift in a lot of departments. You can get a job weaving, spinning, hemming, whatever you want, and on the first, you can help keep up with these kids *and* pay for all they eat."

She had always hated mill work, but the only other jobs she had were as clerks in grocery stores or dime stores, and they never paid much. So she went to the mill office. She had been a weaver in other mills. She came back with a job as a weaver.

They could see part of the mill from the front porch. It made a constant hum, and at night, it put off a luminous glow, and among the smokestacks on the roof was the logo, a huge lighted cannon. Workers were always going and coming. First shift worked from seven until three, second from three until eleven, and the third from eleven to seven. Grandpa and Lucinda were on the first shift; Grandma was on the second. Whistles blew before each of the shifts, prompting people throughout the day about coming to work.

Lucinda didn't like it. "I hate working in that mill, working in the weave room. You get all that crap in your hair.

Takes me an hour to get it combed out when I get off," she told Tony as she sat looking at herself in a mirror on the dresser in their bedroom. "It'll take away my looks. Make my fingers twisted and ugly like Grandma's. You know, a man I didn't know was just walking down the street, and he stopped me and told me I looked like Marilyn Monroe. Said I had great-looking legs." She brushed her blond hair, then filed her nails and tried on two different shades of lipstick while Tony watched. "Which one of these looks better?" she asked him. He pointed to a pink shade. "I think so too." Then she tried on a blouse, cut low and just showing the tops of her breasts. Tony only frowned and looked up at the ceiling.

She was gone a lot and never home on weekends. "Gone again," groused Grandpa. "Down at Myrtle Beach all the time. Doin' God knows what. And when she's here, she don't come home at night sometimes. How many sorry boyfriends has she had just since she's been here? What are those two kids learnin' from her? How to drink whiskey and hell around all the time. That's what."

"She pays us rent, and you ain't no one to talk about whiskey," Grandma said.

"Yeah, but I don't have to like it, and besides, we have to watch these brats of hers."

"Lot of watching *you* do."

"That may be true, but one of these days when she's got old, those looks of hers won't get her nothing but trouble, and we'll be stuck with the kids."

. . .

THE LOOM FIXER

Tony and Mitch sat on the back steps. The houses on the street were on top of a hill that fell away to the street below with a carpet of thick green kudzu vine that went down to the street and almost covered a small group of pine trees on the way. The neighboring backyard was busy with people listening to a radio broadcast of a stock car race. A huge black iron pot sat on a wood fire bubbling with liquid and throwing off steam.

"What are they cooking?" Mitch asked.

"You know. Turtle—cooter."

"Where'd they get it?"

"Caught it in the Pee Dee River is what Mr. Turner told me."

"How?"

"They throw a line way out in the river with maybe four or five hooks on it baited with rotten chicken and bring it in the next morning, and the cooters get hooked during the night. He said you have to be real careful when you try to get 'em off. If they bite you, it hurts, and they won't let go till it thunders."

"Stuff sure stinks. I wouldn't eat it," Mitch said.

• • •

When fall came the first year, Grandma took Tony and Mitch to the nearest elementary school and got them enrolled. Tony would only have one year there, and then he would go to the junior high school across town, but for now, he and Mitch could walk a mile to the school.

"I don't want to go to school," Mitch said the morning they were to go. "I don't know nobody here."

"You'll be fine," Grandma said. "Ever' body around here is just alike. Ain't no rich folks or people with strange religion. We're all just alike. Most ever'body makes the same amount of money, works the same kind of jobs, and lives in the same kind of houses. No airs here. You'll be just fine."

And it was true. After she registered him, she took Tony to Mrs. Winecoff's class. When they stood at the door, the teacher came over and put her hand on Tony's shoulder and introduced him to the class of about twenty students. They were dressed the same in jeans and collared shirts, all of them white, and on this first day, all faces were scrubbed and clean.

Grandma made the boys go with her to church on Sundays, something both Tony and Mitch despised. She made them dress in suits and ties she bought for them at Montgomery Ward. The church was a one-story brick and siding structure several blocks away from the house; it wasn't in the Holler but just on the edge of it. She deposited them in a Sunday school class where they sat for an hour listening to Bible stories about Moses and Joseph. On the wall, there was a roster of the children who were in the class. For every class they attended, the teacher put a gold star beside their names. Grandma had to prompt the teacher to add Tony and Mitch to the roster. They had fewer stars than anyone else.

The teacher spent a lot of time on Genesis. Once, they went five consecutive Sundays and heard the stories all the way from creation through Cain and Abel. Cain was a farmer, and Abel was a herder. The story said that each offered God a sacrifice. Cain offered some of his crop, and Abel offered some "fat portions" of his flock. It didn't seem fair to Tony that God had rejected Cain's offering but accepted Abel's. It seemed that God had insulted Cain and rejected him without a good reason. He asked the teacher to explain. She was a plump middle-aged woman with a mass of brown hair larger than her head. She seemed startled since the children usually never asked questions but were expected to listen quietly. She looked puzzled for a few moments.

She read the passage again silently then looked up and said, "Because God could tell that Cain was a bad person even before he murdered his brother. Think how terrible it was and how God knows everything. He heard Abel's blood crying out from the ground. Think how terrible that was."

"Looks like he was just a farmer. The story didn't say he was bad," Tony said.

"Well. It's the Bible," she sputtered, "and it's the sacred word of God, caused to be written by Him, so it has to be true."

Tony was also puzzled by Adam and Eve and the passage where God says to Adam after discovering what they had done, "Cursed is the ground for thy sake; in sorrow shalt thou eat of it all the days of thy life; Thorns also and thistles shall it bring forth to thee; and thou shall eat of the herb of the field." It was not clear to him. *Before God became angry, they had food provided for them from the garden*, Tony thought, *but now they would have to work for it. Was that the reason for the mill, for getting up in the morning, spending all day sweating and doing some job that maybe you didn't want to do?* But the teacher didn't do any better explaining that passage either.

"You ask too many questions. You should just listen more." Eventually she began to ignore him when he raised his hand.

Grandma waited for them in the dim, musty-smelling hall after Sunday school. From there, she marched them into the church sanctuary for the morning service. The room had dark paneling and a raised dais with three large chairs in a semicircle behind a heavy lectern. A cross with a crucified Jesus was on the wall above the chairs, and there were three small rectangular windows above the cross. Reverend Rogers, a bear-like man with a full beard and wearing a flowing black robe, presided over the service and preached. A choir flanked the altar on two sides. The choir members were also in robes, but theirs were white.

The choir hummed hymns in a low tone while the congregation entered the sanctuary. Reverend Rogers sat in the middle chair behind the podium with an open Bible in his lap and his head bowed, either praying or reading, or perhaps both. After the congregation had filed in, hymns were sung, prayers prayed, offerings taken, scripture read, and then the reverend rose behind the lectern and stared out silently at the assembly. Light, full of motes of dust, streamed in from the windows above the cross so that he was bathed in an aura of yellow, partially blinding the congregation as they stared up at him, waiting to receive the word. When all shuffling was done, all throats cleared, and all babies shushed, when he had their undivided attention, he began many Sundays with these words: "Jesus said, 'I am the way the truth and the light. He that believeth on me, even if he be dead, shall have everlasting life.'" He emphasized the first syllable so that it came out "*Jee*-sus." The sermon would build from there in volume and terror. He reminded them of their sins, what awaited them if they didn't repent, how Jesus was waiting for them to come to Him, that all they need do was repent and accept. Finally, his voice modulated to only a whisper, for by that time the church was as silent as an empty forest in the fog. And with sweat trickling down his temples even if it were winter, he urged anyone who accepted Jesus as their savior for the first time, or if they felt so driven by some secret sin that they wanted to renew publicly their commitment to Him, to come forward and kneel silently in front of the altar. The organ would be playing softly "How Great Thou Art" or "Amazing Grace," and slowly people would begin to file down. As each would kneel with bowed head over praying hands, Reverend Rogers would bend down and whisper something to them.

Some of his classmates from Sunday school went down to commit themselves, but it never occurred to Tony. Grandma recommitted herself several times. He could never make the connection between Jesus and the mysteries of Genesis.

On the way home afterward, Grandma often cried softly and urged Tony and Mitch to listen to Reverend Rogers or they might end up like Grandpa, who never went to church and spent much of his time drinking "likker." She was worried about what they would learn being around their mother.

"She lives in sin. Married but going to those awful places where they drink beer and I don't know what all. She's getting the reputation that she's a cheap hussy. The Lord makes you pay for those kinds of things."

"She's not a hussy. She's doing the best she can without Dad," Tony said. Mitch looked away and said nothing.

• • •

Grandma had four brothers and three sisters. The family had worked in cotton mills since the end of the Civil War. She often told the story about her grandfather, Caleb Keller, who had fought in the war for four years. He was sent to Maryland and Pennsylvania and served with Jubal Early and was captured in the last year of the war. When it was over, he came home and for most of the rest of his life sat on the front porch at the farm and drank whiskey, looking absently over the fields. He had white hair and a white moustache, and Grandma and her brothers and sisters were scared to death of him.

"We come from good families, Kellers and Huffstetlers. Your uncles are high up in the mill, supervisors, and your Uncle Thurman is a vice president." It was true. Her brothers had done well, but after she married Grandpa, the family had little to do with her.

The family was centered around Great Grandma, also known as Grannie. She had been a widow for half her eighty-eight years. She lived in a house across from the mill that was provided for her by Uncle Thurman, the vice president. She couldn't walk without help, and her voice was so soft she could scarcely be heard. Grandma spent all her days in a chair in the living room beside a wood-paneled console radio that took up all the wall space next to her, listening to soap operas and on Sundays a broadcast from the local Methodist church that went out to all shut-ins. She was a revered figure, deferred to, and consulted about ailments and recipes.

Aunt Bessie, the oldest of Grandma's sisters and who had never been married, lived with and cared for Grannie. She brought her water or tea during the day, helped her to the table in the kitchen for her meals, helped her to the bathroom, dressed her, bathed her, and saw to the taking of her medications. Bessie believed in cleanliness. She made chess pies from time to time—pure sugar and butter, intensely sweet—and when grandchildren came on Sundays, it was one of the few things that helped break the tedium of a long, stultifying Sunday in a room clouded with a rank blue haze of cigar smoke when Bessie would ask whatever cousins were there if they wanted a piece of chess pie. But it had to be eaten in the kitchen, and not at the table but over the sink so no crumbs could escape to the immaculate floor.

The family had an annual Christmas party at Grannie's. Names were drawn for gifts. Everyone brought something to contribute to a huge meal. There were hams, turkeys, and barbeque. The uncles kept whiskey down in the basement during the party so their wives wouldn't be offended that they were drinking. At the only party he ever attended, Grandpa was invited to join them, but he got drunk, told them it was the first time he'd ever had any whiskey that wasn't white, and it was sure good. It went down smooth. Later, after the family had eaten, he fell asleep on the sofa and drooled all over his shirt. The next week, Aunt Bessie told Grandma it would be better if she didn't bring Grandpa to any more of the Christmas parties.

• • •

Tony's mother gave him money only to eat lunch at school. He and Mitch never had enough to go to a movie on the weekend, so he got a job delivering the afternoon paper. A truck dropped a stack of papers off in front of the house. He rolled them, put rubber bands around them, and delivered them from his bicycle. At the end of each month, he had to collect money from the subscribers. He got paid from what he collected. It was never much, and collecting was hard in the Holler. He would knock on doors in places where he knew there was someone home but no one would answer, or people would refuse to pay because the paper wasn't thrown on the porch but in the shrubs where they said they couldn't find it. Still, he had more money than he had ever had, so much that instead of eating in the school cafeteria, he sometimes would go downtown at lunch and eat at The Red Pig. They served hot dogs and hamburgers with mustard, chili, onions, and slaw. He could get two of either and a Coke for sixty cents. With the paper money, he could eat there once a week.

THE LOOM FIXER

He even saved enough to buy a small radio at Montgomery Ward. He put it on the table beside his bed. It had a lighted green dial so he could see at night to change stations. His favorite station was in Nashville, Tennessee. It played black music, mostly rhythm and blues by singers like Fats Domino, the Platters, and the Midnighters mixed in with blues by Muddy Waters, Howlin' Wolf, and John Lee Hooker. It even played some white singers like Carl Perkins and Elvis Presley. On Sundays, it played nothing but black gospel music. Even though the reception wasn't good, sometimes fading in and out, he listened to it. During winter nights, he pulled as much cover as he had over him up to his neck, turned the volume down so Grandma couldn't hear it, and listened until he fell asleep.

• • •

When Tony was sixteen and a sophomore at J.M. Black High School in Maple Grove, he quit the paper route and took a job bagging groceries at a supermarket downtown. It meant more money, but it also meant working longer hours and not spending as much time studying as he had before, which was not a lot to begin with. He enjoyed the job. It paid a small wage, and he got an occasional dime or quarter from a customer when he carried their groceries for them.

Because he worked, he was allowed to leave school an hour early to walk up the hill to town and the supermarket. He passed by the middle of the mill complex on the way, the huge mill office that looked like a southern plantation. It was next to the YMCA in a building that looked much like the mill office, only more impressive with winding staircases on both sides leading up to a second-floor porch with massive white columns. There were two residence halls beside the Y, which offered rooms to single teachers in the local schools or to other unmarried women favored by the mill. In front of these buildings was a man-made lake of about two acres. The water from the lake was used in the mill. Next to the lake was a small city park with a bandstand and a memorial inscribed with the names of the town's war dead. Reserved parking places for the executives of the mill surrounded the lake with the names on the assigned spaces.

One cold February day, as Tony was going to work from school and crossing the railroad tracks in front of the offices, park, and lake, he saw a man, a policeman, who appeared to be standing on the surface of the water. As he got closer, he could see the man was standing on the top of a car nearly submerged and slowly continuing to sink. The only thing now visible was the roof and two fins near the rear. The fence around the lake was flattened in front of one of the parking spaces where the car had crashed through it. Other people began to gather, some watching; one threw a line to the policeman, who was now in the water and trying to open the door of the submerged car. He appeared to be losing strength fast in the cold water. A wrecker truck screeched up to the empty space with the flattened fence, and two men waded into the water with a hook, eventually beginning to swim. It slipped away from them in the cold, and they had to start over several times. Tony watched as long as he could but had to leave to make it to work on time. Later he learned that the man driving the car, an executive in the mill, died. He wondered if his fabled Uncle Thurman knew him. *Bad things happen even to rich people sometimes*, he guessed.

• • •

Tony had always been a middling student, not particularly interested in any subject but never failing. He was detached at school, just as he was everywhere else. His looks got him a long way. He was attractive to girls. He was quiet and polite, but he didn't mix much with his classmates, avoided sports, didn't take part in the class activities, and joined no clubs. A girl in one of his classes had asked him to try out for a part in the class play because she said he looked like Elvis, but he had said no. While he knew many people, he had no friends and let no one close to him. Once, the year before, a boy in his class asked him if his mother's name was Lucinda, and when he said yes, the boy said his uncle knew her and then snickered. Tony hit the boy in the mouth, and when he was doubled over, Tony hit him again and bloodied his nose. A passing teacher had stopped him. He was expelled for a week. They hadn't even asked what started the fight, but he didn't care. That was the way things were for him.

Pete, an older boy who lived down the street from Grandpa's and had his driver's license and an old '49 Ford coupe, gave him rides to school every now and then. Pete worked in a car repair shop after school and on weekends. He wore fancy clothes and pants that were tapered at the legs so that they bloused above his shoes. Sometimes he pulled the collar of his shirt up, and his hair was long and swept back into a duck tail in the back. One evening in late spring, while Tony was sitting on the steps, Pete stopped at the curb and motioned for him to come to the car. "Wanna take a ride up to the lake?" he asked.

"Where's that?" Tony asked.

"Just up above Bentley. We can get beer up there. And there are girls at the lake. You can dance with 'em. You know how to dance?"

"No."

"Don't matter. They'll teach you. Or you can just watch. You never know what might happen. You like girls, don't you? Wanna go? Got something you can wear besides those lint-head-looking Red Camel blue jeans?"

Tony went back inside and put on a pair of his church pants. He had nothing else to do. They sped off with Pete gunning the engine. Tires screeched, and gravel peppered the sidewalk. Tony saw the screen door open, and Grandpa came out cussing as they disappeared into the warm night.

Before they got to the lake, they stopped at a service station. The inside was lit by a single bare bulb hanging from the ceiling. A man in a dirty baseball cap and greasy coveralls leaned against a bug-spackled display case full of fan belts and dusty cartons of candy looking as though they had been there forever. A cooler with advertisements for Coca-Cola was against one wall.

"Howdy," Pete said as they entered. The man only nodded. Pete went to the cooler and lifted the top. He reached in and brought out three cans of Pabst Blue Ribbon beer, cold water running off them in small rivulets.

"You old enough to buy that?" the man asked.

"Sure," Pete said. "You wanna see my draft card?" He reached to take out his wallet, hoping he wouldn't have to show a card he didn't have.

"Nah. That'll be a dollar and five cents." Pete handed him the money, and the man put the cans in a brown paper bag. Back in the car, Pete handed Tony two cans and an opener.

"Open those for us. You ever used a church key before?" Tony shook his head. "Hell, have you ever had a *beer* before?" Tony shook his head again. He had tasted Grandpa's moonshine and knew he didn't like that kind of alcohol, but he didn't want to look like some kind of sissy if he didn't try the beer. "Damn." Pete said, "Take the sharp end of the key and punch two holes opposite each other in the can. Nah, just wait. I'll do it."

They had turned off the main road onto a dirt road with woods on either side. Pete pulled onto the shoulder and took the cans and the opener. "You do it like this." He cracked open one of the cans and handed it to Tony. He opened the other, lifted it to his mouth, and took a long swallow. "Ahhh," he said, wiping his mouth, "that was good." He looked at Tony, who was still holding the wet can. "Try it," Pete urged.

Tony put the can to his lips, leaned his head back like Pete, and took a deep swallow. It was cold, bitter, and strong. Foam went up his nose and he coughed.

Pete snickered. "Take it easy. You'll get used to it, and then you'll like it."

But Tony didn't see how he would ever come to like it. It was skunky, sour-bitter, and like nothing he'd ever tasted before. Pete finished his as they went further down the dirt road. Tony took a few more sips then poured the rest out the window when Pete wasn't looking.

They came to a lake about as big as a football field. Along the shore line, there were a few men sitting on stools or overturned buckets, fishing, watching their lines, and smoking. At the far end of the lake, there was a pavilion up on stilts. He could see couples moving in the soft light from some ragged Chinese lanterns that hung from the ceiling, and music wafted across the water, a clarinet and piano. He recognized the song "Moonglow" from the radio. Several couples were in the middle of the floor, swaying back and forth, surrounded by onlookers leaning against the railing under the edge of the roof. There was a jukebox in one corner glowing red and green. Tony followed Pete up a set of steep steps to the dance floor. Pete carried his other beer wrapped up in the brown bag. Several people called greetings to him. Two girls leaning on the railing waved, and Pete led Tony over to them.

"Who's this with you, Petey?" said a dark-haired girl with a pouty pink mouth. Soft looking, her breasts stood out under a thin sweater.

"This is Tony. A friend of mine."

"Ton-eee." She purred his name. "He's cute, but he looks sooo young." She came over to them. "He has beautiful curly hair." She reached up and fingered the single lock above his eyes. "Can you dance, Tony?"

He shook his head no, not trusting words.

"Well, come on. My name's Trish, and I'll teach you." She took his hand and dragged him out onto the floor. Her perfume was sweet and smothering. "It's simple. Give me your left hand and put your right arm around me." She snuggled close to him, putting her cheek against his, and guided him in small movements to the music. She smelled faintly of a spice. "Relax. I'm not going to bite you. At least not yet. Can you talk? You haven't said anything."

"Yeah. I can talk," he said, his chin in her hair.

"Good. Just don't talk now. Just keep doing what you're doing."

They moved slowly across the floor. She pulled his arms down around her waist, and she moved hers around his so that they were dancing in an embrace, barely rocking to the music. She gently put a knee between his legs and moved it back and forth. It was like an electric shock; he was aroused and embarrassed, not sure what to do, so he stopped moving, his entire body rigid.

"My goodness," she cooed. "It's okay, honey. Just relax." She stood on her toes and kissed him on the lips. He could taste the spiciness of her makeup and taste the sweetness of her lipstick all at once. She licked his lower lip with her tongue. Then the record was over, and the next one had a much faster tempo. "Okay," she said, "that's enough for now. Let's go back over to the rail and watch for a while. Just stay close to me, and they won't be able to tell how much you enjoyed that." She took him by the hand and walked in front of him to where Pete and the other girl were standing.

"You looked like a pro out there, pardner," Pete said.

"He's a good dancer and soooo good looking," Pete's girl said before Pete took her out onto the dance floor into a throng of other couples dancing but not clinging together; instead they were holding hands, standing apart, then coming together, twirling, shuffling their feet and turning, going apart again in subtle movements, sometimes scarcely moving. Trish took Tony's hand and moved close to him.

"Did you like it?" she asked.

"Yeah. I did," he said tightly, not sure what she meant.

"I left my purse in the car. Can you walk me to it? It's dark down there." She held his hand.

When they got to the car, she put her arms around him and pushed him against the door. She leaned up and kissed him again, this time forcing his mouth open with her tongue. Her breath became ragged as she leaned into him, kissing him again and again. Then she moved her hand between his legs. At first, he turned slightly away, but her hand was persistent, and he relaxed, tasting her mouth. Suddenly he was wet and embarrassed.

"Stop," he said.

She kissed him, but he was stiff. "C'mon. You're okay. You look all right." And they went back to the pavilion.

"I need to go home," he said to Pete. "Grandpa will be mad as hell if I come in late."

Pete looked at Trish, who shrugged.

On the way back, Tony rolled down his window and kept his head out in the fresh air. Pete leaned over and punched him on his shoulder. "Looks like Trish really likes you," he said. "Says you look like Elvis."

Tony only grunted.

• • •

In English class one morning, Tony got a note from Mrs. Brunner, the guidance counselor, asking him to report to her at the end of class. Her office was in the balcony of the auditorium in what would have been the film projector room, but since they didn't have a projector and space was limited, it was the guidance office. The room was long and narrow, so narrow Mrs. Brunner, a large woman, could scarcely get around her desk. The ports for the film projectors were on the wall above her head. There was only one other chair, and she asked Tony to sit. She explained he had done nothing wrong but that she tried to talk to all the new students as they came in. Sometimes they were not able to get to people as soon as they should, but they did the best they could. She had an open manila folder on the desk in front of her, and she looked down at it from time to time. She asked about his parents.

He told her he hadn't seen his father in years, that he lived with his mother, brother, and grandparents. She arched her eyebrows and said she believed they lived on Pine Street. Was that right? He nodded his head. She was silent for a moment as she looked down at his file.

"Well, Tony, you had all passing grades at the end of the first grading period. They perhaps could have been better, but maybe they were in line with your abilities." She paused and looked down at the folder again. "I don't see that you are a member of any club, and you don't play any sport. Why is that? Just not interested?"

He looked blankly at her, unsure what to say. "Uh, no. I work."

"I see. Where do you work?"

"At Melton's Supermarket. I bag groceries."

She looked at the folder again. "Do you go to church?"

He nodded his head.

"Do you believe in God?"

He had never thought about what he believed. "Yeah. I guess so," he said finally.

"Would you pray with me here?" she asked. He nodded and quickly bowed his head, not knowing if she expected him to speak or if she was going to do all the praying, but with tightly shut eyes, she immediately began. "Dear Lord, please help this young man to live a good and wholesome life and to succeed in his studies. Please help and guide him along your path so that he can prosper in all that he undertakes in life. In Christ's name, amen." She looked up at Tony with a smile.

"I'm so glad we got to know each other. You can go back to class now, and if you ever need to talk to me, don't hesitate to let me know. So do you have any questions?"

He was relieved that it was over and stood up. Then he said, "Do you know why God didn't like Cain?" The thought had popped up in his mind, remembered from those days Grandma had forced him to go to church, and this woman before him looked amazingly like the Sunday school teacher from that time, but he instantly regretted extending the interview. "Seems like what happened wasn't fair," he mumbled.

"Cain?" she asked, looking puzzled.

"Cain," he said. "In the Bible."

"Oh," she said and paused for a moment. "Well, that's certainly an interesting question and one I haven't thought about in a long time." She looked up at the ceiling while she was thinking. "I'm not sure 'fair' has anything to do with it. I think God was testing Cain. Go back and read it again. He asks why he's mad and goes on to tell him that if he gets over his anger and lives a good life, he will be all right, but if he doesn't, then sin wants him and is waiting for him, and God tells him he must overcome it."

"I thought being 'fair' was important." Not wanting to prolong the conversation, he said, "I guess you're right."

Before he could leave, she stopped him, almost as an afterthought. "You go on back to class. There's going to be an assembly after lunch with a speaker you ought to listen to. Do you know who J. C. Penney is?"

He shook his head no.

"Well, he owns the Penney's store in town and all the Penney's stores across the nation, and that's a lot. Mr. F. A. is going to introduce him. They're friends. Aren't you excited?"

"Sure, I guess. Who's Mr. F. A.?"

"*Tony*, Mr. F. A. is F. A. Brown. You know, who owns the mill and who almost everyone in town works for."

He turned red. He only knew about his Uncle Thurman in the mill hierarchy.

"Well, go on then. Maybe we'll talk again soon."

The next week, he got another note from her to come to her office. She looked up from some papers when he came in and said, "Tony, a man from the university is coming to talk to students tomorrow in the small auditorium. I think you should go. I want you to go."

"Why?"

"Because I think underneath your tough-guy act there may be something else. This can't hurt, so you be there."

And so he went to the meeting. It got him out of class for the period. There were football players, student government officers, kids he knew who made good grades, and a few people like him who stood near the back. The man from the university was tall and wore a tweed suit and a bow tie. He had thinning hair and blinked his eyes constantly. He homed in on athletes first and then moved to the lesser people, explaining the charms of the university and how much it would mean to them to get a degree from it; then he went around the room and asked what each of them liked and did and what organizations they were in.

He came to Tony. "What about you, son? What do you like?"

Tony was stunned. He stared for a moment but felt he had to say something. "Well, I'm thinking about joining the drama club," he muttered even though he had no intention of doing this.

"Drama club? You mean act in one of those delicate things, like Shakespeare?" The man extended a limp wrist. Tony blushed. "Well, that's OK for some people, I guess." He looked knowingly at one of the football players. Tony went back to class.

Two days later, he saw Mrs. Brunner in the hall.

"How did the meeting go?"

"OK, I guess." And he turned red thinking about it.

"What happened?"

"Nothing."

"Well, why do you look like something happened? I want to hear about it." So reluctantly he told her. Two weeks later, she called him into her office again to tell him that the university man would be there again to apologize for how he had acted in that meeting. She wanted him to go again, but he refused.

"He's not coming here to say he's sorry to me. He's coming here because someone he works for made him come. I ain't going to college anyway." And that was the end of it.

. . .

Lucinda's old car broke down. The estimate to repair it was $150, and this was from one of her sometimes men friends at T. D. Brown's Paint and Body Shop. She tried to borrow the money from Grandpa, resulting in several loud fights. He was as drunk as Tony had ever seen him; he got out his old double barrel and waved it around, telling her to leave with her snot-nosed kids who were eating him out of house and home anyway.

While she could walk to work, loss of the car meant she couldn't take trips to the beach or see her men friends when she wanted. When she wasn't working, she spent all her time in her room, crying and sipping from a pint of flavored vodka. She had grown increasingly remote, leaving Grandma to get the boys ready for school and see that their clothes were clean. If they had questions about schoolwork, they kept them to themselves.

One rainy afternoon before Tony had to be at Melton's, he stuck his head in the bedroom door. The room was chill and the walls gray and damp in the dim light from the window. She was a lump under a pile of covers, hair sticking in all directions on the pillow. The head rose slightly.

"What, honey?" she asked. "Come here." She motioned to him. The room smelled like sleep and vodka. "You're such a good-looking thing. I want the world for you." She reached out to touch his arm. It was more than she had said to him in a month.

"I want to help you with the car," he said as she ran her hand through his hair. The hand stilled on his head.

"Oh, honey, that's so sweet." She began to cry quietly. "But how will you do that?"

"I can give you part of what I earn at Melton's."

"I can't let you do that." She snuffled.

But she did. He started giving her ten dollars a week, thinking she would save it until she had enough, but week after week went by and nothing happened with the car. One afternoon, he looked in the dresser drawer where he knew she kept money when she had it, and it was empty. There were two pint bottles of vodka resting on a stack of blouses.

Grandpa had seen him giving her money. "You think she's gonna save any of that to fix that old trap? You got another think coming, boy. She's taking you for the same ride she's taken ever'body else for. She cain't handle money. Never could. Keep your money, boy."

She worked less and slept more and came in later and later. If she could get the car fixed, things might be different. He thought if the car could be fixed faster it would maybe keep her home more often, although there was no real reason to think that. But what he earned at Melton's wouldn't be enough to get the repairs done sooner.

• • •

There were four checkout lines at Melton's, manned by four women cashiers. A bagboy was assigned to each to put the groceries in boxes or bags as they were rung up by the cashier. All of the women liked Tony. He was their favorite, good-looking, polite, and quiet. From time to time, the cashiers would walk away from their registers with the drawers left open for a moment to get change or to find something in a purse left at the office cubicle. Tony had seen the stacks of bills in the open drawers—twenties, tens, fives, ones—all arranged in descending order from left to right. One of the Melton brothers usually sat on a stool at a desk in an elevated enclosure overlooking the checkout lines, but they took breaks too.

One slow afternoon when only two lines were open, both checkout girls and the watching Melton were gone at the same time with the drawers open, waiting for change. Tony moved quickly and took two tens from each register before anyone got back. That evening as he was cleaning up and mopping the floor, Mr. Melton called the two cashiers to the cage, and they all talked for a few minutes. No one was smiling, and heads were shaking as the meeting broke up.

The opportunities didn't present themselves often, and he was cunning enough to realize he couldn't take advantage every time or he'd be caught, so he limited his pilfering to once or twice a month and didn't take the same amount from each register if two were left open.

Eventually he had accumulated $160. He took it to T. D. Brown's and told them to fix the car. They charged $10 to tow it to the shop, so he covered everything. Three days later, when it was fixed, his mother drove off to Myrtle Beach and didn't come back for two weeks. The Monday after she left, Mr. Melton told Tony he wouldn't need him anymore. He didn't say why, and Tony was afraid to ask. He just took off his apron and left.

There were other grocery stores in town, so he applied at all of them, but they told him they didn't need anybody, yet he knew people that had got jobs shortly after he had been rejected. He even applied for his paper route again but was turned down there too.

Mr. Jordan, who hired for the paper, took him aside. "You're too old for a paper route, son, or I'd hire you." He paused and looked down at the floor. "I heard what they say happened at Melton's. Gonna be hard for you to get a job around here again unless it's in the mill. They pretty much forgive everything. You'd have to quit school for that. Not a good idea. You need to have a high school diploma no matter what you want to do."

. . .

He spent his time after school, watching the pool players in the basement of the Y, bored and with no money. Grandpa nagged him all the time about getting a job so he could pay for the food he and his brother ate and the electricity, water, and heat they used.

Pete saw him at the Y and told him Trish was asking about him. "She wants to see you, man. She don't care if you don't have any money. Might even give you some . . . of both," he laughed.

T. D. Brown gave him a job in the car repair shop. It was greasy, aggravating work made worse by Brown's temper. He worked some days hungover, smelling like the previous night's whiskey and ill as a hornet. Tony didn't know enough about car repair to do more than fetch things and hand them to Brown or the other mechanics when they were under cars or bent deep down into an engine. If he brought the wrong wrench, they cursed him, called him a dumbass, and told him he was useless. Worse, payday was on Friday, and Brown would often not come to work that day or leave early so Tony and the other employees would have to wait for him to appear or not get paid until the next Monday. He hated the job and Brown.

He saw Trish again. Their relationship had changed since he first saw her at the lake. She was older and then seemed much more knowing than Tony, but now he was less unsure of himself. He met her several times for the late show on Saturday night at the Rio theater in town. It was one of the few things to do on Saturday night, and he could walk there from Grandma's. The theater was across the street from the Baptist church. There was a long concrete wall on the church side of the street. Moviegoers, almost all high school kids, gathered across the street before the movie started at 10:00 p.m., sitting on the wall and watching their friends go by slowly in cars. The cars made a circle around a traffic island further down the street then turned and came back by the wall again. Some of the cars were lowered in the rear with fender skirts and mufflers that growled and popped if the driver revved the engine. Police standing at the street corners kept an eye on the wall and the cars.

The theater was always packed with people. At the concession stand, they popped popcorn, its delicious smell wafting all over the theater. They saw *Three Coins in the Fountain* twice. He thought it was sappy, but she liked it. She snuggled close to him in the dark and reached up and kissed him on the cheek every now and then.

She asked him to come to her house one Saturday night. She lived across town in a section of small homes not owned by the mill. He hitched rides most of the way and walked the rest. She let him into a small living room. There was a record player on a table by the sofa. Through a door, he could see a man and a woman seated at a table in the kitchen. She closed that door and all the others so that they were alone in the living room. Then she put on a record—a slow song, "Only You"—and stood in front of him so close so close he could feel the warmth of her breath as she hummed with the music. She put her arms around him and pulled him close.

"You remember how to dance, don't you? Like I taught you." And she moved gently but firmly against him. "I thought Mom and Dad were going out tonight and we'd be alone, but they're not. So we can't do all the things I wanted. Too risky. But we can have fun anyway."

After a while, they collapsed on the sofa, and she snuggled next to him. She pulled his head down and kissed him. She cut off the record player and turned the radio on so she wouldn't have to keep changing the record. When she sat back down, she pulled him to her and enveloped him in a long kiss. She put her tongue in his mouth. He stiffened but then got accustomed to the sensation. She tasted like spearmint. She pulled a blanket from the back of the sofa and covered them with it. She moved his hand up under her sweater and placed it over her breast; then she took it and moved it up under her skirt guiding him to where she wanted it. "Right there. Yes, yes. That's it," she whispered. Then she was groping at the fly of his pants. There was a faint knock on the door behind them.

A woman's voice came from the other side of the door. "Trish? Would y'all like some popcorn, or a drink?"

"Damn," Trish muttered and tried to clear the hoarseness from her throat. "No, Mom, we're fine." She listened for a second, and when she was satisfied that her mother was gone, she grabbed at him again, but he sat up on the edge of the sofa, letting the blanket fall away.

"What's the matter? Don't you like doing this?" She looked up at him. "You're funny. Good-looking, but funny."

"I don't want your folks to catch us."

They spent the rest of the evening on the couch with her showing him what she wanted him to do to her and him clumsily complying, but when she touched him, the feeling was warm, and he was amazed at the sensations but hesitant for fear of her parents coming in.

The next week Pete told him Trish thought he was good-looking but maybe funny in a strange way. "She's not sure you like her. You got to be careful about these girls, Tony, and if they start talking to you about going to Rock Hill, you start making tracks."

"What's Rock Hill?"

"It's a town in South Carolina where they all want to go to get married."

"Why do they want to go to South Carolina to do it?"

"Don't you know *shit*? Up here it takes a lot longer to get a marriage license. They have to check you for disease or something. Takes at least a week. But down there, you can do it in one day. Just apply for the license and go to a justice of the peace or a magistrate. Used to be you went down there when she was knocked up and you wanted to do it real fast. Nowadays most of 'em do it cause it sounds cool or something."

"I ain't going to Rock Hill. That's for sure," Tony said.

• • •

What he earned at the auto shop was not enough. He never had any spare money. Grandpa now insisted that since Tony was working, he pay something more for rent and food for him and Mitch. His mother was around less and less, and she gave him and his brother nothing. Her car that he had worked so hard to have repaired, even been fired for, was broken again with grass and weeds growing around its wheels in the side yard. Grandpa grumbled and complained all the time. Tony made sure he didn't get home until Grandpa was either drunk or asleep.

One day he was in a local department store after school and before work. He needed a shirt and was looking at some, but then he saw some women's blouses and it was near his mom's birthday. Their prices were way more than he could afford. He looked around. There were no clerks and no customers in sight, so he stuck a blouse under his windbreaker and walked toward the revolving door leading out to the street. He reached to push the door open when someone behind him grabbed his shoulder.

"Just a minute, kid." A burly, ugly man held him fast. "Let's see what's in that jacket."

Tony tore away and tried to push through the door, but the man caught him again. Then other clerks were rushing toward them, and a uniformed cop came in off the street.

He called Grandma from jail. They released him into her custody. She cried all the way back to Pine Street. "What are we gonna do? What are we gonna do?" she muttered all the way home. "You know you come from good people. All your uncles are high up in the mill. Your Uncle Thurman is a vice president. I'm going to see him. Maybe he can help. Oh, Tony, why did you do that? Why?" But he couldn't answer that question. He wouldn't have stolen a shirt for himself, but somehow doing it for Lucinda made it all right. He knew the difference between right and wrong, but doing it for her made it less evil. It blurred the lines.

There was no one to attest to his good character at his juvenile hearing. Grandma asked the people at the grocery store, but they all were too busy. Grandma went to the mill office after her shift to see Uncle Thurman. She waited for an hour until the office was almost ready to close before she was admitted, but his uncle, who didn't remember Tony, said there was nothing he could do. None of his teachers came. T. D. said he would come, but he didn't. So, the judge, probably having heard rumors in a small town about missing money at the grocery store, sentenced him to a year at the training school.

Grandma cried quietly and hugged him before the deputies took him away. She kept saying over and over, "Oh, Tony, oh, Tony," then just lifted her hand and waved as they hustled him out the door.

• • •

If work at the repair shop had been dirty and the people he worked with degrading, then life at the training school was an absolute hell. The staff brutalized the captives verbally and bodily. Half of their time was spent cleaning the place, but even with hard work they couldn't remove the age-embedded grime. The wards were cold and dirty in the winter and hot and dirty in summer. When someone from Raleigh came for an inspection, they were lined up beside their bunks and lockers and told how to answer any questions in advance. The dignitaries, men or women, whisked by in a blur.

The only peace he got was the few hours at night when he was on the thin mattress, covered by a rough horsehair blanket in winter and a filthy sheet in summer. He kept his mouth shut, made no friends or enemies, put up with unspeakable behavior by the staff. Even if it was only a year, it seemed like an eternity. He wondered about Trish. Would she be there?

She wrote to him every month, even though he only wrote back once in a while. He struggled with what to say to her and he carefully formed the letters and words.

The letters were short: "Dear Trish, This place is bad. I work all day except for the time I go to class. I maybe can graduate here. How are you? Tony."

Lucinda had written him twice. Once she sent him five dollars.

He finished high school inside. It was the only good thing that happened there. He could at least get a job in the mill when he got out.

There was no one waiting to meet him outside the gate when his sentence was up. The warden didn't think this was remarkable. "You'll probably be back," he said, "Most of you are before a year's up, but I reckon next time you'll go to Central in Raleigh. You'll be too old for here. Good luck, and here's ten dollars from the state to last until you get a job or rob somebody."

• • •

Now he was returning to Maple Grove, and he had nowhere else to go except Grandma and Grandpa's, so he went there. His mother's old car was still in the yard after a year, weeds growing up around the tires. He took the key from under the flower pot on the front porch and let himself in. His bed was in the same place, and Mitch's meager things were there, but his mother's closet was empty, the door open, and nothing but empty clothes hangers in it. It was after three o'clock, and Grandpa would be home soon. He didn't want to see him, but he had to have a place to sleep at least for tonight. Then he heard the front door open. Grandpa looked as though he had aged much more than a year. He shuffled and had white stubble on his face. He walked past Tony and didn't see him even though he couldn't have been more than three feet away.

"Grandpa?" Tony said.

The old man stopped and whirled around, his arms up to ward off an attacker. He peered at Tony. "What're you doin here?" the old man muttered finally.

"Came to see Mitch and Ma."

"Well, she ain't here. I'm still puttin' bread and meat into your brother, but she's gone. And I ain't planning to have you back. No criminals here."

"I just want to stay long enough to see Mitch and get my things together. Just one night."

The old man glared at him. "Make sure it ain't no longer, and you ain't got no *things* here that I know of."

Tony and Mitch sat out on the front porch in the early evening so they could talk without being overheard by Grandpa or have to listen to his never-ending grumbling. The only sounds were the constant throbbing of the second shift at the mill and the cars going by on Pine Street.

Mitch said, "She's down in South Carolina near Myrtle Beach. Conway or Loris. She was goin' to look for Dad. I don't know why. He sure don't give a shit about her or us."

"When's the last time you heard anything from her?"

Mitch thought for a minute. "Last month, just after July fourth. She called here. She was at Ocean Drive. Sounded tight. Didn't make much sense."

"You don't have an address?"

Mitch shook his head. "She might be stayin' at Uncle Stan's. Least that's where she probably started. They might know where she is now."

"That's where I'll start."

"When are you leaving?"

"In the morning. He won't let me stay here more than tonight."

"Grandma could take care of that. He ain't as strong as he used to be."

"Nope. I don't want to stay any longer. Tired of his complaining about us all the time. He always mistreated Mom, and now he's worse."

A car that had come by earlier came by again and pulled slowly to the curb in front of the house. They could see cigarettes glowing from the dark inside. "Toneeee, you're home. Come over here and see me," said a girl's voice from the car.

"For somebody who don't seem to like girls, you got more pussy chasing you than Elvis," Mitch said.

Tony walked to the car and leaned into the passenger-side window. Trish was in the front passenger seat. She sat up and moved toward him.

"Aren't you going to kiss me?" she asked. "I haven't seen you in a year. Thought about you all the time," Trish said in a low voice. The girl driving the car snickered. Trish leaned into him and kissed him wetly. Feeling him stiffen, she said, "It's OK, hon. Seems like I'm saying that to you all the time."

He relaxed, reached in, and pulled her head toward him and kissed her again.

When he let her go, she pulled back and said, "Well, *dayum*, that was more like it. Maybe they should put you away for another year. Get in the back seat, hon. We'll take Marge home and spend some time catching up."

He waved to Mitch as he got in the car. "I'll be back in a little bit," he said. When they got to Marge's house, Trish wanted him to drive, but he had no license. As they sped off, she reached over and took his left hand and put it between her legs.

"We're going to have a good time," she said.

• • •

He left the next morning after Grandma had fixed him breakfast. He'd stayed in bed until after Grandpa had left. She didn't want him to leave. She cried quietly as she fixed the bacon and eggs. He could hear her praying to herself. When he had finished eating, he took the little plastic bag they had given him at the school, put his few belongings in it, and walked out the door toward the highway that led toward Charlotte and eventually Myrtle Beach.

Grandma gave him a twenty-dollar bill as she hugged him when he left. "Try to be a good boy, Tony. You know the difference between right and wrong."

He was lucky and made it to the South Carolina line in two rides, the last being with a driver who couldn't have been much older than himself. He was driving a green late model Ford. The car had been coming fast, and when it pulled over to pick him up, its rear end hiked up off the road. They took off, and the driver gunned the engine and changed gears using a lot of force. He had a short blond crew cut with sideburns an inch below his ear and a blunt, flat face. The radio spewed the roaring sound of a stock car race with the announcer naming the race leaders over the din.

"Where you headed?" he asked, but Tony shook his head that he couldn't hear over the radio. The driver turned the volume down. "Usually don't have races on weekdays, but this one was cancelled 'cause of the rain. Ford's gonna kick ass. So where you goin'?"

"Myrtle Beach, Ocean Drive, just the beach," Tony said.

"I work the second shift at Plant Three in Maple Grove, but I didn't feel like working for the rest of the week. Called in sick and took off. It's getting toward the end of the season. Need to see the beach as much as I can. Name's Willis." He looked at Tony. "Don't talk much, do ya? You must have seen me around town. You ever go to the Oasis?"

"Nope. Where's that?"

"Man, you don't know nothing. It's north of town, just over the county line so they can serve beer." He looked up in the rearview mirror at a car behind them that was closing on them fast. "Some fucker in a Chevrolet behind me coming up like a scalded dog. Let him get up close then we'll see what's up."

The other car came right up on Willis's rear bumper then pulled into the outer lane to pass. The other driver looked over at them and grinned and gunned his motor to finish going around them, but Willis suddenly pushed in the clutch and jammed the gear shift up into second gear. The engine howled, and the Ford shuddered but edged in front of the other car. It dropped back behind them. Willis laughed and looked over his shoulder, pushed in the clutch, and yanked the gear shift to third. There was a loud clanging sound, and the Ford began to lose speed.

"What the hell?" Willis said.

They pulled off onto the shoulder. The Chevrolet came even with them and stopped, idling and rumbling on the black asphalt. It was red and had a radio aerial on each of its rear fenders. It appeared to be slightly lower in the rear than the front.

"Need some help, cracker?" the driver asked.

"Shut up, asshole," Willis said.

"Pieces o' crap like that shouldn't screw with real cars. There's a station a couple miles up the road. Have a nice walk." He gunned the car and left a long rubber mark behind him.

Tony and Willis started off walking along the flat sandy right of way, heat rising in waves off the asphalt. Willis muttered about poor workmanship in the Ford. Tony was quiet. No one came by to offer them a ride, so they walked all the way to the concrete block building with a Gulf emblem on a pole. There was a hand-lettered sign on the wall next to the door that said "meckanic on duty-24hrs." A middle-aged man with two days of beard got up off a ratty upholstered sofa and asked, "What can I do fer you?"

The man had to call his cousin down the road who had a tow truck. Tony thanked Willis for the ride and said he'd start thumbing again. As he left, he heard Willis telling the man about the poor workmanship in the Ford.

Tony thumbed for a long time, but there were few cars and the rides he got only took him a short way. It was late in the afternoon, and a thunderstorm was rumbling off behind the thick woods. Pockets of cold air wafted through the trees. He hadn't seen a car in over an hour, and the storm was getting closer. Then, in the direction he had come from, he saw a faint car shape in the late afternoon shadows. It got closer, and he recognized Willis's green Ford. It slowed and came to a stop next to him.

"Me again. Ain't you lucky?" Willis grinned from the now dim interior.

Tony got in and smiled. "Glad to see you," he said. "Glad you got it fixed."

"Took all my damn money, but I'll take care of that soon enough."

A road sign told them they were thirty-eight miles from Myrtle Beach. Just outside a small town, they went past a ramshackle store with a red ball painted on the side. Willis turned the car around in the road and went back toward the store.

"What are you doing?" Tony asked.

"Just watch me. It's Friday evening. Little liquor store. That place might be flush. Didn't see anybody around neither." He reached under the seat and pulled out a pistol, a black automatic. He looked over at Tony and grinned. "Got to fill the bank up." They pulled into the parking lot, and Willis got out. "Won't be but a minute."

He went in and after a few minutes rushed back out, leaving the black screen door swinging before Tony could think of what to do. He slammed the car door and threw a wad of bills on the seat between them as he started the car and roared out onto the road.

"Won't they call the cops?' Tony said in a tight voice.

"Didn't see a phone. We'll be past Conway and almost there before anybody else knows about this," he said. "Count that money."

"Sixty-eight dollars," Tony said when he was finished.

"Good haul from a little place like that. Take a ten and give me the rest."

Tony hesitated, but he had only fourteen dollars without any prospect for more unless he found a job. It was late in the season so there was not much chance of that.

"Thanks," he said and stuffed the bill in his pants pocket.

Willis snickered. "Now you're as guilty as me. Aiding and abetting. That's what they call it."

Tony looked out the window into the sandy pine forest. He shrugged his shoulders.

They came into the town of Myrtle Beach in the early evening. At first, they passed small businesses, fruit stands, and car repair shops. As they got nearer, they could see a Ferris wheel on the horizon. They passed seafood restaurants and stores selling inflatable beach toys, rafts, and bathing suits.

Willis drove them right to the center of the resort where there was an enormous barn-like pavilion with a high ceiling; it was full of pinball machines and booths selling hot dogs and hamburgers smelling like fried onion and peppers. It faced a long sandy beach, and the ocean with a purple and pink sky over it was on one side. There was an area with a jukebox and concrete dance floor covering as much space as a small house. It was still early in the evening, and not many people were there except some children playing the game machines.

"Where you want off? I'm headed to a trailer down the road a ways where I have sleeping rights."

"Here's good," Tony said.

"You got a place to stay?"

"I'll be OK," Tony said, not wanting to tell him he had an uncle nearby. He got out of the Ford and thanked Willis for the ride. The car slowly pulled into the traffic cruising up and down the main road in front of the pavilion and all the bars, juke joints, and saltwater taffy places.

Tony walked down Ocean Boulevard toward where he remembered his uncle's house was. It was in an area slowly going from houses to businesses. Uncle Stan was his great uncle. He was Grandma's brother. He drank a lot, had been in World War I, and claimed to have been gassed in France. He had a shock of white hair, a hook nose, and always a gray stubble. He had a gravelly, hoarse voice and coughed a lot either from the gas or from cigarettes. He was married to his third wife. The other two had died. The current wife, Bertie, always dressed in baggy shorts and a T-shirt. She was pear-shaped, with most of her weight in her rear and stomach, and had a visible line of hair on her upper lip. She came to the door when he knocked. After he had managed to explain to her who he was through the locked screen, she opened it and yelled toward the back of the house, "Gaynelle's grandson is here." He heard violent coughing and throat clearing.

"Who?" came a response through another fit of violent coughing.

"Gaynelle's grandson," she yelled again. "Go on back to the porch. He can't hear me. Tell him who you are." She was a big woman. Her waist spilled low over the top of the shorts she was wearing. She wheezed softly after any effort.

Uncle Stan was sitting in a rocking chair. Beside the chair was a small table with an ashtray full of butts and a burning cigarette. There was a glass of clear liquid on the table. Uncle Stan peered at him through thick glasses. "Now who are you, son?" he asked and coughed as he took a drag on the cigarette.

"My grandma is your sister, Gaynelle. She lives in Maple Grove up in North Carolina. My mother is Lucinda, her daughter."

The old man bobbed his white head up and down. His hair was cut short but combed straight toward his face so that it came to a point at his forehead. "Oh yeah, I remember now." He paused and blew out smoke. "How's Gaynelle? Still married to that ornery turd?"

Tony grinned. "Yessir. I reckon she is."

"So what brings you down here?"

"I'm looking for my mother."

Uncle Stan looked puzzled.

Bertie stood in the doorway behind him. "She came by here a month or so ago. Far as we know, she's staying in a trailer over behind the Fish Hook. It's a bar and café out on the highway," she said.

"Can you tell me how to get there?"

"Sure, you want to go?" she asked. He nodded his head yes. "Have you got a place to stay?"

"No, ma'am."

She sighed. "Well, we rent the room in the basement, and nobody's in it. Guess you can stay there for a while. Nothing permanent, you understand?"

"Yes, ma'am."

"What did you say?" said Uncle Stan.

She ignored him. "You hungry?"

"Yes, ma'am."

She shuffled off.

"You come down here to fish?" Uncle Stan asked. "Had a good fishing season in the spring. Spottail bass ever'where. I caught two over twenty pounds last day I fished at the pier." He coughed again. Then he dropped his chin to his chest and breathed raggedly, his face red under the white stubble. After he took a sip from the glass, he said, "Catch 'em right in the surf, right where the waves are breaking. Most folks don't understand that and fish too far out to do any good."

Bertie came to the door behind them. "Come in the kitchen and eat," she said.

Tony followed her into a small kitchen. There was a plate with a sandwich, a bowl with steam rising from it, and a glass of tea on a small table covered with a flowered oil cloth. "Sit and let's talk a little." She sat down heavily in a chair opposite him and wheezed. "Your grandma called here earlier today. Don't know how she was able to make a long-distance call without your grandpa finding out about it. She's worried about you and wants you to come back to Maple Grove. Says the mill's shorthanded, and they'll give you a job." She paused and wheezed a little more. "Your mother's taken up with the man that runs the Fish Hook. He's pretty sorry, if you ask me, so when you go over there, be prepared. You want me to call her and let her know you're here?"

"I guess so," he said as he ate. The sandwich was bologna and cheese, but it was the first food he'd had in a day. The bowl was pinto beans full of a rich white broth with a few flecks of raw onion floating in them. A piece of yellow-white corn bread was beside the beans. He had to force himself to eat it slowly and not show how hungry he was. She had leaned back and stretched her legs out away from the table so that he could see her feet in a pair of shower shoes.

"Eat those beans," Bertie said. "They'll stay with you all day."

"Bertie? Where'd that boy go?" Uncle Stan yelled from the porch.

She shook her head and fanned herself with a paper napkin. "He sits out there all day, smoking and drinking gin, coughing and yelling at me," she said. Turning toward the porch, she yelled through the door, "He's in here eating."

"When he's done, send him back out here. I was telling him how to catch spottail bass." He coughed some more.

"Right in the surf where the waves are breakin'. That's where you catch 'em."

Aunt Bertie showed Tony the small room in the basement and told him how to get to the Fish Hook. He lay down and rested for a while before leaving to look for his mother, wondering about Willis and what had happened to him, whether he had got caught, and remembering the money in his pocket that had come from the robbed store.

. . .

Tony left as it was getting dark. He'd heard Bertie talking in a hushed voice on the phone before she told him how to get there. It wasn't hard. The place was on the long strip of highway that ran behind all parts of the coast. There was the ocean and the highway, and everything else was in between; all the buildings, amusement parks, and homes were locked into that narrow strip between the water and asphalt. He went south along the highway, catching one ride and then walking until he saw a neon sign on top of a flat-roofed building. It flashed on and off and said "F-sh Hoo" in gapped letters.

It was early yet, and there were few cars in the lot. Tony pushed his way through battered double doors leading into a dim interior. A few couples were sitting at scattered tables and a Patsy Cline song was playing on the jukebox, the steel guitar fragments disappearing into the smoky corners of the room. There was a long steel-covered bar off to the right. A rail-thin balding man stood behind it and eyed Tony as he approached. "You old enough to be in here, boy?" he asked.

"How old do you have to be?"

"Eighteen."

"I'm old enough."

"Got proof? A draft card?"

Tony fumbled for his billfold.

"Never mind. Kids as young as you don't usually come in here. You ought to be down at the pavilion or up north at O. D. This place is for a more raggedy, *experienced* crowd."

"I'm looking for my mother."

"Name?"

"Lucinda Pettyjohn."

The barkeep's face went blank. Then he smiled slightly. "Didn't know she had kids."

"Is she here?"

"Out back in the trailer. You can go down the hall there and through the back door. She know you're coming?"

"I think so."

"I *hope* so," the barkeep said.

Tony made his way down the dark hall and pushed through a battered door into the yard behind the bar. There was a gray single-wide trailer a short distance away in a grove of scruffy pine trees. Concrete steps not completely attached to the structure led up to the door. Rusty cans, scraps of paper, and broken pieces of wood littered the yard. He stood on the first step and knocked on the door. There were shuffling sounds inside, and the door opened a crack, then completely, and his mother was there in a bathrobe, her hair up in curlers, a dark circle under her left eye.

"Hello, sweetie," she said. "Come in, come in. What are you doing here?" She put both arms around him in the doorway. He could smell her perfume. "You look so good, grown so much." She cried a little. "I'm sorry I didn't come to see you at the school, but"—she stopped and waved her hand weakly—"things have just been so hard. I was sick."

"It's OK," he said, looking away from her at the cluttered inside. The kitchen area had a sink full of dirty dishes; clothes were strewn everywhere on the floor among battered furniture.

"What are you doing here?" she asked again.

"I came to see you. What are *you* doing here?"

She sniffled again and pulled him toward a couch.

"What happened to your eye?"

She ignored the question. "I couldn't stand living with Pa anymore, so I came down here to try and find a job and start over. Then I met Sonny. He owns the bar. He offered to let me stay here until I got on my feet." She shrugged her shoulders. "So here I am. I wait tables here. I don't make much, but I'm looking for something else."

"He live here too?"

"Yes, honey, but it's not like you think."

He stared at the floor.

She punched him on the shoulder. "What's wrong?" she asked.

He shook his head.

"Do you have some place to stay?"

"Aunt Bertie's letting me stay there for a few days. Do you know where Dad is?"

She didn't answer. Then she asked, "Do you have any money?"

"Some," he said. "Enough," he lied.

"I'd let you stay here, but there's not much room."

He shook his head again. There was noise outside, and the door swung open. A squat, ruddy-faced man with dark hair swept straight back from his face stood in the doorway and looked hard at Tony.

"Sonny," his mother said nervously, "this is Tony, my son. He's come to visit for a little bit."

Sonny grunted, went past them to the refrigerator, and took out a beer. "How long's a 'little bit'?" he asked.

Tony felt tightness in his throat and a hot feeling in his head behind the eyes. For a moment, he wasn't sure he could speak. But he stood. He was at least an inch taller than Sonny.

"Guess I better be leaving," he said.

She followed him out the door and stood on the concrete steps as he walked away. "Don't go like this," she called after him. "We haven't even talked. He's OK. He's just tired."

As Tony was walking away, he looked back, but she was gone. Then he heard Sonny yelling from the trailer. There was a thump, and he stopped but didn't go back. He was through the bar and out on the highway, fighting the urge to return.

• • •

He stayed one night at Uncle Stan and Aunt Bertie's. There were only two weeks before Labor Day, and the beach shut down for the most part after that, so there was little chance he could get a job. He went back to the Fish Hook one more time to say goodbye. This time she opened the door and came out onto the steps without asking him in. She had the black eye and now a swollen lip. When he started to speak, she put her finger to the cut lip to shush him and motioned with her head toward the inside. He could see purple bruises on her arms. They talked only for a moment, and she gave him a slip of paper. "Call me ever now and then at this number. Best to do it in the morning."

Then there was a bellow. "Bitch, git in here."

"Why are you staying with this bastard?" he asked. "Come back with me."

But she only hugged him and hurried back inside before the hot, embarrassed tears came to him.

Not wanting to but with no other prospects, he made his way out to Highway 17, stuck his thumb out, and headed north. Around midday, he caught a ride that took him past the store that Willis had robbed. The screen door was hanging open just as Willis had left it before they took off. He wondered if Willis had done more than take the money. Maybe he had killed the owner. There had been no sound of a shot, but maybe Tony had been too excited to hear it.

Late that evening, he got to Maple Grove. He walked from the highway to Grandpa's, hot and tired. Grandma hugged him at the door. She took him into the kitchen and made him a sandwich. He wolfed it down. "What's the rush?" Grandma asked.

"I got to get out of here before he wakes up. He won't let me stay here," Tony said.

"You never mind what he said. He don't remember half the time anymore what he has and has not said. It' that likker. You stay here if you want. At least for a little while. Let me take care of him. You're supposed to see Mr. Striker at the mill hiring office tomorrow morning. He knows all about you. He's a kind man. He's always helped us because he knows your uncle."

Grandpa was snoring in his chair, the television mumbling in a low hum. Mitch was out.

• • •

The next morning, he sat in a hard chair in the hiring office and waited for Mr. Striker. The man came in looking through a file and stood for a moment behind the desk, still looking at the file before he sat down. He was tall, rumpled, thin with gray hair and a harried face that seemed to come in and out of concentration on something every ten seconds.

He looked at Tony. "I've talked to your grandmother, son. She's worried about you. I know you've been in some trouble before. Happens to a lot of kids. Look, I know the first thing on your mind right now is not your prospects in life, but if you can, you need to think about these things. Your family has always been involved with this mill. Your uncle is a vice president. You probably won't ever be a vice president, but this is what you need to think about: This ain't a bad setup here. You can make a living wage, live in a good mill house, buy your water and power from the mill and all of that for cheap. You know what the rent is on a mill house near town? Near the Number Three Weave Room? It's twenty-five dollars a month, and they repair it if anything goes wrong and even paint it for you every five years. All you got to do is live in it, mow the grass, and pay the little bit they charge you for rent, electricity, and water. Anywhere else and those things alone would eat up a third of your wages, and the house would be a little more than a shack. You got a girl? You can get married, work hard, and who knows? Maybe one day you'll be a superintendent. I can start you as a cloth boy."

Tony took all this in, sometimes nodding his head in agreement, but really thinking about other things—about how to work things out *now*, how to get Lucinda back. He knew that Sonny was dangerous. He wasn't thinking about what would maybe happen ten years in the future, but taking cloth off looms couldn't be any harder than what he had been made to do in the school. Renting a house? It had never crossed his mind. He had one goal and that was getting his mother out of that trailer in Myrtle Beach.

• • •

So he began working as a cloth boy in the weave room on the third shift. He worked in a space that seemed as big as a football field. It was painted a dull green and had high ceilings with a network of hoses suspended over the machines that sprayed a slight mist of water every few minutes to keep the thread moist so it wouldn't break so easily. The looms were loud. All night and all day, they made a rhythmic "clacka, clacka, clacka." To be heard, Tony had to yell. There was an enclosed rectangular space at one end of the room where workers went to smoke. One break an hour was OK. He had never smoked, but he took it up so he could rest each hour. All night long, he took full rolls of cloth off long rows of chattering looms under the watchful eyes of the weavers and replaced them with empty rolls.

The job wasn't as easy as he first thought it might be. He walked up and down the aisles between the looms dragging a cart behind him. The finished cloth came off the looms and wound onto a roller. When the roller was full it was his job to take the full roll off and replace it with an empty roller, but the loom had to be stopped first. While the loom was running a shuttle flew back and forth through the threads to weave the cloth. If it wasn't stopped just at the right moment, it would fly through the strands, ripping them to shreds and stop the machine. The weavers were paid by how much cloth they wove, and sometimes it would take the loom fixers hours on their hands and knees using picks to rethread and retie the broken threads to get a stopped loom running again. Until he learned when to stop a loom, there were a lot of hard words and sharp eyes turned on him.

. . .

Each morning when he got off, he was covered in cotton lint. There were people in the department who had done that job all their lives. He tried to imagine that life: he'd eventually marry Trish, who would also work somewhere in the mill. They'd have children. He'd go fishing on the weekends, drink beer on Friday and Saturday nights, go to church on Sunday, and eat Sunday dinner at her parents' house. Maybe one day he'd be a foreman in a spinning room in charge of maybe ten or twenty workers and oversee them spinning thread all day.

He saw Willis on his way in and out each day. One evening in early spring, after Willis had asked him a number of times, Tony finally rode with him on a Friday evening to a place called the Oases to drink beer even though Tony really didn't like beer. They sat alone at the bar. There was a room behind them separated from the bar area by a curtain of glass beads where people were dancing to music from a jukebox. Mitch was probably back there. He had become a good dancer.

"You ever think about our ride down to Myrtle last summer?" Willis asked.

"Not much."

"We need to go together when the weather gets better in a couple months."

Tony thought about this but said nothing.

"We're a good team," Willis said.

"How do you mean?" Tony asked.

"Took care of that little store, didn't we?"

"Don't remember it that way. Seems like *you* took care of it."

"Yeah, but I can tell. You got a feel for that kind of thing too."

"Don't think there's much future in it. I spent time at the training school once, and I don't want to do it again."

"Stick up a store or go to prison?"

"Either one. I need to go."

"Let's leave this Thursday and take a long weekend drinkin' a little beer, chasing a few girls."

"Can't, man, I'm working Thursday."

"Leave anyway."

"Yeah, and get fired. I need the money."

"You ain't been around here long enough to know how it works. You won't get fired, and even if it happens, they'll take you back in a week or two. I know a guy who drove a cloth dolly who walked off in the middle of a shift and left the whole damn thing tyin' up the plant and still got hired back a month later."

"Not me, not now."

Willis left him on the curb in front of Grandpa's, but before he pulled away, he said, "We could do OK knocking off a little country place just every now and then. Think about it." He gunned the car away from the curb and was gone. Thinking about doing another robbery made Tony uncomfortable, but nothing had ever come of the first one, and maybe Willis was just blowing smoke and wouldn't really do another one anyway. Tony went inside. Grandpa, who had been asleep in front of the TV, drooling slightly, awoke with a start.

"Where the hell you been?" he said, wiping his mouth. "Have you paid me this week's rent?"

Tony didn't answer. He went to his room.

• • •

Tony called his mother once at the number she had given him. They only talked for a minute, her with a hushed voice, before he heard yelling in the background.

"I've got to go, honey," she said quickly. "Call me again."

He fell into a routine of work through the week and weekends at Trish's house. He was comfortable with her, but he remembered the warning about going to Rock Hill, and he didn't want that—not right now, anyway. He knew that if she got pregnant, he was there forever, but he had no other place to go, nothing else to do with his weekends.

He thought about his mother and Sonny. He thought about Sonny a lot.

Tony bought a car, a 1949 Ford. He took it to T. D. Brown before he bought it to have him check it out. T. D. chuckled after looking at it a few minutes and told him there was no real way to tell how many miles might be on it. "One good thing about these Fords, they almost never die completely. Might run for another fifty thousand miles."

It was all Tony could afford, so it was either that or nothing. He went to a finance company and borrowed a couple hundred dollars and took that and his savings and bought the car.

"I don't want that piece of crap parked it my yard and dropping oil all over the place," Grandpa said. "You want to keep it here; I'm charging you an extra five dollars a month rent." Before he had tolerated Grandpa, but now he had begun to hate the sight and smell of him. More and more, he walked away from him without answering or acknowledging anything he said.

The car was a distraction from the ordinary flow of his life. It was fun driving it in the country with Trish sitting close beside him, leaning her head on his shoulder. He drove it to the Oases several times and met Willis. In the car, he felt free, knowing he could get it in and go wherever he wanted. Maybe he would go somewhere for good and never come back, after he had helped Lucinda.

It broke down two months after he bought it. T. D. said it would cost a couple hundred to fix it. He didn't have the money, so the car sat in the side yard, and weeds began to grow up around the wheels like Lucinda's old car. Trish offered to help him pay for it, but he didn't want to take money from her; he didn't want to feel anymore obligated to her than she already made him feel because, as she said, she had given herself to him. He wondered how many others she had given herself to.

He came home at midnight one Saturday late in the spring after leaving Trish's. Grandpa was drunk, slumped in his chair watching a wrestling match. He seemed to drift off to sleep, and Tony changed the channel to a movie, but the old man started awake.

"What the hell? Where's wrestling?"

Tony got up to change the channel back, but the old man lurched to his feet and shuffled off toward the back of the house. Tony was standing in front of the television just before turning it off when he heard Grandpa muttering behind him. He turned to see him holding his old double-barreled shotgun and waving it slightly in the air. "Show you, show you," the old man mumbled.

"Grandpa? What the hell are you doing?"

But Grandpa didn't answer. Instead he raised the barrel, and Tony ducked. There was a deafening boom, the sound of glass breaking and shot ricocheting all over the room, and the smell of burnt powder.

"You shot the damn television, you old fool!" Tony said, and, realizing that there was another barrel, he lunged and grabbed the gun, pushing Grandpa to the floor.

Grandma had edged out of the bedroom door, peering into the smoky room. "What in the world! What in the world!"

"Go to bed, or I might kill you," Tony muttered at the old man, but Grandpa had slumped into his chair again, a white spot of spittle in the corner of his mouth.

Grandpa's hands gripped the chair arms, and he swiveled toward Tony, his head bobbing up and down slightly. "You don't know shit about what's in front of you. I've worked in that mill over there for fifty years. Since I was sixteen. Ever'day I go over there and do something to keep getting paid. I don't know what it's all about. What's it all about, huh?" He looked up at the ceiling. "Why does anybody have to do this? Ever'day. When I started, I was a sweeper. Then a cloth boy. Then I was a weaver. Then I fixed looms. Got fired twice but they always take you back. Is that a good thing or a bad thing? Have to be able to eat, but it looks like there could be a better way. Your grandma says the reason we have to work is because of Adam and Eve and all that shit. Says the Bible says because of eatin' the apple we're cursed to work all the time." Tony struggled to make sense of this. He hadn't thought of the Adam and Eve story in years and couldn't remember the details. "If they hadn't of ate that apple, food would just grow on trees, she says. What about clothes, I say. She says we wouldn't of needed clothes 'cause we wouldn't of knowed the difference if they hadn't ate that apple. What about radios and cars? Would they have growed on trees, I say. She don't say nothing to that. So much horse shit if you ask me, but what other reason is there?" His head dropped to his chest and for a moment he nodded off. Then with a start, he looked up. "That's what you got to look forward to. 'Less of course you wind up in jail, which you might again. Go on." He pointed to the door. "Get out of here but think about what I said." It was like a curse. Grandma, still standing in the doorway to the bedroom, shook her head.

"Blasphemy. Awful, awful. God will punish the old fool for all he's done."

"Go to bed, Grandma. I'll clean up the mess," Tony said.

• • •

Tony couldn't stay there after that, so he got a room in one of the rooming houses across the railroad tracks from the mill. It cost ten dollars a week, but that included supper in a common dining room. His room was small, but the landlady, Mrs. Overcash, kept the place clean and well run. The meals were simple: hamburger steak, fried chicken, mashed potatoes, and biscuits. He didn't eat breakfast and bought a sandwich for lunch from the dope wagon, a cart that came around through the departments with sandwiches, soft drinks, candy bars, and cigarettes. He didn't even buy a drink at work. He drank water from the tap. He had enough money left over each month to pay for small things. But there was little room for anything else. He spent a lot of time after work lying on his sagging bed staring at the high ceiling, and listening to other shift workers snoring or talking in their sleep through the thin doors and walls. He walked to the YMCA sometimes and played pool or ping-pong, and he went out with Trish. She paid for them to go to the movies when he didn't have enough. It made him feel cheap. Like he was worthless or less than he should be. He had left the Ford in the yard beside Grandpa's. He itched to get it fixed.

Tony had seen Willis between shifts once or twice; then one day he saw him coming into work the next shift. "Let's go to the O after work," Tony said.

"Sure. I'll pick you up," Willis said and smiled.

Tony was standing by the curb when Willis pulled up. There was something dark and shiny on the seat between them—a pistol, an automatic. Small enough to fit easily into a pocket.

"Where'd you get that?" Tony asked.

"It was my uncle's. I bought it from him." Willis put the car in gear and pulled off. "Oases is where you want to go?"

"Sure. Can I hold the gun?"

Willis nodded. Tony picked it up, feeling the cold weight of it. "I been thinking about what we did. Maybe we could do a couple more jobs. In South Carolina, I mean." Willis turned in his seat and looked briefly at Tony.

"You go from being sort of righteous about not doing this to all of a sudden sayin' we ought to do a few. I don't get it," Willis said. "What caused the big change?"

"I dunno. I need some money. Still making payments on the car that ain't runnin', paying rent too. No better jobs around here than what I've got, and no one would hire me anyway 'cause of the reform school time. I mean, I don't want to do it a lot, but it would help right now."

"OK. Maybe now you're just *half* righteous," Willis said and snickered. "Yeah? Well, maybe we can do a couple. Can't do too many. Too dangerous."

"And I need you to do me a favor," Tony said.

"Yeah? What kind of favor?"

"I need you to lend me a couple hundred bucks so I can get the Ford fixed. You can keep my share of the money when we do a job."

"I don't know. What if I lend you the money and then you back out?'

"I ain't never backed out on anything, and I won't on this."

Willis lent him the money, and the Ford was fixed. Then one evening they passed each other at shift change, and Willis called him aside. "Time to take a trip to the beach. Let's do it this Friday."

"Sure."

And so they left the next Friday late in the afternoon, and by dusk, they were over the line into South Carolina, passing budding peach trees and pine forests. They came to the outskirts of a small town. A small flat-roofed cinder block building with a red circle on its side came up on the left.

"Looks like a good one," Willis said and slowed down to pull over. "A liquor store."

"It's Friday night," Tony said. "Is that a good time to go into a liquor store?"

"Don't see anybody." The car was stopped but still running. "Let's go."

"You want me to go in?"

"Yeah. Since I lent you money from this, I want you to be more 'n an abetter."

"A what?"

"I told you before. An abetter. It's somebody that don't do the stick up but maybe looks out or drives the car."

They opened the screen door and peered into the gloom. There was a narrow corridor between shelves of whiskey bottles leading to a counter in the rear with a cash register. Behind the counter sat a woman. Her hair was gray, falling raggedly below her ears. In the dim light, Tony could see an enormous pair of glasses on her but no other features. She continued to sit while they pretended to look for something on the shelves, making sure no one else was there.

She kept her seat and said, "Can I help you with something?"

Satisfied that she was alone, Willis pulled the gun from under his shirt and walked to the counter in front of her. Even looking at the gun, she remained seated, and then Tony saw she was in a wheelchair.

"I'm going to come around behind the counter and get the cash out of that register, ma'am. You just stay right where you are and you won't get hurt," Willis said.

"Mister, if you take that money, it'll ruin me. This is the first good week I've had in months," she said. Tony could see tears glistening below the glasses. Willis got the register open, found a brown paper bag under the counter, and scooped bills into it. The woman sniffled and sobbed as they rushed out the door. Willis gunned the engine, and they were gone down the black asphalt.

"Count it," Willis said, handing the bag to Tony, who took the bag but looked back toward the store that had now disappeared. He looked down at the bag.

"Go on. Count it. What are you waiting for, Mr. Righteous?"

"Three hundred and eighty-two dollars," Tony said.

Willis whistled softly. "Umm. That's a good night's work. You keep fifty and gimme the rest. That pays me back plus a little for overhead with the car. OK?"

"Sure." Tony took the money, stuffed it in his pocket, and handed the bag back to Willis. They sped on down the road.

"So far, so good," Willis said, looking up in his rearview mirror. "Don't see anything and don't hear anything." He turned the radio on and twisted the dial until he found Elvis singing "Heartbreak Hotel" and turned up the volume. "You like Elvis?" Willis asked.

"He's OK." Tony shrugged.

"You're a funny guy. What *do* you like?"

• • •

They found a cheap place to stay in Ocean Drive. The next morning, they went to a diner for breakfast. Someone had left a morning paper on the counter near where they sat. Tony picked it up and scanned it.

"What are you doin'? Looking for a write-up about us? It'll be on the second or third page from a little burg like that," Willis said.

Tony found it way down on the third page.

Chesterfield. June 5, 1958. Last night an ABC store outside of this small town was held up. The owner described the robbers as two white males between eighteen and twenty-two years of age. They used a pistol and got away with over three hundred dollars. The owner thought they were driving a late model Ford but was unable to get the license number. Police are investigating.

Tony showed it to Willis, who said, "See? Slick as a whistle. Don't even know what state the tag was from."

"Sometimes they don't always tell you in these things what they know, or sometimes they even put wrong stuff in here, so you won't be suspecting it," Tony said.

"Bullshit. You watch too much television. Relax. Let's have a good time."

They spent the day at the pavilion at Ocean Drive, looking at girls and playing pinball. Willis drank a lot of beer. Tony had one. There was a jukebox on a concrete dance floor that overlooked the ocean. After three o'clock, a small crowd gathered there to dance and watch others dance. Some girls eyed them. Willis made small talk with one of them. The other, blond, freckled, and named Audrey, asked Tony to dance; she even took his hand and led him out to the floor. The jukebox was playing a song by the Platters. He felt awkward, but they shuffled back and forth among the small crowd.

"You don't talk much like your friend does," she said. He looked down at her. "Where are you from?" she asked.

"Up the road in North Carolina," he said. She smelled like suntan lotion, and he could see the tan lines from her bathing suit on her shoulders. "How old are you?" he asked.

"Eighteen," she said, pretending to be angry. "How old are you? Anybody ever told you that you look like Elvis?"

They danced some more. Willis and the other girl had disappeared, so Tony walked Audrey through the pavilion and through the amusement park, looking for them among the rides and Ferris wheel.

"Maybe they went down on the beach," she said. They walked down to the sand but still didn't see them. She talked him into taking off his shoes and walking along the surf line. By this time, she was holding his hand and leaning against him as they walked. "You sure don't talk much."

"Don't have much to say."

"Do you work? Go to school?"

"I work. Finished school last year."

"I'm still in school. I'll be a senior next year. Can't wait to get out and leave Podunk."

The sun was beginning to set, but there was still no sign of Willis.

"Where the hell did he go?" Tony muttered.

"What's the matter? You don't like me? Not pretty enough for Elvis?"

"*Sure* you are. Just wondering where he is. That's all." He was thinking about his mother and had planned to ask Willis to borrow the car so he could see her. "Are you staying far from here? Maybe they went there."

"It's a couple more blocks this way. We're staying with Joyce's folks. They've gone down to Murrell's Inlet to eat. Won't be back for a while. Maybe they did go there. We can go look, but don't get any ideas, Elvis. I'm going steady back home, and I don't know anything about you."

"Don't worry," he said.

She got angry at this, dropped his hand, and walked apart from him. "You engaged or something? If you don't want to be with me, then you can go back," she said.

"You're going steady, you said."

"Yeah, but I can still have some fun."

Tony wanted to find Willis, so he moved closer to her and took her hand again. He bent down and kissed her on top of her hair, smelling the good scent of it. They walked a little further, and she pointed toward some steps in the dunes going up to a house and led him up to the steps and toward a screened porch. From a window, they could see into the living room. Willis and the girl were on the couch with Willis holding her, one hand on her thigh and talking. Beer cans were on the end table next to them and several more on the floor.

"Holy shit," she said. "If her parents come back and catch them like this . . ." She moved to open the door, but Tony stopped her.

"Leave 'em alone. C'mon, let's you and me go back on the beach and sit for a while."

"But what if they get caught?"

"Their business." He took her by the elbow and led her back out toward the dunes. There was a bench along the rail just before the steps, and when they got to it, he turned her around and bent to kiss her. She resisted slightly at first, but then she put her arms around his neck and opened her wet mouth onto his, then she pulled away.

"I didn't think you liked me," she said.

"Sure, I do. Sure, I do."

They walked back down the beach toward the pavilion. Before they got there, they found a big piece of driftwood and sat down on it. They kissed, and he tried to put his hand down her blouse, but she pulled his hand away.

"Just a minute, mister. I'm not that kind of girl."

He didn't try again. After a while, he asked if she'd like a Coke, told her to wait right there, and walked up to the pavilion to get the drinks. But he didn't buy drinks. He left and headed for the rooming house. He remembered that Willis had left the car keys on the dresser. He could take it and make the short drive down 17 and see Lucinda, maybe get a chance to talk to her and get her to go back with them. The girl on the beach could stay there. Nothing would ever come of it anyway. "Not that kind of girl. Right. Good for her."

• • •

Tony turned the car toward Highway 17 and the Fish Hook.

It was crowded. He stopped just past the entryway and looked over the mostly country-looking crowd. The skinny bartender he had seen the first time was working the center of the bar. He saw Tony at the door and waved him over. "You here again? Not a good time."

"My mom here?"

"Haven't seen her all day, but she's probably in the trailer. Sonny's been drunk for a couple days. I wouldn't go back there."

But Tony went anyway. Down the dark corridor and out into the gloom between the building and the trailer. He stood on the steps and knocked softly on the metal door. After a few minutes, the dirty louvered window on the upper part of the door opened slightly. Lucinda looked out, dressed in the same bathrobe, her blond hair straggling around her shoulders. She opened the door wide enough to step out. She put her arms around his neck without saying anything and held him. They went down the steps, and he held her away from him and looked at her. This time, there were no bruises or split lip, but she kept looking up at the door.

"You can't stay here long, and I've got to go back inside, honey. If he wakes up and I'm not there, he'll be mad as hell," she whispered.

"Why don't you leave with me right now? What's keepin' you here?"

"It's not that easy."

"Why? You in love with him?"

She looked down with her arms crossed, holding the robe together. "I owe him money," she said.

"How much? For what?"

"Keep your voice down. It don't matter, and it's too much."

"We can go back to Maple Grove. I've got a job. You can get a job. We don't have to live with Grandpa."

There was a stirring inside. "Cinda? Where are you?" With a noise, the door flew open. Sonny peered out at them, no shirt, huge belly draped over a pair of dirty shorts, his eyes puffy and red. He reached down and grabbed her by the arm, pulling her up the steps. The top of the robe flew open to her pale breasts. She pulled away and covered herself again.

"Go, go," she hissed, motioning with her hand.

But Tony lunged toward Sonny. "Keep your fuckin' hands off her," he said.

Sonny half tumbled down the steps, shoved her to the side, and swung a roundhouse at Tony, hitting him in the neck. Then he swung again and hit him full in the face. Blood splattered from a cut lip, and Tony staggered back, still trying to breathe from the blow to his Adam's apple.

Sonny moved slowly toward him with his fists still clinched. "You come around here again and I'll kill you and beat her ass good, or maybe I'll kick her out and let you take her. Worthless anyway," he said.

His mother pushed past Sonny and ran up the steps into the trailer, closing the door. Tony bent over with his hands on his knees, clearing his head, and trying to catch his breath. He spat blood on the ground.

"Don't you worry, fucker. I'll be back," he said and backed away slowly.

"Yeah. You come back. See what happens to both of you!" Sonny shouted at his back.

Tony pushed through the crowd in the Fish Hook. People stood to the side when they saw his face and shirt covered with blood, leaving a wide space for him to get to the door. He found some napkins in the glove box of Willis's car and held them to his lip as he drove. When Tony pulled into the sandy drive way in front of the rooming house, Willis was waiting on the steps. He came down to the car.

"Damn. You took my car. What happened to you?" He looked in the car in the dim light of the overhead. "Shit. You got blood all over my seat covers. I almost called the cops. Thought somebody had stole the car."

"Would have been real smart," Tony muttered.

"I didn't say you could take it. I gotta find something to get that blood off." He ran up the steps. Tony slowly followed him and sat down in a chair outside the door. Willis came out again with a balled-up shirt dripping wet with water. "If I can't get this blood out, you're paying to have them replaced." He ripped open the door and began rubbing furiously. "It got on the fabric. It ain't coming out."

"I'll get it out or get it changed. Don't worry," Tony said quietly.

Willis came up the steps, still swearing under his breath. "Where did you go? What the hell happened?"

"I went to see my mom. Had an argument with this guy she's staying with."

Just then, a light went on in one of the rooms next to the porch. The door opened, and a small woman with a dried-up face and clutching a robe around her peeked out the door.

"You boys have to be quiet out there," she said just above a whisper. "It's two o'clock in the morning. You're waking the whole house up."

"Yes, ma'am. We will," Tony said.

She closed the door, and the light went out. The bleeding had stopped from his nose and lip. His neck was swollen.

"You gonna be OK?" Willis asked. "Man, did you piss off that girl, Audrey, or whatever her name was. You just left her on the beach? You could've done all right there."

"I had to see Mom."

"Yeah, well I was doing more than OK with the other one. Then yours came back after you left her, mad as hell, and screwed me up. Now I can't go back there because of you dumping on her friend. Shit."

"I'm going to bed," Tony said.

He slept hardly at all, his mind racing over Sonny. What to do?

After they ate breakfast at Hoskins, they headed north for home, Willis grumbling about the stains on his seats and his wasted opportunity with the girl. Tony wanted to leave, but he also knew he would be back and it would not be long. On the way home, he offered to buy the gun, but Willis wouldn't sell it. "I know where maybe you can get one. Maybe even cheap. There's a pawnshop over south of town, and sometimes they have used guns."

• • •

After work one day the next week, Tony borrowed Willis's car and drove to the pawnshop. The display window was full of guitars, diamond rings, and even a wedding dress on a mannequin in one corner. There was no one behind the counter when he went in. A man in a dirty white shirt bloused over his pants came out of a door behind the counter. He wore wireless glasses with smudged lenses. His face was covered with black-and-gray stubble. Tony could smell onions and hot dog chili.

The man was picking his teeth. "What can I do for you, bud?"

"Looking for a gun," Tony said.

"Shotguns are right over here."

"No, I'm looking for a pistol."

The man paused and sucked his teeth. "Have to have a permit for that. Takes a while. How old are you?"

Just then, a phone on the wall behind the counter rang.

The man turned his back and picked up the phone. He listened for a moment and said, "I sent that yesterday." He grunted several more times then hung the phone up and briefly stood looking down at the floor. "Pistols are over here," he said and moved to another section of the counter. "How much you want to spend?"

"I've got a hundred and fifty dollars."

The man reached under the counter and pulled up a dull blue revolver with a broken wooden grip wrapped in black electrical tape.

"I can let you have this one for a hundred fifty. It's a .38 special. Used to belong to a cop. It's a good deal." He paused and sucked his teeth. "You give me the cash, and we'll forget about the paperwork."

And it was done. He got a box of shells for it at the same time.

· · ·

Tony called Lucinda the next day from a phone booth in town. When Sonny answered, he said nothing but held the receiver for a moment before hanging up.

"You little shit. I know it's you. I'll beat the hell out of her if you don't stop callin' here. Put that phone close to your ear and listen to this." There was a pause and then a muffled thump, fist on flesh, and he heard a moan. "How's that? Huh? Ever'time you call here, I'm gonna hit her. You hear me?"

Tony put the phone down as quietly as he could.

• • •

Tony got his car fixed, left work, the rooming house, and Maple Grove and headed south for his mother and Myrtle Beach. He tried to think through what his life was going to be like after the next few days—what all of their lives would be like—but it was too confusing. It was better just to know that this had to be done for her and for his own pride, no matter what happened afterward. He got there much faster than he thought. It would be less dangerous to do it during the day before the club opened so there would be fewer people to worry about.

He didn't know Sonny's habits, when he came and went, so Tony would have to find a good vantage spot and wait. It was two o'clock when he got to the front of the club. It was in a clump of run-down businesses, including a tire shop, a beauty parlor, and a pizza place. He walked past them and then down an alley that led to the rear and the trailer. The stores looked empty. The gravel alley opened up to a jumbled area with trash cans and strewn with litter. The trailer was to the right, and just before it was an old Chevrolet with a cracked windshield and weeds growing around the wheels. There was a good view of the entrance to the trailer from the car. It was perfect. He tried the passenger door on the right side. It resisted for a minute and then creaked open. The seats were dusty and covered with leaves, but he sidled in and eased the door to without closing it completely. He took the gun out of his jacket pocket and checked the loads. He waited. Nothing moved in the alley but rats scurrying around the trash cans. Someone from the pizza place behind him dumped trash into one of the cans. He dozed off and on, tired from the trip down.

The rear door of the Fish Hook opened abruptly and woke him. Sonny came out and made his way to the trailer steps. Tony opened the car door and stood silently, his hand on the gun in his pocket.

Sonny paused and looked at him. "Well, I'll be damned. Look who's here. Come to see the whore, or do you want some more of what I gave you last time?"

"I came for her . . . and for you."

"You can't have either, asshole. Come back in a month or two after I'm done with her and you can have her or what's left." He took a knife from his pocket and stepped toward Tony. "Come on, bud. I want to smash your nose again."

Tony raised the gun and fired twice. One shot hit the stomach. The other hit Sonny in the neck. He slumped and put his right hand over the blood oozing from his throat. He fumbled at the wound on his stomach with the other hand. He looked quizzically at Tony, as though he were seeing him for first time. "Damn," he said. "You shot me." Then he fell face forward into the gravel, body on top of his hands.

The shots had been so loud that Tony could hear nothing but a roar. There was mucous dripping from his nose onto his lip. He was crying and thinking about that story, how the blood cried out from the ground; then the door to the trailer flew open and Lucinda stumbled out, looking first at the body and then at Tony. Her hands went to her mouth. "Oh my God, Tony, what have you done?"

"I came for you," he whispered and almost sobbed.

"What were you thinking? What are we going to do? People heard the shots. They'll be here in a minute. Oh my God!" She took steps toward him then went back. "Here, help me drag him behind the trailer. Maybe we can buy a little time." They pulled the body over the gravel and weeds, stumbling and jerking. There was a muddy blue tarp crammed under the trailer. They took it and covered the corpse. They kicked gravel over the blood at the spot where the body fell. She grabbed Tony by the arm and pulled him inside. "Wait a few minutes. Nobody's coming. Then take off. Go home. Go somewhere, but you have to get out of here."

"You're coming too," he said.

"How? You didn't think this through. How long do you think we'd last without them catching us?"

Outside they heard voices, people talking about the noise. "Probably a truck backfiring. Don't see nothing," someone said.

Lucinda said, "Soon as it gets quiet out there, you have to leave."

"What about you?" he asked.

She looked much worse than when he had last seen her: circles under her eyes, a scab on her swollen lip, bruises on her forearms. "I'll come later. Soon as I can figure out how. Maybe tomorrow I'll catch the bus. Can't wait longer than that. Someone will want to know where he is." She put her face in her hands and sobbed. "Go. Now." She pushed him toward the door.

"OK. But I want you to come home." He hugged her.

"I know, baby. I know."

He went to the door and peered out through the small window at the top. The alley was empty. He hugged her again and left, driving north on Highway 17 toward Maple Grove. There was no traffic, so he pulled over onto the shoulder and threw the pistol into a tidal pond on the side of the road.

• • •

Tony looked into his rearview mirror the entire trip, sure that sooner or later they would come for him, but he made it to Maple Grove. He pulled into a parking space behind Mrs. Overcash's place late in the evening and went to bed, his mind racing the whole night with visions of Sonny lying on the ground, his mother clutching the robe closed around her. When dawn came, he got up and splashed water on his face and headed to work.

The rumble and clacking of the weave room was comforting to him in a way, and it made him feel that somehow he could get lost in the great maw of the mill and nothing would find him. He went from loom to loom, rhythmically taking off the rolls of cloth and loading them onto a dolly, then emptying them at the drop-off point. He took regular smoke breaks and bought a ham sandwich and a soft drink from the dope wagon. It was the first time he could remember eating in a long time.

He was in the smoke room when he saw Mr. Striker motioning him to come out.

"Uh-oh, you're in trouble now," the man next to him said.

Tony felt his heart stop and his throat get dry. He stumbled as he got up and made his way through the door, knowing that this would be the end of life as he had known it, never imagining that he would miss it but knowing he would now.

"Tony Pettyjohn," Mr. Striker said as he put his hand on Tony's shoulder, "you've been doing a good job here since you came. How would you like to train to be a loom fixer and get a raise?"

Tony's mouth fell open, and he stuttered, "Sure . . . sure, Mr. Striker. Yes."

"OK, then you finish up on the cloth tonight, and tomorrow you start following Pete Wilson fixing looms and learning how to do it."

"Thank you. Thanks." Suddenly his eyes were moist.

"Well, son, didn't mean for you to take it that way," Mr. Striker said with a big smile. "Here, you'll need this." He handed Tony a tool; it was long with a shaft like a skinny screwdriver but with a hook on the end. It had a tortoise shell handle. Tony took it and turned it over in his hands.

"It's a loom pick. You'll learn how to use it soon."

"Thanks." He wiped his eyes.

"Well, go on and finish up your last shift as a cloth boy."

• • •

Tony drove to Trish's that night. She came to the door, not smiling, her mouth downturned. "Haven't seen you in a long time. You haven't even called."

"Sorry. I had business down south I had to take care of. You gonna let me in or should I go?"

She opened the door and stood aside. When the door was closed, she lunged at him, put her hands around his neck, pulled up, and covered his mouth with hers.

When she leaned away, she said, "You asshole. Why do I put up with you? You come around every day for two weeks, then I don't see you for three weeks." She put her arms around his neck and nestled against his shoulder. He could feel her crying.

"I'm sorry. What I had to do was important." He hugged her awkwardly. "I got a promotion . . . and a raise. I'm going to be a loom fixer." He felt a hollowness as though he were imagining the whole thing, and then he was quiet again. She was still and said nothing for a moment as though considering what this meant for her and them.

"That's *great*." She moved him toward the sofa, and they collapsed onto its familiar softness. She pulled away from him. "Have you found your ma? Is that settled? Look at me."

"Yeah. Yeah. It's settled. She's coming home soon."

"Is that good or bad? Are we going to see more of each other or less when she comes?"

"It's good. Yeah, I want to see you . . . I want to see you a lot."

She hugged him again. "I'm going to tell Mom and Dad."

"Tell 'em what?"

"About your promotion and raise."

He leaned back into the sofa and closed his eyes as she went into the kitchen. *Jesus, please help me*, he thought. *I don't deserve this.*

The next morning he started as a loom fixer and followed Pete Wilson the entire shift. They worked on one fouled loom for more than half the shift. Wilson said almost nothing. He grunted things. An hour into trying to retie the hundreds of broken strands, he finally motioned for Tony to have a hand at it. He fumbled with the pick, but after long minutes, he was successful in getting one strand back as it should be. Wilson mumbled and moved him out of the way so he could get to the rest of the shredded strands. When it was all done to his satisfaction, he reached for the lever to start the loom again, the weaver anxiously watching him as he did. "You have to make sure the tension is just right or it'll start and then rip all them threads to pieces again. Nothin' like doing one loom the whole shift. Plus it pisses her off," he said, motioning with his chin at the watchful weaver. "Gits paid by the piece. You know that, don't you?"

Tony nodded his head. "Yeah, I had that explained to me a bunch of times when I was taking off cloth," Tony replied.

The weaver smiled. She came over to them; she had dark brown eyes and brown hair with a gray fringe of lint. She took Tony's arm and patted his butt, then said to Wilson, "Elvis here learned fast. One of the best. Now we'll get a jerk we have to train again. Least he'll still be around."

Tony sat on the floor beside Wilson smoking a cigarette after they had eaten lunch. Mr. Striker was standing outside the door as they came out. "How's he doing?"

"Gonna be OK, I think." Wilson replied.

Striker put his hand on Tony's arm and said, "Good. I'm proud of you, boy, your grandma will be too. Just keep at it."

For a moment, he was happy. No one had ever said things like that to him, and then he remembered what had to come. What would they say? How would they feel if he was caught? And he *knew* he would be, so this was just a little break before a disaster, before he got what he deserved. And he had heard nothing from his mother.

He felt good at the end of each day like he had accomplished something, getting the balky looms to run again, figuring out how the jumble of strands fit after one had shut down, feeling the gratitude of a weaver when the loom was running again because of him. It was like he had a feel for them and the machines responded to him. He liked the feel of the cloth, and he liked the colors, the red or blue stripes in the towels and washcloths.

He saw Trish more. She asked more questions about their future, and he felt less threatened when she did. He could almost visualize it. Living in a good mill house at first, having kids, buying a boat, going to the beach when the mill stood for the week of the Fourth. It seemed possible to him. Maybe even help out his mother.

They went to a couple of football games at the high school stadium. The game had always been big there. She clung to his arm as they made their way down the concrete stairs and looked for a good place to sit. People waved, mostly at her, but he felt included, feeling like maybe there was more now than just waking up tomorrow.

Then one evening after work he was looking through the local newspaper. There was a small article on page two down near the bottom of the page under "South Carolina News":

Myrtle Beach, SC. The body of Clarence "Sonny" Murphy was found yesterday behind the trailer where he lived behind the bar he had run for many years. Police suspect his former girlfriend, who has disappeared. No other information is available at this time.

It was like an icepick into his heart. Tony couldn't see for a moment. It was all about to come to an end. He didn't know how to get in touch with Lucinda; there was nowhere to call. He would have to go there and look.

He aimlessly went through his shift the next day. Just before the next shift came in, he looked for Mr. Striker. "I have to be gone for a while," he said, looking down, nearly in tears.

"Why, son? We need you right now. We're running six days a week."

"I know. But I can't help it. I think my mom's in trouble, and I have to find her."

Striker sighed. "I remember your mother. Are you sure you want to risk your job to look for her?" He looked down. "I'm sorry. I shouldn't have said that."

"I just have to."

"I'll hold the job for you as long as I can. Hurry."

• • •

Tony didn't say goodbye to Trish, knowing she would be angry and crying and clinging, so he threw some clothes in the Ford and headed south. He'd try to fix things with her when he got back—if he ever did.

It rained the whole way to Myrtle Beach, a cold, depressing rain. He was afraid to go to the Fish Hook but didn't know where else to start, so late afternoon, he pulled into the gravel lot, sat for a moment thinking in the car, and then went in. It was nearly deserted in the period when regulars were getting home from work and doing those things they did on Tuesday afternoon after work and before going to drink a few. The skinny bartender was putting beer in the cooler. He looked up and paused for a moment, looking surprised. Tony walked to where he stood behind the bar.

"I'm looking for my mother," he said.

The bartender leaned on the counter. "You ain't heard then?"

"Heard what?"

"They arrested her yesterday for murder. Found her all the way down in Florida. You knew about Sonny?"

"Where is she?" he muttered.

"Don't know for sure if they've got her back yet, but when they do, she'll be in the local lockup until she's tried. Best thing for you to do is go down to the jail and find out when they expect her. If she waives extradition, it won't be long." He paused, and his face softened. "I know this ain't gonna be easy for you. Sonny was a rat-fucker. Nobody liked him. Maybe she can beat this," he said as Tony walked toward the door.

"How do I get to the jail?" he asked.

• • •

Lips moving, the deputy behind the counter was reading a newspaper when Tony walked in. He continued reading for a moment then dropped the paper far enough to look at Tony.

"Help you?" he asked.

"Trying to find out about my mother."

"Name?"

"Tony Pettyjohn."

"No, bud, I mean your mother."

"Lucinda Pettyjohn." The deputy sat a little straighter and put down the paper. His voice went down a notch, becoming official.

"As I understand, she's waived extradition, and she'll be here tomorrow from Florida."

"When can I see her?"

"Well, she'll have to get processed in before she can have visitors. She'll see the judge first thing she gets back. Enter a plea and all that. Then you can prob'ly see her."

"Can I call her or something?"

"'Fraid not. Best thing for you to do is get a place to stay and start lookin' for her a good lawyer. She's gonna need one."

"I don't know anything about lawyers," he whispered.

"If she don't have no money, they'll appoint one for her. If y'all have money, then you need to get one. I recommend Snake Lawson for this kinda stuff. He's the best, but it'll cost you."

Tony left but didn't know where to go. He didn't want to spend all his money, since he didn't know how long he would have to stay. He decided to go to his uncle's. It wouldn't be pleasant, but it would might be free.

Aunt Bertie came to the door. "I thought you'd be here sooner or later." She let him in and sighed heavily. He could hear Uncle Stan coughing on the porch.

"Who is it, Bertie?"

"Gaynelle's grandson, Tony. You remember him?"

"Who?" There was coughing.

She shook her head. "Sit down for a minute before you go talk to him. I don't think he knows. He can't see to read the paper anymore and falls asleep before the news come on TV."

Tony slumped in a chair in the kitchen. She sat across from him and wheezed from the effort of walking. "I know Lucinda is in bad trouble. But I just can't imagine her killing somebody." She paused.

"I don't think she did it. Mom wouldn't kill anybody no matter how mean they were."

"What are you going to do? Have you seen her?"

"No. Can't see her until tomorrow. Don't know what to do. Try to get a lawyer, I guess."

"Gaynelle called yesterday. She's so tore up she could scarcely talk. Wanted to know if you'd been here. Said to have you call if you came." She paused and looked down. "Have you got any money? For a lawyer, I mean?"

"Some. Probably not enough. The deputy at the jail told me to see a lawyer named Snake Lawson. You heard of him?"

She nodded. "Yeah. He's pretty famous around here. Represents all the murderers, thieves, and drug dealers. Knows all the judges and I 'spect he contributes when they run for office. But I'm sure he ain't cheap. Lives in a big house in the ritziest part of town. Drives a Cadillac and is married to his third wife who's fifteen years younger than him."

"Who are you talking to in there, Bertie?"

She got up heavily. "Go on out there and talk to him while I make you something to eat, but don't say anything about Lucinda."

He went out onto the porch, Uncle Stan peering at him through his thick lenses. "I'm Tony. Lucinda's son. Gaynelle's grandson."

The old man seemed to think for a minute. "Yeah. You were here not long ago, and we talked about fishing for spottail bass, but you left before we could go."

"Right."

"You see, you fish for 'em right in the surf. Most people don't know that and fish too far out. But that's where you catch 'em. Right in the surf." He stopped and tried to catch his breath. Then he lit another cigarette from the one he had in his hand. "We need to go fishing this time."

"He ain't been fishing in ten years," Bertie grunted from the doorway. "Couldn't stand up long enough to fish now."

"What's that? What?" Uncle Stan paused, his face red, and caught his breath again.

"There's a sandwich on the table in the kitchen. Let's go in and talk for minute."

Although Tony wasn't hungry, he sat at the table in front of the food.

"Here's a hundred dollars," Bertie said. "It probably won't be enough to hire Lawson, but maybe he'll at least talk to you and you can work something out."

"Aunt Bertie, you don't have to do this."

"I want to, for Gaynelle's sake."

• • •

Lawson's office was in a house in a part of town that had been residential but was becoming commercial. The waiting room, which had been a living room, was lined with fifteen or more straight-backed chairs that were all occupied but two. A secretary sat at a desk that took up most of a wide door between the place where people were sitting and what must have been a dining room with walls now lined with gray filing cabinets.

She looked up from her typing when Tony came in, and when he paused at the door, she motioned him forward.

"Can I help you?"

"I want to see Mr. Lawson."

"And it's about what?"

"My mother."

"What about your mother?"

"She's in jail."

"For what?"

"Murder, I reckon."

"What's her name?"

"Lucinda Pettyjohn."

"Oh, yes. Read about that. And what's your name?"

"Tony Pettyjohn."

"Just have a seat, Mr. Pettyjohn." She nodded toward one of the empty chairs.

He sat among the others who were dozing or reading magazines, trimming their fingernails, or staring at the floor. After a while, the door on the other side of the file room opened and a tall, silver-haired man wearing horn-rimmed glasses and a white shirt with a bow tie stood imperiously in the door without coming out. He looked to be about sixty and had a pear-shaped body, heavy around the middle, smaller at the shoulders. His long face fell away to a weak chin with a wattle, which merged into his neck. His gray hair, thinning on the sides, was combed back above a big forehead. The thick lenses magnified his eyes so that they filled the glasses.

THE LOOM FIXER

He ushered a small scruffy man out and in a booming voice said, "I'll see you in Conway next Thursday. Make sure you're on time and dressed in the best you got, and I'll need this before I go in there with you." He handed the man a slip of paper. "OK?"

The man looked at the paper and shook his head slowly from side to side then shuffled toward the door.

Lawson pointed toward another seated client and motioned him into his office. Tony waited for two more hours with several people who had come in after him being invited into the office before him. Finally, with it being almost dark and the waiting room empty except for Tony and one other person, Lawson stood in his door, looked down at a piece of paper the receptionist had handed him, and motioned for Tony to come in. He pointed at a chair and went behind a desk piled high with files and papers and a scattering of coffee cups. A flag of South Carolina was in one corner and the US flag in another. Diplomas hung on the wall together with licenses and pictures of Lawson with politicians alive and dead. The color of the place was sepia with dust and cobwebs everywhere. Only the area in the center of the desk appeared to be used.

Lawson leaned back and put one foot on the edge of the desk. He looked down at longish fingernails on one hand and said, "You might have noticed that I didn't take people in the order that they came in the door."

Tony nodded his head.

"Reason for that is that I been doing this long enough to be able to look over a crowd of people and tell which ones have money, which ones don't, and which ones will git it if they don't have it. That's the reason you're almost the last person coming in here." He looked intently at Tony, took a small knife from his pocket, and ran the blade underneath the nails on his left hand, and then he inspected what was on the blade and wiped in on a file on his desk. "Was I right or wrong?"

Tony looked down at his lap and felt his face begin to burn.

Before he could speak, Lawson went on. "You know why I let you in here even though I knew you didn't have any money?"

Tony shook his head.

"Because of the nature of your matter. Your mama is in big trouble, and it's going to be a big thing around these parts. Fairly young, attractive woman guns down a none too popular semi-thug a lot of people would just as soon have dead. It could get a lot of press. And when that happens, more clients follow. I reckon I've done fifty murder trials. Half of the defendants walked. That's pretty damn good. The DA knows me. I'm worth a lot of fee." He paused again, looking at Tony and down at his nails again. "How much money do you have? And what else have you got or could get?"

"Two hundred dollars. And I've got a car."

With this, Lawson looked up at the ceiling and smiled. "What kind of car?"

"A '49 Ford."

"Shit, son, that wouldn't get you through the arraignment, but bring the car here tomorrow so I can see it."

"Does this mean you'll take the case?"

"Hell, no! I need to think about it and talk to your mother. Just bring it around. How old's your mother? Like to see what she looks like up close."

"What difference does that make?"

A small smile played at the corner of Lawson's mouth. "It makes a difference to the judge, the jury, and me. You bring that car on around. I'll try to see your mother tomorrow. We can talk more after that. Out is that way." He pointed to the door.

. . .

Tony got to the jail at ten o'clock. The deputy at the desk told him that visiting hours started at eleven and lasted for an hour. He was told to wait in a dirty room with two long benches along the wall. It was crowded with others waiting, dozing, or staring at the grimy walls. Children sniffled and chased each other over stretched-out legs. Mothers and grandmothers scolded and snatched at them. The room had an odor of sweat, dirt, and misery. The benches were tattooed with carved and scratched messages and names: *judge carter sucks*, *lawyer moore is a lyin bastard*, *tommy & rita*, too many *fuck yous* to be counted.

Eleven o'clock came, and a bailiff began to call names and let them in. The room was half full when he heard his name called. Eyes turned to him, and there was a small murmur. He followed the man through a dismal corridor. They came to a room that had six cubicles enclosed in thick plexiglass so that everything could be seen from the outside. There was a chair and a ledge with a telephone in front of a thicker plexiglass wall with an identical ledge, phone, and chair on the other side. The bailiff told him to take a seat. His mother would be brought in shortly.

A door opened in the room on the other side, and she shuffled in. It took him a moment to recognize her. She wore an orange jumpsuit with "prisoner" stenciled across the front; it could have fit someone three times her size. The cuffs were rolled up over a pair of white rubber slip-ons that were so big she had to slide her feet to keep them on. Then he saw she was wearing leg irons. Her blond hair was tangled and knotted; circles were under her eyes. The deputy unlocked her handcuffs so she could use the phone, indicated the chair, and left.

Just then, a deputy opened the door to his side and said, "You got ten minutes, son. I'll knock on the door when you got two minutes left."

"Hey, baby," she said and put her hand against the plexiglass, letting her sleeve fall back as she did, showing a thin forearm. His eyes burned, and he fought not to cry. "We don't have much time so we need to hurry."

"I'm gonna tell them it was me."

"Don't do that yet, baby."

"What else can we do? I don't want you in here. I saw a lawyer yesterday."

"What did he say? You didn't tell him what happened, did you?

"No. He only wanted to talk about money."

"How much?"

"He didn't say, but it's going to be more than we've got. Said this was going to be a famous case, like maybe he wanted it even if we didn't have enough money. Where did you run to?"

"They found me in Jacksonville, Florida. Damn, what a terrible place. Was there for five days before they sent me up here. I hated it so much I waived extradition." She cried slowly. "It's been awful, honey."

He looked at the purple circles under her eyes and her rough lips. "I'm taking my car for Lawson to look at this afternoon. I guess if he won't represent you, they'll give you another lawyer that they pick."

"It's hard for me to think right now, but don't tell him what happened. Let's wait and see how this works out."

There was a knock on the door.

"OK, Mom. I love you. I can't stand for you to be in here on account of me."

"I think it's on account of *me*, baby."

The deputy came and took her away.

. . .

Tony took the Ford to Lawson's office the next day. He waited for an hour with the other clients for Lawson to talk to him. All heads would lift when his door opened, all anxiously hoping it would be their turn. He was wearing a string tie and a loud red-checked sport coat and had a clipboard in his hand. He motioned for Tony to come outside with him.

"Where is it?" he asked.

"Around back in the lot."

Lawson did a slow tour around the car, making notes on a paper on the clipboard as he did. He grimaced each time he came to a dent or a scratch. He stooped and inspected the tires, measuring the tread with his finger. He stood and looked down at the clipboard, making a few calculations.

"Shit, boy. This clunker ain't worth more than a couple hundred dollars, if that. Is there a lien on it?"

Tony shook his head no.

"Well, I need to think long and hard about this. Gonna take a lot of time. I might get some money from the state if I can get the judge to rule her indigent."

"Rule her what?"

"Indigent. Means she's broke. State will pay for her lawyer, but it don't pay much. I'm not on that list. It's just mostly young lawyers or drunks, but I know the judge. I might be able to work something out. I need to talk to your mother. Need to see her. What's her name again?"

"Lucinda. Lucinda Pettyjohn."

"I'll try to get over there tomorrow. Got a little preliminary hearing for another murder trial today. Problem is if you get into these things—I mean, like your mother—you can't get out no matter how long it takes or how bad it gets. I'll decide after I see her."

. . .

The local newspaper and television stations ran stories every day about the killing of the local bar owner by his live-in girlfriend. The paper ran a picture of Lucinda taken several years earlier. She was slim and blond, wearing sunglasses and a tight T-shirt. There was a picture of her after the arrest with her hair tangled and her hands hiding her face. They discovered that she had worked as a dancer in a fancy men's club in the north part of the beach some years ago and had now nicknamed her the "Go-Go Killer." Several tabloids had sent reporters to interview her. They tried to talk to Tony, but he avoided them until one offered him $500 for a story. But the reporter managed to get so little out of Tony that he gave him only a hundred dollars.

Tony went back to the jail to see her after he met with Lawson. "Has he been here?" he asked.

"No. What did he say?"

"Wants to see you and talk before he decides, I guess."

"I need some better clothes and some makeup before he comes. They won't let me have the clothes, but I need the makeup and a good hairbrush. Can you get it? Like this afternoon and bring it to visiting hours tomorrow?"

"I guess. I don't know what to buy, and it'll use up money to pay for his fee."

"Just get the brush and some brown mascara and tell the lady in the store I'm blond and need makeup for a blonde. And get some pink lipstick. When you come tomorrow give it to the bailiff, and he'll bring it to me, I hope. I'm not gonna see Lawson until I have it."

"Why?"

"Baby, I've been around men for a long time and I know what works. Just do it."

On his way out, he passed through a line of TV camera people and reporters who shouted questions at him. Lawson was standing on the sidewalk. He had on a wide straw fedora so big it was almost an umbrella. He wore the string tie again. "Your mom's attracted quite a crowd," he said with a slight smile. "I'm gonna try and see her tomorrow."

"Maybe you better wait. She don't feel good today. Day after tomorrow might be better."

"She dope sick?"

"No. She don't do that stuff. Just doesn't feel good."

Lawson nodded his head still with the smile and walked toward his office.

• • •

Tony called Trish from Uncle Stan's. The phone was in the hall with doors opening to all the other rooms so he had to keep his voice low. Her mother answered, and when he asked for her, she paused as though she had to think about it. Finally she sighed and said, "Wait a minute."

After a long time, Trish came to the phone. Her voice was small. "Where are you? Why didn't you call sooner? I been worried to death."

"Myrtle Beach. Mom's in trouble with the law. She's in jail."

"We know. It's been in the papers up here."

There was a long silence. "She didn't do it."

She didn't respond.

"I've got to help her. Get her out. Do something."

"Mr. Striker saw Daddy in the mill two days ago. Said you been gone for a couple days and he can't hold your job much longer. Tony, come back. You've got a good start. Loom fixer's a good job, and Striker likes you. And what about *us*? I thought . . . I don't know what I thought."

Tony could hear Uncle Stan coughing on the porch and Aunt Bertie was shuffling in the kitchen. It seemed she shuffled louder the longer he talked.

"I've got to hang up. This is long distance, and I got to pay for it. Tell your dad to tell Mr. Striker I'm doing the best I can and I want my job. I miss you. I'm gonna come back just as soon as I can."

"Is that the best you can do? I *miss* you? A lot of guys up here want to go out with me. How long am I gonna have to wait for you to get serious?"

"I gotta go. Bye." And he put the receiver down carefully.

Aunt Bertie was in the kitchen.

"I'll pay for the call, Aunt Bertie. Just let me know how much it costs," he said as he went by her.

"Wait a minute before you slip out of here. We need to talk," she said. He leaned against the door jamb and looked at her. "We need to rent that room you're in. We don't have all that much money. Any idea how much longer you'll be here?"

"I'm gonna pay you."

She waved her hand in dismissal.

"I should know in the next couple days how much longer. They ain't gonna give her bail since she ran once already. So she'll be there until the trial or unless something else happens. Soon as we find out when the trial is I'm going back to my job. We need the money. I'll come down on the weekends. All depends on Lawson. If he decides not to take the case, then it's a different story."

"I don't know why he'd want the case," she said.

"Maybe he sees it as a way to get his name out or something. I don't know."

"Hummph! Your mama can still be a good-looking woman if she gets cleaned up. What is she now, thirty-six? The man has a reputation, you know, and not only with being able to spring criminals. He's a real ladies' man. You be careful what the two of you are getting into with him."

He didn't answer her. He went to the local drug store to buy a hairbrush, pink lipstick, and the other things Lucinda had asked for, then he delivered them to one of the bailiffs and asked that they be taken to his mother.

• • •

THE LOOM FIXER

When Tony went at visiting hours the next day, they wouldn't let him in. "Already had a visitor today. Still in there. She can't see no one else until tomorrow."

"Who's seeing her?"

The bailiff looked down at a clipboard. "Lawyer Lawson," he said with a smile.

Tony waited outside the jail. An hour passed, and still Lawson had not come out. Finally, he came out swinging his briefcase, smiling and whistling under the straw hat. He was wearing a bright red bow tie this time. Tony stood as he approached, but a reporter who had been waiting outside stopped Lawson first and they talked while Tony waited on the sidewalk. Lawson patted the woman on the shoulder as she left, scribbling on a pad. "Anytime, you hear? Anytime." Then he turned to Tony.

"You see my mother?" he asked.

"Oh, yeah. I did."

"How come you were in there so long and I only get to stay fifteen minutes?"

"I'm a lawyer and the deputies know me. I give 'em all a little something at Christmas."

"Are you going to take the case?"

"I reckon I might. She looks pretty good to have been through all she's been through. Mighty nice."

"Is that yes or no?"

"Damn, sonny, you're demanding." He took a cigarette out of his shirt pocket and lit it with a silver lighter then blew a cloud of smoke in the air. "Yeah, I'm gonna take the case. Her prelim is tomorrow morning."

"What's that?"

"Where they charge her and she enters a plea of not guilty and I tell 'em I represent her."

Tony was silent for a moment. "What about the money?"

"Oh, we'll work something out. Don't worry about it for right now. I'm thinking since Judge Porcher is on the bench tomorrow I got a good chance of getting her out on bail."

"Why would Judge whatever-his-name-is do you a favor and set bail for her? Don't that cost money too?"

Lawson dropped the butt on the sidewalk and ground it out with his black-and-white shoe. "You pronounce the name 'Puh-shay.' It's Huguenot, and, son, you're worrying too much right now. Let's take one thing at a time. Right now, you go on home and rest up. Tomorrow will be a big day. Hearings start at ten o'clock. Don't know where we'll be on the calendar. You need to see about getting your mama a place to stay if she gets out. Any idea where?"

"Her aunt and uncle live in town."

"Well, now that's a start."

Tony could almost see Aunt Bertie's face when he presented her with this news.

• • •

Court opened at nine o'clock. Tony hadn't been in a courtroom in a long time. It was the same as he remembered it from home: dirty smelling, crying children, filthy benches, and miserable people. The dirt and filth all disappeared at

THE LOOM FIXER

the rail separating the common people from the lawyers and court staff. On the other side of it, there was order, and things were clean with clerks in nice dresses busily making notes in files and lawyers in suits and ties whispering to one another and smirking over some private joke.

He took a seat as close to the front as he could. Lawson wasn't there.

A bailiff entered through a side door and said in a loud voice, "All rise. Hear ye, hear ye, the circuit court for the county of Horry is now in session, Judge Porter Porcher presiding."

The judge swung in with robes swishing, climbed the stairs to the bench, stood for a second peering over the crowd, and sat down. He was a diminutive man with a sharp face, his dark hair parted severely and shiny with some type of hair dressing. He wore reading glasses and had a stern look on his face. He looked down at a notebook before him.

"This is the criminal session of the circuit court for this county," he began in a high-pitched voice. "Today we will have arraignments and motions. Mr. District Attorney, you may call the calendar and call it for the week."

The district attorney stood with the calendar in his hand. He was a tall, skinny man with thinning hair, most of it brought over from the side of his head to cover the balding area on top. His round face had a disgruntled look about it. He wore steel-rimmed glasses that glinted when they caught the light. His name was Toy Ravenel, also a time-honored South Carolina Huguenot name. He looked briefly around the room and said, "Your Honor, we have three arraignments:

Lucinda Pettyjohn, Elwood Smith, and Jose Carpenter. They'll be brought in when we begin."

The judge nodded, and the DA began to call the remainder of the calendar. After each name was called, an attorney responded or there was silence. If there was no response, the matter was carried over to next term. It was a long calendar, and with the pauses and brief exchanges between the parties, it seemed to take forever, and Lawson was still not there. Finally, it came to an end.

The judge looked up from over his reading glasses way down on his nose. "All right, let's do the arraignments. Bring 'em in, Mr. Bailiff."

At that moment Lawson came sweeping in from the back. He pushed through the gate at the bar, surveyed the courtroom with a smile, ran a hand through his hair, and took a seat as though the place belonged to him.

The DA stood again and motioned for the bailiff to bring in the prisoners for arraignment. Tony's mom shuffled in wearing leg irons, handcuffs, and the same orange jumpsuit she had worn since the first day he had seen her. But today she looked much different. Her blond hair was combed and fell in neat waves around her neck. She wore makeup and the pink lipstick he had got for her. She looked fresh and not hungover, as attractive to men as she always had been, he thought uneasily. Heads turned, and a murmur went through the onlookers.

"This is case number 15-07985, the State of *South Carolina versus Lucinda Marie* Pettyjohn. The charge is a violation of South Carolina Criminal Code 14-02, murder." Ravenel paused and looked over his shoulder toward the lawyers seated in the wooden chairs behind the two tables before the bench. "Is the defendant represented by counsel?"

Lawson was immediately on his feet behind defense counsel's table. "Your Honor, Sidney Lawson of the South Carolina and Horry County Bar," he said in a booming voice. "I represent the defendant."

This all seemed like some kind of theater to Tony, as though it were planned well in advance. He and the spectators behind the bar were watching a play that they could not alter or affect.

The judge pushed his reading glasses up on his nose. "Stand up, Mrs. Pettyjohn." His mother slowly rose and looked intently at the judge. "How do you plead to this charge, Mrs. Pettyjohn?"

She looked over at Lawson and then said in a small but clear voice that could be heard all over the now quiet courtroom, "I plead not guilty."

"Madam clerk, let the record indicate that the defendant is represented by counsel and that she has entered a plea of not guilty. We now need to proceed with setting this case for trial. Perhaps this would be better suited to be done in chambers. That suit you, gentlemen?" He looked from the DA to Lawson.

"The State agrees to that," the DA responded.

"The defendant also agrees to that, but Your Honor, we would like to be heard as to the matter of bail."

"We can do that right now, Mr. Lawson. You may proceed."

Lawson turned slowly and looked at his client. "Your Honor, my client is a single mother from North Carolina. She has raised two boys without the benefit of a father. One of them who was an honor student in high school and now works as a loom fixer in the mill there is here in the courtroom to support her." He turned to look over the crowd for Tony. When he spotted him, he motioned for him to stand.

Tony blushed and hesitantly stood amazed at the outright lie Lawson told about him being an honor student. His fellow onlookers murmured again, some basking in their proximity to stardom. He sat down quickly.

Lawson spoke again. "My client has lived in our community for in excess of a year. She was caught in an abusive relationship with the person who will be identified as the deceased in this matter."

At this point, the DA jumped to his feet. "Your Honor, I hadn't planned to try this case this morning. What we are trying to determine at this point is whether the defendant is entitled to bail and whether she is at risk to flee the jurisdiction, and from the fact that she left after the murder, it is highly probable—"

"I object to characterizing this as a murder at this time," Lawson, flushed and stuttering, interrupted.

"Oh, Jesus, Lawson. What do you want me to call it?" The DA shook his head. "All right then, let's just say that his client lit out for Florida after the dead body was found behind the trailer where she lived with the deceased, which resulted in her being charged with murder, and if that ain't evidence that she's a flight risk, then I don't know what is."

Lawson looked down and shook his head back and forth. "May I continue, Your Honor?"

"Please go on, Mr. Lawson, remembering that there are other matters to come before the court this morning besides this." Looking at the DA, he added, "Let's cut down on the histrionics, both of you, please."

"As I was saying, the defendant has no prior record of arrest or involvement with the law except for minor traffic offenses. Other than that she has lived, if not an exemplary life, then at least one that was a combination of raising children, working, and doing the best she could. She regularly attended church near where she lived. She has an aunt and uncle who live here in Myrtle Beach. She can stay there while the trial is pending, and it would certainly make it easier to prepare her defense. And in addition to those matters, for all the State knows, my client went to Florida on a vacation and didn't even know there was a body behind that trailer. We ask that the bond be set at an amount that she has a reasonable chance to make. Thank you."

"Your Honor," Ravenel began, "this defendant is charged with capital murder and disappeared immediately after the event and was found three hundred miles away in Florida and, as Mr. Lawson says, for all we know, she might have been trying to get to Mexico. And her record is not as pristine as Mr. Lawson has represented. I see a number of convictions for drug use and one for solicitation. I think nothing more needs to be said except that she should be denied any bail at all. Thank you." He sat down and turned to another file, apparently confident that the matter was settled.

Judge Porcher looked down at his book and seemed to study it for a while. Then he looked up at the dingy ceiling. Finally he turned his gaze to the lawyers. "Ever now and then in your career, you see matters come up that look a lot more important than they turn out being. I think this may be one of those cases. The defendant, while charged with a heinous"—seeming to like the sound of the word, he repeated it—"a heinous crime, seems to otherwise be nonthreatening in appearance and reputation."

At this, the DA slowly rose with an expression of disbelief on his face.

"For that reason, I am going to set this defendant's bond at twenty-five thousand dollars."

"Judge Porcher," Ravenel said in a choked voice, "this woman is charged with murder and has already fled the jurisdiction once. The people object. This bond is woefully inappropriate." At this, he slammed a file down on the prosecution's table, causing the water pitcher and glasses to jump and rattle.

Judge Porcher's face turned red. He rapped his gavel twice and, glaring at the DA, said, "Mr. District Attorney, don't forget where you are and whose court you're in. I can hold you in contempt as easily as I can anyone else. I suggest you calm down."

The DA put both hands on the table and muttered something under his breath.

"What did you say?" Porcher asked.

"I said I'm sure you're right, Your Honor."

"Good. We need to move on. Will there be any pretrial motions that either of you know of at this time?"

"Your Honor, the defendant will be making a motion to dismiss this case for lack of evidence in the very near future," Lawson said.

"The State welcomes the opportunity to argue the motion, Your Honor," Ravenel retorted.

"Very well, gentlemen. Is there anything else we need to discuss about this case at this time?"

Both answered in the negative.

"Then, Mr. DA, call your next case. No, wait. Let's take a fifteen-minute recess." Judge Porcher dismounted from his elevated bench and disappeared through a door to the side. Before he had entered the door, the mass of onlookers began a loud chatter and rose to stretch their legs or go outside for fresh air or to smoke, marveling at what they had witnessed.

"Snake Lawson did it ag'in. Prob'ly tappin' it as well as gittin' paid by the state," one man said to another as they moved out. He smirked at Tony as he passed.

After the bailiffs had taken Lucinda back to the jail, Lawson stood looking over the bar and motioned to Tony to come forward. He had a triumphant expression. He was wearing a dark striped suit, solid red tie, and a pair of snakeskin cowboy boots that added to his already considerable height—modest compared to his normal dress. Some of the audience came close and spoke to him, and he acknowledged the greetings almost regally. He ignored most of them to talk to a tall man wearing a ten-gallon hat and a badge and uniform. "Good to see you, Rowdy. How you been keeping?" Lawson said. His name was Clarence Brown, known to all as "Rowdy" for his exploits in earlier times. He was the sheriff of the county and had been a pretty good halfback on the state university football team fifteen years ago with a reputation for drinking and partying. He'd had one game against the school's biggest and most bitter rival where he had run back a punt with only seconds left to win the game. Voters remembered it long enough to get him elected sheriff after a short pro career. The sheriff leaned in and whispered something to Lawson then he moved off with the other spectators, mingling among them and shaking hands.

When they were finally alone, Lawson asked, "Do you understand what just happened?"

Tony shook his head.

"Well, I just hung the moon for your mama. Normally she would have been denied any bail, but for me, ole Porcher set it low enough for you to pay it."

"Twenty-five thousand is too much for us to pay." Tony said.

"Hell, I couldn't get him to make it any lower. He's got to get reelected. I gave a lot to his campaign last time, but he can't set it at *no* bond."

"I can't pay that."

THE LOOM FIXER

"No, son. You don't have to pay that much. We get a bondsman, and he'll charge you ten per cent of that, just twenty-five hundred."

"I can't pay that either."

Lawson rolled his eyes. "How much can you pay?"

"I told you. I've got five hundred that I was gonna give to you for part of your fee."

"Son, that five hundred dollars ain't gonna come close to paying even a little of the fee I would normally charge for a case like this." He thought for a moment. "OK. I know a bondsman, Gabe Lewis, who owes me a bunch of favors. I've sent him a lot of cases. I can talk to him and see if he'll bond your mama for less."

"I don't understand. Why are you doing this for Mama?"

Lawson smiled slightly. "Let's just say I feel it's my duty to take cases ever now and then where people can't pay my usual fee. And I like your ma."

. . .

Tony saw Lucinda at visiting hours that afternoon.

"Is he gonna get me out of here?" she asked.

"Don't know. Says he knows a bondsman who owes him a favor and maybe we'll only have to come up with five hundred dollars or something to pay your bond. He said he'd know later today." He stared through the plexiglass at her for a long time. "I don't understand," he said. "Why does he want to do anything special for you? He brags about all the big cases that he's won and all the big fees he gets. What makes you different?"

She looked away. "He's a middle-aged man who wonders whether he can still attract younger women. And if he attracts them, can he satisfy them? And I guess there's other reasons. Publicity. I don't know. You don't understand these things yet. Seems like women always stuck to you, but you didn't care whether they did or not." She looked at him and smiled. "What's that girl's name you were seeing? Whatever happened to her?"

"Trish."

"Yeah, Trish. She was after you like a duck on a June bug, but I never thought you cared one way or the other. You still seein' her?"

"Yeah. She wants us to get married. I didn't tell you this, but they moved me to loom fixer at the mill. I was doin' pretty good till this happened."

She began to cry. "Oh, baby. I'm so sorry. You go back there right now. This is working out good for you. They're totally convinced that I did this. Aren't even considering any other possibilities. Show you how stupid cops and sheriffs can be. Worst that's going to happen here is that I go to jail for some time. I know it won't be for life or anything like that."

"I can't leave you here alone with these people."

"I've been pretty much alone with people like this all my life. Truth be told, I guess I'm one of them. It's the best way. Get out of here and they won't think of you again. Hang around and something might go wrong."

. . .

The next few days were filled with trying to convince Aunt Bertie to let Lucinda stay in her house until the trial. She didn't want the newspaper or TV people hanging out in front all the time. Where was the money for rent to come from? Tony assured her that he and Grandma would send it.

A bondsman that Lawson referred to as Stowe agreed to provide the bond for five hundred dollars, almost all Tony had. Stowe was a grizzled little black man who wore a pork pie hat even indoors. He didn't have an office, but Lawson told Tony where to find him: a barbeque place in town in the third booth on the right. That was his office. He was affable, usually smiling. Tony always thought bondsmen were scary people who came after their clients who ran with a vengeance and brought them back so that they lost no money. But Stowe was different, not menacing, and he didn't look like he could catch a stray dog. They made the deal, and that afternoon, he picked Lucinda up and took her to Aunt Bertie's and Uncle Stan's.

It took much explaining over all the hacks and coughs to make Uncle Stan understand who she was and why she was there. "*Oh*, Gaynelle's girl. Haven't seen you since you were a teenager and you used to come down here for the week of the Fourth when the mill stood." He gasped for air between coughs. Then he took a deep breath and another drag on his cigarette. "Gaynelle still married to that dried-up little turd?"

"Stanley, watch your language."

"Do you fish, Linda Sue?"

"Stanley, it's Lucinda, and I'm sure she ain't interested in fishing," Bertie said and motioned to Lucinda for them to go into the kitchen where they could talk.

When they were alone, his mother took Tony's hand and looked intently at him. "You go on home now. There's nothing more you can do here, and the further away from here you get, the better off you are. They haven't even thought about you, can't connect you up to this anyway. So go."

"I don't want to leave you alone down here with nobody but the lawyer," he said.

"You go back to Trish and that job you need. I can take care of myself. My life is already pretty much a wreck. Yours is just starting. Have you got enough money for gas to get back?"

He nodded his head.

"Then go."

He went to the basement bedroom, put his clothes into his cheap plastic bag, and got in the Ford.

Before he went north, he stopped at Lawson's office and waited for two hours to see him. When he finally was admitted into the dingy room, Lawson was leaning back in his chair, hands behind his head, smiling at the ceiling. "What can I do for you *now*?" he asked.

"I'm leaving. When will the trial be?"

"Don't know that yet, son, but I'll be sure and let you know in plenty of time for you to get down here and help. I want Judge Porcher to hear this case. I'll want you to testify as to what you saw the deceased did to your mother, what he said. All that."

"What do I do about your fee?"

Lawson put his feet down, took a business card from his desk drawer, and handed it to Tony over the desk. "You send as much money as you can to this address every month." He smiled. "You might be sending it for the rest of your life."

The secretary stuck her head in the door. "Your wife's on the phone."

"Tell her I'm busy."

"Already done that three times. Says she has to talk to you."

"Shit. OK, Mr. Pettyjohn, you need to get out of here. Have a safe trip."

He headed north for home.

• • •

Tony was sure they would have given up his room at the boarding house, since he paid by the week and hadn't paid for some time, so he found an empty parking place outside the mill and fell asleep in the car in the dim light of the lint-covered windows, listening to the steady muffled chatter of the looms inside until it was time for his shift to start, hoping he still had a job.

He walked in with the shift change and worked his way to No. Three Weave Room. When he walked in, Mr. Striker was standing by the office cubicle. He smiled when he saw Tony and came to him with his hand extended.

Tony took it, and Striker put his arm around his shoulder. "I'm glad you're back, son."

Tony coughed and looked down feeling his face get red. Then he stiffened, nodded, and said, "I want to go to work now."

"Sure," Striker said and pointed to the rows and rows of looms with weavers bent over them in the dim air clouded with lint. "It's waiting for you."

After work he went by to see Mrs. Overcash to ask about his old room in the boarding house. It was open, then he went to see Trish. Instead of inviting him in, she insisted that they go out.

She asked, "Have you thought about what I said on the phone?"

"I can't remember."

"I said other guys want to go out with me and I don't know where we stand." She paused, but he said nothing. "Well?"

"Trish, there's a lot I got on my mind right now."

"I got a lot on my mind, too, and *us* is one of them. Why don't you drive over to the quarry and we can talk instead of just driving around?"

"Where's that?"

"It's where people go to park and make out. You never been there? Sometimes I think you're on another planet or something, Tony."

He followed her directions off the paved road eventually taking a gravel path into some woods until they came to what looked like a huge pit surrounded by jagged teeth of rocks, ghostly pale in the moonlight. Several hundred feet below the edge was a lake covering several acres, the water smooth in the faint light. He parked, and she pulled him roughly to her almost as soon as they stopped.

She took his hand, put it on her breast, then took her mouth off his. "Don't you want me?"

"Sure I do," he whispered.

"Then do something. Put your hand down there. I don't understand you." She was leaning against the passenger-side door, one leg up on the seat, the other spread on the floor. Hair hung over her forehead, her face dim in the moonlight, her eyes dark pits. Then she said, "That's right, ohhh, that's better. Yes." She unbuckled his belt and put her hand on his crotch. She stroked him slowly. "Don't get too excited. I want this to last." She struggled to yank off her panties, slid back down on the seat, and opened up her legs again. "Come here," she said, her voice deep, and he did what she asked.

• • •

For a few days, he lived his life as it appeared that fate had decided he should: going to work, getting stopped looms working again, seeing Trish almost every evening. It became a routine, pleasant, but always on the edge of consciousness there was Lucinda, what he had done, and him wondering how it would be resolved. She was in trouble for what he had done and was willing to protect him, and it gnawed at him. It wouldn't let him completely enjoy anything without worming itself into his mind.

One Friday night, he took Trish to the Hav-a-Burger restaurant, a place on the highway that was usually full of high school kids. But there were also a few people like them, remembering how it had been before graduation and real life caught up with them. After they ordered, Trish put her elbows on the table, rested her chin on her hands, and stared at him.

"What?" he asked.

"I'm thinking about us. Where we're headed."

"What do you mean?"

"Well, is this what it's going to be like all the time?" She paused. "Are we ever going to get married?"

He looked down at the table.

"I mean, we could get married, and I make good money. We could rent one of the nice little houses near GI Town, you know, that little section the mill built after the war for the guys who came back. They're little houses. We could afford that. Or are you not thinking like that? What *are* you thinking?"

"I don't know. I'm thinking about Mom. I think about it all the time."

"I know you do. But you can't let her take up all your life. What about me? What about us?"

"I ain't thought that far. It's hard. You don't know. There's a lot of stuff you don't know about me."

"Like what?"

He was silent.

"I don't care about the other stuff. You haven't shot anybody in the face that I know of. I just want a life for us." She began to cry quietly.

He reached across the table and took her hand. "Don't do that. Please," he said.

"We could go to Rock Hill and get married quick." She sniffed.

He froze at this, not knowing what to say, his eyes narrow, his mouth a hard line.

"Why would we go to Rock Hill?" he asked. "That is, I mean if we was to do this."

"Cause my daddy wouldn't let us do a regular wedding. We'd have to run off to do it."

"Why? I thought your dad liked me."

"It's not that he doesn't like you." The waitress brought their hamburgers. Trish asked her to bring a bottle of ketchup for the French fries. "He says you have a history."

"What's that mean?"

She picked up the fries one by one and dipped them in a blob of ketchup before eating them. "He knows about your mom, like everybody else in town. Knows what she was like before all that happened at the beach. He knows you were in the training school."

"That was a long time ago."

"He says you never had a dad either. And he knows your grandpa."

He looked down at his untouched food while she continued to push her food around on her plate," then he said, "I never been close to a lot of people. Never felt anything like *love* that they talk about in the movies. My mom is the closest thing I've ever come to caring about something." He paused thinking it was not what he wanted to say. "But I feel good with you. I feel like maybe I belong with you." Then he stopped. "But I ain't going to Rock Hill. I just can't do that now with mom and all." He hesitated. "Plus, I ain't had time to think it all through. Maybe you can do that."

She sniffled all the way back to her house. He walked her to the door and left without going in. She stood on the steps and watched him drive away.

• • •

The trial was to start in mid-March. Until then, Tony worked, and after a lapse of several weeks following the Hav-a-Burger evening, he started seeing Trish again. There was no more mention of Rock Hill or getting married. He talked to Lucinda at least once a week, but she discouraged him from coming to see her. He was surprised sometime in February when Aunt Bertie called to ask if he knew where his mother was.

"Thought she was living with you?"

"She left about a week ago without saying anything. Took her clothes and left in the night. I thought she would have told you where she was going."

He told her he'd find out and let her know, and they hung up. He called the number he had for her, but that was Bertie's number, so he called Lawson's office and asked that Lawson call him as soon as he could. But instead of Lawson, Lucinda called him late in the day. He had to talk on the common phone in the hall at the boarding house.

"Aunt Bertie says you ain't living there anymore."

"Baby, I meant to tell you, but I just haven't had time. I couldn't stay there anymore. They were always watching me, and I just had to move out."

"Where are you living?"

There was a pause. "I'm staying at the Howard Johnson's out on the highway."

"Where you getting the money to do that?"

"Lawyer Lawson says I'm going to be able to sell this story, and he's lending me the money. I can pay him back later."

"Mama—" he started.

"I know, I know—"

"You don't know," he interrupted. "What else are you doing for him? He's a shit, Mama. A shit."

But she had hung up. He slammed the phone down on its cradle.

Tony visited her once before the trial started but it was awkward. She didn't want him there. "They don't have any reason to suspect you, honey, so the further you are from here, the better off you are."

But he knew the real reason was she understood how much he disliked Lawson and how it grated on him to see her around him. So he waited for the trial to start before he went down there again.

• • •

It was warm the second week in March with trees starting to bud and flowers coming up. Shirtsleeve weather. Tony got permission to leave work for a week. Mr. Striker knew about his mother, so he agreed to cover for him. Tony felt like he had bothered Bertie and Stan enough, so he got a room in a cheap motel out on the highway. On Monday morning, he went to court with the disheveled crowd of defendants, witnesses, and relatives. The day was reserved for calling the calendar and arranging the schedule for the balance of the week. It droned on and on, the assistant district attorney calling the names of defendants, asking about whether or not they had a lawyer, and having summons issued for the ones who did not show up. Midmorning, the judge called a recess.

Tony got up to stretch his legs and went out front to the lawn where others had gone to smoke and gossip. He leaned up against a tree and overheard conversations.

"I heard Lawson was taking out his fee with the Pettyjohn girl in the sack."

Laughter. Snickering.

"Knew that would happen sooner or later. Old Snake Lawson. Gotta hand it to him."

Tony flushed and turned to the men but stopped. For now, he would abide the insult. He had done it all his life with her. People began to shuffle back inside. The assistant district attorney had turned the proceedings over to her boss, a change causing murmuring in the crowd.

The judge gaveled the proceedings back into order. "Please proceed, Mr. District Attorney."

"Thank you, Your Honor." The DA looked down dramatically at the papers in front of him and turned. The crowd quietened. "First on the calendar is *State versus Pettyjohn*, which we are prepared to try at this time. The defendant has entered a plea of not guilty and is represented by Attorney Lawson."

Porcher turned to Lawson, who stood at the defense table with Lucinda by his side.

"Are you ready to proceed, Mr. Lawson?"

"We are, Your Honor."

Tony was surprised at how his mother looked. She was dressed in a plain dark blue suit and a pair of flat black shoes. No earrings or other jewelry. Her blond hair was pulled back in a slight bun, and she wore only the slightest gloss of lipstick. She stood with her head slightly bowed.

Judge Porcher looked over his reading glasses toward Lucinda and Lawson, then he turned to Ravenel. "Please proceed, Mr. DA."

Then began the long process of picking the jurors. The pool sat in the jury box—all seats were filled. No one seemed to want to miss the opportunity to hear this case. It promised to have everything. There was an equal number of men and women in the pool. Most of the women prospects looked like housewives, plainly dressed and seemingly churchgoers, but there were two younger-looking women who looked like they might work "outside the home," the phrase used by Lawson and the DA as they questioned each one. The men, for the most part, looked like farmers or mill hands. They were dressed in overalls; one had a toothpick in the corner of his mouth. Several looked like they were professional jurors, maybe picked by the bailiff if someone hadn't shown up.

Tony had a seat immediately behind the defendant's table so he could hear some of what Lawson whispered back and forth to Lucinda as each potential juror was examined. During the period when Lawson was asking general questions to all the jurors, he asked the panel if any of them would think that an accused who did not testify would be admitting guilt in some way. They all answered no. He told Lucinda that he had asked this question to pique the jury's interest, to let them think about what might happen during the trial and speculate among themselves, as he knew they would.

The first female juror, who looked unlike a housewife, brought intense attention from both Lawson and the DA.

"Miss . . . or is it Mrs. Campbell?" he asked.

"It's Mrs.," she replied.

"So, Mrs. Campbell, you're married?"

"I am."

"And do you work outside the home?"

"I work at First Bank."

"And what do you do for them?"

"I'm a teller." She was tall, perhaps forty, and dressed in a gray suit. Her hair was brown, shoulder length with a slight curl. She was composed.

"And what does your husband do for a living?"

"He's a long-haul truck driver." She paused. "He lives in Maryland. We're separated."

"I see."

And so the examination continued through how many children she had. Two. And they lived with her and were in grade school. Did she know either the defendant or the deceased? Did she know the DA or anyone connected with the case? She didn't. Had she ever been in court before? She had. Her divorce had taken a long time. Could she serve on this jury impartially? She could.

Lawson bent over to consult with Lucinda. "I like her," he whispered loud enough for Tony to hear. "I checked in the clerk's office. Her ex has a couple convictions for assault on a female. Probably her. What do you think?"

She nodded agreement.

"DA won't like her cause of the divorce, but he may be in a box because he's used all his peremptory challenges." Lucinda looked puzzled. "He can only challenge a few witnesses without having a cause for the challenge, and he's used his, and there's no reason he can show this witness might be prejudiced."

The DA passed her. Eleven jurors had been picked. There were two other women besides Mrs. Campbell who were unthreatening housewives. Among the eight men jurors, who were mostly farmers or mill workers, several had keen eyes for Lucinda, but Lawson didn't know whether this was good or bad for their chances. There was one final juror to be picked among three candidates. Lawson knew one of them to be a part-time preacher in a nondenominational church. He definitely didn't want him on the jury. One was a man who had been on the other side of a divorce proceeding in which Lawson had represented the wife and could be challenged for cause. So their choices were the preacher or the wizened little man Lawson now began to examine. The man slumped slightly in his chair and propped his chin in his hand, resting his arm on the chair.

"Mr. Boyce, how are you this morning?" Lawson asked in his most unctuous voice.

"Ok, I reckon," Boyce responded in a low voice, almost inaudible.

"I'm an old guy, Mr. Boyce, and don't hear so good, so you'll need to speak up some."

Mr. Boyce nodded his head. He had been a weaver in a local cotton mill. He had worked there for forty years and was now retired. He didn't know the defendant but had seen the deceased because he occasionally went to the bar he owned but had never spoken to him.

This gave Lawson pause. "How many times a week would you go to that bar?"

"Didn't go ever week. I'd go maybe twice a month."

"And you never had occasion to speak to the deceased, Sonny Murphy?"

"Nope."

They went through the other questions without uncovering anything serious. That Boyce visited the Fish Hook was unsettling, but Boyce was better than the preacher or the other man, so Lawson approved him and hoped the DA would also. It made no difference because the DA had sent Boyce's brother away for larceny ten years ago, so the DA challenged him for cause. It left the preacher and then the two alternate jurors they would have to turn to if the preacher was challenged, but Lawson had no reason to challenge him, and he had no peremptory challenges left, so they took the preacher.

. . .

The wait for the restless audience was finally about to be over after two days of jury picking. At last, they were going to hear the lurid details of the crime.

Judge Porcher looked up from his papers. "Mr. DA, do you wish to waive opening arguments?"

"No, Your Honor. Although we customarily waive, in this instance, Mr. Lawson has informed me that he wishes to make opening, so I will also."

"Then please proceed."

The DA stood and walked slowly to the front of the jury box, head down, seeming to ponder what he was about to say. The jurors, still fresh, all followed his movements attentively.

"Ladies and gentlemen of the jury, this case is simple. Sonny Murphy, the deceased, lived in a trailer behind the Fish Hook Bar and Grill with the accused, Lucinda Pettyjohn. She had lived with him for several months and was unemployed. On the afternoon of May 15th, 1961, the State will prove that the accused, Lucinda Pettyjohn, maliciously and with premeditation shot Sonny Murphy to death outside the trailer they lived in, dragged the body behind the trailer, then fled the state to escape the law and was caught in Florida and returned here for prosecution." He paused and looked up at the ceiling. "You will hear testimony from the state medical examiner's office with regard to the cause of death. You will hear testimony from the sheriff who was first on the scene to investigate. You will hear testimony from employees of the Fish Hook with regard to arguments between the deceased and the accused. All of these things will convince you of the accused's guilt, for which she should receive the maximum penalty prescribed by law: death."

The jurors looked gravely at Lucinda.

"This is a simple case, and without going on and on, I'm sure you will hear this evidence and do your duty. Thank you." He returned to his seat at the State's table.

Lawson rose slowly with a wide grin on his face, shaking his head from side to side. He slowly strutted to a position in front of the jury box, put one hand on the rail, and said, "The DA is completely right about this case being simple, and the reason he didn't go on and on about the facts is that he doesn't have any facts." He laughed and surveyed the jurors, slowly giving them the benefit of his good humor. He pushed away from the rail and walked slowly toward the defense table. "Ladies and gentlemen of the jury, what the uncontroverted facts in this case will show is that on the afternoon of May 15th of this year the deceased, Sonny Murphy, was found dead of multiple gunshot wounds behind a trailer where he lived with the accused, Lucinda Pettyjohn."

Here he stopped and put his hand in a fatherly gesture on Lucinda's shoulder then turned and walked back toward the jury. "Several employees in the Fish Hook heard loud noises from the direction of the trailer, but they were busy and thought it could have been a truck or car backfiring from the highway in front. At some time in the afternoon, it was necessary for one of them to talk to the deceased, so Mr. Black, a bartender, went to the trailer to find him. When he got there, the door to the trailer was open, and no one was there. On his way out of the trailer, he noticed what looked like blood on the ground near the left of the front door. He didn't stop at that time to inspect it further and went back inside thinking he would see the deceased later. After the passage of some amount of time, another employee, the bookkeeper, Ms. Dorner, also went to the trailer to look for him. Black had alerted her that he had seen what looked like blood on the ground by the trailer, so when she got there, she looked closely and saw that the bloodstains appeared to continue to a spot behind the trailer. She followed them and discovered the body of the deceased in the weeds covered by a tarp."

Lawson reached the bar again and paused to let the jurors digest this.

"Now, all of these folks will testify at some point that the accused lived with Mr. Murphy in the trailer and she had been there for some months. There is no question about that. But none of them will testify that they saw the accused that day at the trailer with the deceased after midmorning." He put one arm behind his back and looked up at the ceiling, seeming to think hard about what to say next. "You will hear testimony that the deceased suffered two gunshot wounds, one in the lower abdomen, the other in the head over the left eye. These came from a .38-caliber pistol." He stopped and stood midway between the seated jurors and put both hands on the bar. Looking intently at them, he said, "No one has produced the weapon that took Mr. Murphy's life. There are no fingerprints, nothing. This is the flimsy evidence that the State has used to charge this poor woman"—here he turned and gestured toward Lucinda—"with murder and ask that you take her life." He looked earnestly at the jury again. "I'm sure that you will do your duty here and return a verdict of not guilty. Thank you." And he returned to his seat.

There was a lull of a few minutes while the judge appeared to make some notes. It started in silence and then finished with a rumble of low murmuring as the courtroom relaxed and discussed the morning among themselves. Tony noticed a man and a woman sitting in the first row of seats behind the bar and the State's table. They were older, maybe the age of Grandma and Grandpa. The man looked like Grandpa with overalls and a face weathered either from work or alcohol. The woman was plump and wore a dress that would have been referred to as a "church dress" in this town. It was dark blue, faded with little white flowers. Their faces were stern, staring straight ahead toward the judge, DA, or witnesses. The woman held a ball of tissue tightly in her fist. They were surrounded by four or five people who looked as though they could be relatives or friends. From time to time, the couple whispered to them, and they all leaned in to hear.

Judge Porcher then announced that the court would take a fifteen-minute recess. "Mr. DA, will you be ready to proceed at that time?"

"Yes, Your Honor, the State will be ready."

. . .

The first witness called by the State was the coroner who examined the body of Sonny Murphy. He was a local undertaker, not a medical doctor, who owned the largest funeral home in the county. His name was Orville Arthur. He looked like a mole, wearing thick glasses over a face accented by a pointed nose that was perhaps useful for digging over a thin moustache. He peered intently at his notes while describing the wounds to the body of the deceased. The DA showed him pictures of the body and asked him to confirm that he had taken the pictures and asked if they illustrated the location and severity of the wounds. He answered all of these questions in the affirmative. Then the DA offered the photos into evidence and passed them to the jury for inspection. They passed them in turn to one another; some grimaced, some had no reaction. Arthur described the gunshot wounds in grisly detail. The bullets had been flattened and made huge exit wounds. He described the blood loss, the pools around the body. Tony listened and thought about the Cain and Abel story. He had never thought of himself as Cain. He offered nothing. But what had Sonny offered but pain and evil? It was at least some consolation for having killed him.

"Coroner Arthur, were you able to determine the time of death?" Ravenel asked.

The mole chuckled a little and stroked the whiskers under his sharp nose. "No, we're not that precise, but I'd say he'd been dead about twenty-four hours from the time of the exam." He sniffed and stroked the whiskers again.

"Which would mean he died, in your estimation, on May 15th. Is that correct?"

For the sake of theater, Lawson objected that the DA was now testifying. The objection was overruled.

"It would be about then, yes," the mole said, his eyes slits, whiskers twitching.

The DA then stated he had no further questions and passed him to Lawson, who stood and said dismissively that he had no questions for the witness.

The State's next witness was Ernest Black, the bartender. He testified that they were running short of change that morning and that he went to the trailer to find the deceased and get him to open the safe, and while there, he saw the accused drinking coffee at a table while he was talking to the deceased. He then testified that later in the afternoon he needed the deceased's signature on a receipt for a shipment of whiskey and that he went to the trailer, but the deceased was not there and nor was the accused. He saw something that could have been blood on the ground in front of the trailer but he was in a hurry and didn't stop to inspect it. "Your witness, Mr. Lawson."

Lawson took the bartender through his background, how long he'd lived in the area, what he did before moving there, and how long he had worked at the Fish Hook. "So you have known the deceased ever since you've been working there for, what is it, a little over two years?"

The bartender nodded his head and answered "yes" in a barely audible voice. The judge admonished him to speak up so the court reporter could hear him.

"And would you say the deceased was a dangerous and violent man?"

At this point, the DA was on his feet, red faced. "Your Honor, I object. I don't see where this is going, and we're not trying the deceased here."

"Judge Porcher, if you will bear with me a little longer, I think everyone will see how this is relevant," Lawson responded.

"You may proceed for now, Mr. Lawson."

"So, Mr. Black, as I was saying, would you say the deceased was a dangerous and violent man?"

"How do you mean?" Black looked uncomfortable, squirming a little in his chair.

"Did he have a bad temper? Have you ever seen him strike anyone?"

"Well, it wouldn't do for you to try and beat a bill in the Fish Hook. He'd get pretty mad about that."

"Ever seen him hit someone over a matter like that?"

"Yeah."

"How many times?"

"I dunno. Maybe ten or fifteen."

"Well, lessee. If you saw that ten or fifteen times and you've worked there a little over two years, that means it happened at least maybe every other month. Right?"

"I reckon so. Never been too good at math."

The jury snickered.

"Mr. Black, did you ever see him hit the accused?"

The DA was on his feet and blustering.

"I object. He's trying the deceased. This is not relevant, Your Honor, and it's highly prejudicial and wasting time."

"Overruled," Porcher said.

"No, I never seen him hit her."

Lawson looked theatrically perplexed for a moment, then he said, "Have you ever seen the accused in the Fish Hook when it looked like someone had hit her? Like with a black eye, a swollen lip?"

Ravenel, standing at his full, skinny height, bellowed, "I object. This is outrageous. Even if she did come in there looking beat-up, there's no telling where it happened or who did it. I object."

"You can bring that up on redirect, Mr. Ravenel. Besides that, you've made your point to the jury." Then he looked sternly at Lawson. "Mr. Lawson, you're getting out on the edge of my patience and the strictures of evidence law here." He paused. "But I'm going to let you go on for a while and then rule as to whether the testimony is permissible."

"But, Your Honor," Ravenel spluttered, "after they hear it, there's no way to get it out of their minds. That's why he's trying to get it in."

"Proceed carefully, Mr. Lawson."

The DA folded himself disgustedly into his chair.

"I'll repeat the question for you, Mr. Black. Did you ever have occasion to see the accused in the Fish Hook when it looked like she had been beaten?"

After a little more squirming, Black said, "Well, I seen her a couple times with a black eye and a busted lip."

"Mr. Black, were you ever told that the deceased was selling the accused's sexual services and was holding her captive in that trailer?"

At this, the courtroom erupted in low murmuring that rose in volume so much that the judge had to bang his gavel. Ravenel stood, arms outstretched, livid, his mouth working but with no sound coming out.

"Your Honor," he screamed, "this is outrageous! Even if it weren't prejudicial, there's no foundation for any of this, nothing in any of the pretrial matters where Mr. Lawson mentioned this."

"Your Honor, we just learned of this last evening. I would certainly have disclosed it to Mr. Ravenel beforehand if I could have."

"I think I need to see you gentlemen in my chambers right now. Mr. Bailiff, we'll take a fifteen-minute recess. Come with me, gentlemen."

At first, Tony struggled to understand what Lawson meant. When he realized that Lucinda could have been selling herself, he flushed and squirmed over smelly bodies and feet to get to the aisle and outside, away from the eyes following him. For the first time since it had happened, he felt no remorse for killing Sonny. There was an unfocused kernel of anger building in him, directed at Lawson for bringing this to the attention of the world. Then there was Lucinda. He had loved her and protected her as best he could all of his life, and now this.

He stood outside the courthouse, a dignified building three stories tall with white columns in front. It was surrounded by palmettos and live oaks with a statue of a Confederate soldier in the midst, black and green with pigeon droppings on his slouch hat and rifle. Clumps of people surrounded the statue, smoking and discussing the case among themselves. He felt that all were staring at him, but none approached him. The old couple he had noticed and their friends stood slightly apart from all groups and talked in low voices among themselves, occasionally making cutting glances toward Tony. The street in front was lined with one-story flat-roofed brick buildings, narrow single offices with the names of lawyers in black on the doors or windows. One office advertised a bail bondsman in white lettering on the door. Like bookends, there were two restaurants on either end of the street enclosing the other offices. The Tick-Tock advertised three vegetables and a meat for $2. The other, The Tasty Pig, sold barbeque, hot dogs, and hamburgers.

There was movement at the entrance to the courthouse, and spectators began shuffling back in. This time, Tony did not take a seat. He stood in the back of the packed room and leaned against the wall. Judge Porcher, the court reporter, and the bailiff came back in through door behind the bench, and Lawson and Ravenel followed them in.

"Ladies and gentlemen of the jury, at this time, we're going to take our noon recess since it's already eleven forty-five. We will recess until one-thirty, at which time, Mr. Lawson, you will conclude your examination of witness Black, and Mr. DA, you will put on your next witness, which I believe will be the bookkeeper, Ms. Dorner. Is that correct?"

They both spoke in the affirmative.

"All rise," intoned the bailiff, and the judge left the courtroom. Lawson was on his feet, turning toward the crowd and peering until he saw Tony. He gestured for him to approach the bar. Tony made his way through to the bar.

Lawson came close to him. "We're going to lunch, and your mother wants you to come with us," he said, almost whispering. "Meet us at my car, the black Lincoln, across the street. We can't go to either of the close places 'cause there'll be a lot of these people there. We'll go to a place across town. OK?"

Tony nodded and left to find the car. He was leaning against it when he saw Lawson and his mother coming across the street.

When they reached him, she grabbed his arm and pulled him close. "Oh, honey, I need to talk to you so bad."

He didn't respond or return her hug. He looked down at his feet.

"I know it sounds awful, but I can explain everything," she said.

"C'mon," said Lawson, "before somebody sees us."

They drove in silence down Highway 17 in the direction of Georgetown and Charleston until they came to a restaurant called Mollie's Crab Shack. Tony followed Lawson and his mother into the building. It was dim inside, the light absorbed by the dark wood paneling. Shells and seahorses and plastic crabs of all kinds were caught in the mesh hung on the walls. A plump waitress with blond hair cut short hustled up to them. She wore a starched white uniform with a red sash at the waist. She wore a tag that said "Margie."

"Y'all sit anywhere you like. Good to see you this week, Mr. Lawson. I'll get some menus."

Lawson picked a round table in a corner already set with placemats that were for children to color and draw on.

"I think we're doing fine so far," he said. "Now, son, we need to talk about that last part of the testimony about—" But before he could finish, Margie was back with the menus.

"Y'all ready to order, or should I come back in a minute?"

"I think we're ready," Lawson said. "I'll have the shrimp basket and so will she," he said, pointing at Lucinda. "What do you want, son?"

Tony stared hard at the menu, not really seeing it.

"The oysters are really good this time of year," Margie said to him. "But anything on the menu is good. Just ask Mr. Lawson."

"Guess I'll have a hamburger," Tony finally said.

"Oh, you'll love it," said Margie. "Want French fries or tater tots with it?"

He shook his head no.

"Ever'body want tea?" Margie asked.

"Yes," said Lawson.

"I want a Coke," said Tony.

Margie gathered up the menus and swished off toward the kitchen.

"Now, back to what I was saying. Your mom was not working as a hooker out of that trailer."

"Then why did you say she was?"

"I didn't say she was. I asked him if he had ever *heard* that she was. There's a difference. Anyways, I can't go on with it. Judge won't allow it without some evidence, but the point is I got it in front of the jury, and they'll think about it. I think we've got this one in the bag as weak as the State's evidence is. Sheriff did a terrible job of investigating this case. Spending too much time looking at the bottom of a whiskey glass, I expect. But let's be thankful for that. Can't believe they never looked for the gun. Never interviewed any witnesses outside of the Fish Hook. If we play our cards right, I think we got this."

Tony said nothing and stared intently at his hands.

"What's wrong, honey?" Lucinda asked. "If I beat this, nobody will remember anything about it in a year or two. They'll forget all about it." She patted his arm, but he was stubbornly silent.

Margie came bustling up holding three plates, one in her hand and two balanced on her arm. She deftly put them down and went off to get the drinks. There were French fries on Tony's plate.

"Ma'am," he said when she returned, "I didn't order the fries."

"I know, but I thought you'd like 'em. No charge. Just enjoy 'em."

They busied themselves with salt, pepper, ketchup, and cocktail sauce and then ate in tense silence. Tony ate a few bites of the hamburger and one or two fries. Lawson and Lucinda finished their shrimp.

Lawson pushed his plate back. "You ain't said anything much since we been here, son. Guess you're not happy."

"No, I'm not happy," Tony said.

"Son, your momma's getting ready to walk away from a murder here and, I think, maybe scot-free. You oughta be happy, delighted, not pissed off about something that will help the case and be forgotten after everything settles down."

Margie came back at that moment.

"Y'all need anything else? How about some peach cobbler?" She looked at Tony's plate. "Hon, you didn't hardly eat a thing. Didn't you like it?"

"Yes'm. It was fine. Just not too hungry."

Lawson asked for the check and leveraged his bulk out of the chair to go to the men's room.

Lucinda clutched Tony's arm and spoke just above a whisper. "Honey, he doesn't know the story. He thinks maybe I shot Sonny, but he doesn't know. Said it wasn't his business to know whether I was guilty or not. Said it was his job to defend me. Has no idea it was you. Just be calm and everything will be OK." She leaned close and peered at his eyes. "OK?"

He nodded his head yes. Then Margie came back with the check and Lawson appeared at the same time.

"I want y'all to come back again whenever you can." Looking at Tony, she said, "Next time, you'll eat all of your dinner. Bye now."

They went to the car and headed back to town and the afternoon session.

Tony made his way into the courtroom. When he came to the row where he sat that morning, those who were already seated moved over and made room for him, treating him like a celebrity. He turned his attention toward the front. The judge had not yet returned; then he felt a hand on his shoulder. He turned to see Grandma and Trish in the row behind him. Grandma had on her Sunday clothes, the blue hat, and a severe black dress. She looked diminished. In her left hand, she had a wad of crumpled tissue, which she used to dab at her eyes frequently.

He motioned for Trish to lean toward him. "What are you doing here?" he whispered.

She motioned for him to go outside, and they made their way over the others to go through the double doors in the back. As they were going out the door, the bailiff intoned, "All rise." And the judge came back and settled himself in his high-backed chair. When they got outside, Trish hugged him.

"We can't talk now," he said as he gently pushed her away. "They're starting again. Why are you here?"

"Your grandma called me. Said she had to come down here, and I couldn't let her go by herself." She shrugged. "So here I am. Plus, I guess I'm here because I love you no matter what you do or how you treat me."

He wanted to say something to her but couldn't. Not many people had done anything for him without expectation of some return, money, or a favor, but she wanted something he had never given, didn't know how to give. He took her arm and led her back inside.

"The witness is still with you, Mr. Lawson," the judge said.

Lawson looked over his papers for a moment and then rose. "Don't believe I have any more questions for this witness, Your Honor."

"Mr. Ravenel, he's your witness on redirect."

Ravenel got the bartender to confirm that even if he had seen the accused with black eyes and a split lip, he had never seen the deceased hit her and it could have been done by someone else. He also confirmed that he knew nothing about any prostitution being run from the bar or the trailer.

On recross, Lawson asked if Black had ever heard the deceased yelling at the accused or threatening her.

"I heard him yell at her a time or two, yes."

"How much is a time or two?"

"Dunno, maybe three or four."

This got Ravenel on his feet again. "Your Honor, it's obvious that this man doesn't have any real recollection of any of these accusations by Mr. Lawson. I object and urge us to move on."

"I agree, Mr. Ravenel. Counselor, you have established that the accused showed evidence of some battery being committed on her by the bruises and wounds to her face. But you have got nothing but your own testimony in the form of a question with respect to the other matter, and I have given you more leeway than I should to go into these matters. And I remind you that you have not pleaded self-defense. So, unless you have some more good evidence, not speculation, I want you to move on."

Lawson ended his recross.

Next the State called the bookkeeper, Mrs. Dorner, who testified that she had seen blood on the ground near the trailer when she went to look for the deceased to get his signature on a check. The blood trail had led to the back of the trailer where, to her horror, she found the body of the deceased partially covered by a tarp and looking as though animals had got to it at some point. On cross Lawson asked her a few perfunctory questions: Did she see the accused there? Did she see a weapon anywhere? All those questions were answered in the negative. Lawson asked no further questions but reserved the right to recall the witness. Judge Porcher announced that he had another matter to attend to, so he recessed court for the day.

The State's next witness was Clarence Brown, the sheriff. In his life after football he had become fleshy, jowly, and now, balding. His face and cheeks were red and striated with veins.

He radiated good humor, smiling and crinkle-eyed. No one could dislike him. He had never been the most diligent law officer. A local religious group did a little research and discovered that over half the people stopped for drunk driving in the county were never prosecuted because the tickets disappeared, and of those who were prosecuted, only a quarter were convicted. The rest either were allowed to plead to a lesser charge or their cases were pending forever. There was also the botched investigation of a grisly homicide several years back where the accused, who had done it without a doubt, was not properly informed of his rights and walked away scot-free. Rowdy weathered a bad uprising in the next election, but he was able to squeak by because he and his friends spread rumors that his opponent was a pederast. It wasn't true, but enough people believed it to get him reelected.

He settled himself into the witness chair and smiled at the jury and the courtroom. Ravenel got him to identify himself and asked a few questions about his background. Rowdy liked to talk about his past, so this lasted for a while before the DA moved on.

"Mr. Sheriff Brown, were you called to the Fish Hook on the afternoon of May 16th?"

"I was."

"And what was the occasion for the call?" Ravenel took Rowdy through identifying the body, where it was found, the wounds, and how it was dressed.

"Was there anyone else at the scene or in the trailer?"

"No."

"Did you enter the trailer?"

"Yes. We went in the trailer. No one was there."

"What did you see there?"

"Well, there was a bunch of dirty dishes, cups, saucers. Dirty frying pans. Looked like nobody had cleaned up in a month."

"Did you see any evidence that someone had left the trailer in a hurry, like open drawers or clothes . . . ?"

Lawson stood. "Your Honor, he's completely leading the witness. Please tell him to let the sheriff testify on his own."

The objection was sustained. Ravenel paused to gather his thoughts.

"Sheriff, when you were examining the contents of the trailer, did you find any evidence that someone else lived there?"

"We found unopened mail on the dresser in the back addressed to Lucinda Pettyjohn. Also mail in the box out front addressed to the same person."

"Was there any other evidence of a woman living there?"

"Yes."

"And what was that evidence?"

"Uh, there were panties and brassieres on the floor in one corner."

The courtroom snickered quietly. Rowdy enjoyed getting a response from the audience, so he added, "Looked like they'd been used."

The laughter got louder, causing Judge Porcher to bang his gavel. Tony squirmed in his seat. *Nothing here but sorry people*, he thought, *even Mom. Trish has come a long way because of me. She deserves more from me than what I've given, more than Mom.*

"And did you determine who else was living there?"

"Yes. We asked the people who worked in the Fish Hook who else lived there, and they told us the accused had lived there for a couple months."

Lawson objected to hearsay and that the question had described Lucinda as "living" there. Ravenel responded that he could call the employees who would confirm Rowdy's testimony, but it would be a waste of the court's valuable time. Lawson withdrew his objection, and Ravenel took the sheriff through the steps that had led to Lucinda's eventual arrest, the all-points bulletin, and the arrest in Jacksonville, Florida, at a bus station.

"Now, Sheriff Brown, did you interview the accused after she was returned?"

"Yes, I did."

"And did you question her about the murder?"

"Yes. We read her rights and got her to sign the paper. Then we questioned her. She only would say that she was sorry it happened."

Ravenel turned the witness over to Lawson. The man composed himself and smiled a little, not wanting to offend Rowdy or appear too aggressive with a witness so obviously admired by the jury. He reviewed his background, how long he'd been sheriff, and how many murder cases he'd investigated in his career. "So, Sheriff Brown," he asked when he had finally decided to get to matters about this case, "has there been a determination of what type of weapon killed the deceased?"

"Was a .38-caliber pistol."

"And did you conduct a search of the scene to find the weapon?"

"Yes, we did."

"And did you find such a weapon?"

"No, we did not."

"And when you arrested the accused, did you search her person and possessions for the murder weapon?"

"Yes, we did."

"And did you find a weapon?"

"No."

Lawson, who was standing, put his hands on his hips and looked down at his notes, seeming to decide what to do next. "How many days had passed between the alleged date of the murder and when you took custody of the accused in Florida?"

Rowdy's face clouded. He screwed up his mouth and looked up at the ceiling.

"I . . . I think it was three, but might have been four."

"And to the best of your knowledge, were any tests performed on the accused for traces of gunpowder?"

"No, but that stuff only stays on—"

"Please just answer the question, sheriff," Lawson interrupted.

Ravenel objected. "He's entitled to explain his answer, Your Honor."

"Sustained. Sheriff, continue please."

"Gun powder evidence lasts a short period of time. We didn't see any need for a test 'cause of how long it had been."

"So," Lawson said, "there's no evidence of the defendant being near a weapon?"

"Move on, Mr. Lawson," Porcher growled.

"OK. Sheriff, let's move to something else. Were you able to determine when the accused left the trailer?" Rowdy looked puzzled, so Lawson added, "I mean, Mr. Black testified he saw her there in the morning, but was she seen after that? Did you ask from the employees or any neighbors when was the last time they had seen her?"

"No, we didn't ask."

"So she could have left right after Mr. Black saw her with the deceased?"

Ravenel objected that the witness was being badgered. The judge overruled the objection, and the sheriff admitted that they didn't know when the accused had left the trailer.

"So, Sheriff Brown, when you interviewed Mrs. Pettyjohn, you say she would only say that 'she was sorry it happened'?"

"Yep, that's correct. She was crying the whole time. Must have gone through a whole box of Kleenex."

The jury snickered, and Brown swiveled around, enjoying his effect on them.

"Sheriff, did you ask her if she knew what happened to the deceased?"

Brown nodded his head. "Said she didn't know."

"Did you ask her whether she killed Sonny Murphy?"

"Yeah. She just cried and said she was sorry he was dead."

"But she never said she killed him?"

"No."

Lawson was satisfied.

"No more questions of this witness at this time, Your Honor."

Judge Porcher looked at Ravenel and told him to call his next witness, but Ravenel stood and announced that the State rested.

"You mean you have nothing else, Mr. DA?" the judge asked.

"That's correct, Your Honor. The State rests."

There was murmuring among the crowd, which rose to the level requiring the judge to bang his gavel. He looked at his watch and announced that since it was nearly twelve o'clock and that the court would recess for lunch and return at one-thirty.

"Mr. Lawson, you will commence the defense at that time."

"With pleasure, Your Honor, and I will be making a motion at that time also."

Outside, the family and Trish came together standing in embarrassed silence and awkwardness at seeing one another again. Grandma timidly approached her daughter, put her arms around her neck, and cried softly into her shoulder. Lucinda returned the hug and murmured something to comfort her.

Lawson looked on the scene mutely at first but then as it appeared that it would go on for longer than a few moments, he cleared his throat. "Folks, I hate to break this up, but we're going to be putting on our defense when court starts again, and we need to eat and then make a few plans."

Lucinda pushed Grandma back and introduced her to Lawson.

"Pleased to meet you, ma'am," he said, scarcely looking at the little woman. "Let's all go over to the Tick-Tock. It's quick, and they've got a room in the back where we can talk without all the looky-loos bothering us."

He made to herd everyone in that direction, but Tony and Trish held back and said they would go to the Tasty Pig. There was no need for Tony to be included in the plans, since he had very little influence on what had been done so far. There were booths in the back, and they took the last one, passing curious groups on the way. They both spoke at the same time, each deferring to the other to start, when the waitress, an older lady with gray hair pinned up in a bun, came up with two menus, and bustled off after they both told her they wanted sweet tea for drinks.

"And what can I get for you two?" she asked after she had returned with the tea, leaning her hip against the table. They ordered and she left.

He reached across the oil-cloth covered table and took Trish's two hands in his, trying in his inarticulate way to show his gratitude for her presence. He was grateful and thankful, and he also felt indebted, a feeling that was just on the edge of his consciousness. Trish bent her head slightly, and two tears dripped down onto the table.

"What?" he said in a low voice. "Why are you crying? Seems like that's all you do when we're together."

She sniffled some and took one hand from his and wiped at her tears. "I'm just so glad to see you," she said, continuing to cry. "I want this to be over. I want you to come home."

"Reckon we could go to Rock Hill," he said. There was a moment of silence as she stared at him.

"What did you say?" she asked, her mouth open and eyes wide.

"Maybe we could go to Rock Hill."

"Oh, Lord. Oh, Lord," she said.

He was nodding his head up and down, and she was crying, and just then, the waitress brought their food. Before putting it down, she looked at Trish.

"Are you all right, hon? You look like you seen a ghost."

"Yes, yes," Trish mumbled. "I'm fine, just fine."

The waitress put a sandwich and a drink in front of each of them, placed the fries in the middle between them, and asked, "Anything else, now?"

They shook their heads no.

"Then y'all enjoy and let me know if you need anything."

They stared quietly at the food. Neither ate.

"Yes, yes, yes," she finally said. "But I don't understand. You know I've wanted this for a long time . . . so why now? I thought you just didn't want to."

"Never been that. Just some things had to be cleared up before I could do anything. Mama being in trouble and all.

Now I think it may be OK." He took some of the fries and ate them slowly. "And . . . I've done some bad things in my life. This here has caused me to think hard about 'em."

"Like what?" she asked.

"I don't want to tell you everything. I don't even like to think about some of it. Some of it was a long time ago. Seeing you and Grandma just made me think about where I might be headed is all and what I've got. Sounds stupid, I guess, but I started thinking about all that stuff when I was a little boy and Grandma would make us go to church. Cain and Abel, all that stuff." His voice trailed off.

"What made you think about Cain and Abel?"

"It's just stupid stuff. Let's don't talk about it anymore. You don't mind if we don't do it right away? Like maybe could we do it in a couple months? Would your parents let us? Do we have to go to Rock Hill?"

She wiped her nose with a paper napkin, then her eyes. "Let me figure that out. First of all, you have to get back to your job before Mr. Striker lets it go. You know that, don't you?"

"Yeah. This thing ought to be over this week. Maybe today. Can you get word to him that I'll be there next week?"

"Even if I have to go to his house, I will."

They picked at the rest of the food, and then he said, "We need to get back. It's been an hour. C'mon."

Spectators were filing back in as they got there. They found seats next to Grandma. She gripped Tony's arm. Everyone was in place when Porcher made his way in and the bailiff intoned his entrance.

When he had settled himself in his chair, he said, "Mr. Lawson, please call your first witness."

Lawson arose, hands on hips and spreading his jacket out so that he looked more pear-shaped. He looked up at the ceiling and stroked his chin.

"Your Honor, at this time, the defense makes a motion pursuant to code 15A-1227 (1) to dismiss this case for insufficiency of evidence." Porcher instructed the bailiff to take the jury back to the jury room.

Lawson began again. He paused between numbers of the statute and looked down at his notes to get them right. "There is nothing here to connect the accused with the death of Mr. Murphy except the fact that at one time she lived in the same trailer with him. The State has not shown that the accused was in the trailer at or near the time the coroner says the event took place. There is no murder weapon, no evidence that she had fired a gun. The bare grounds of the State's case are that she left town and was found in Florida after Murphy was killed, and it is the defense's contention that this simply is not enough to try her for murder. Thank you, Your Honor."

The judge turned to the DA. "Mr. DA, what say ye?"

Ravenel rose. "Your Honor," he began, "Mr. Lawson knows full well that there is enough here for this case to go to the jury." He went on largely repeating himself. When he had finished, the judge announced that they would take a fifteen-minute recess. Lawson got the group together at the bar after all had gone out.

"He won't dismiss it," Lawson said. "Would put too much heat on his reelection chances next year."

Lucinda had agreed to take the stand. She was reluctant at first, but Lawson thought she could be a sympathetic witness with a little help from him, and they could play to the divorcee bank teller juror to help them.

"All we need is one of them to hang the jury, and I don't think Ravenel wants to try this again." He turned to Lucinda. "Now, you're going to do just fine," he said as he put his hand on her shoulder, standing close to her. "The men like you. I've watched them, but you have to be innocent looking. Take a little more of your lipstick off."

She wiped her mouth with a tissue that Lawson provided. He looked intent. "That's right. Looks better."

Irritated, Tony looked away, angry at Lawson but also at his mother.

"You'll know how to do this," Lawson said, smirking.

At this, Tony walked away from the group. Grandma followed him, as did Trish, but Tony motioned her away. When they were out of earshot of the group, Grandma said barely above a whisper, "I'm so afraid, Tony."

"Why, Grandma?"

"She's killed a man. She's going to hell. She hasn't been in a church in years." Here, she cried so hard her shoulders shook.

"She says she didn't kill him, Grandma. Don't you believe her?"

"I don't know. I just don't know. If she didn't, then who did? And even if she didn't, she's been living down here in sin with that man. We come from a good family. I never taught her to do these things. I tried to raise her right, took her to church until she wouldn't go no more. Then she married that no-account father of yours."

Tony's face began to flush, and he shushed her. "It's OK, Grandma," his voice nearly a whisper. "She didn't kill that man. I promise you she didn't."

She looked up at him and started to ask a question, but just then, the judge strode back out and took his seat. When the room had quieted, he raised his head and looked magisterially over the scene. "Mr. Lawson, I'm going to deny your motion at this time. You may renew it again at the close of all the evidence, if you wish. Are you ready to proceed with your defense?" Lawson replied that he was. "Then, please do so."

Lawson began the defense by recalling Ms. Dorner, the bookkeeper, who had found the body. He took her through the history of her employment at the Fish Hook, how long she had known the deceased, and how long she had known the accused. Then he led her through her earlier testimony, that she had seen what looked like blood on the ground and it led her to the corpse. She said again that she had not seen the accused earlier that day or when she made the discovery.

"Now, Ms. Dorner, you had known the accused for some months, is that correct?"

She nodded her head and was prompted by the judge that she must answer so the court reporter could hear her.

"Yes, I knew her for maybe three months."

"And did you have occasion during those months to observe any interactions between the accused and the deceased?"

"I'm not sure what you mean by interaction."

"Did you have a chance to see them so that you could tell whether they were arguing or fighting?"

Ravenel was on his feet at this. "Your Honor, I don't see where this is leading. Her defense is that she wasn't there. What difference—"

He was cut off by Lawson's interjection. "This goes to the entire environment between these two people. It gives the jury an idea of how they lived and is certainly relevant."

Whether relevant or not, or perhaps because the judge wanted to hear any salacious details, he allowed Lawson to go on. Ravenel rolled his eyes to the ceiling, ran his hand through his hair, and sat down.

"Ms. Dorner, did you ever see the deceased hit the accused?"

Again, Ravenel objected. Porcher overruled it.

"Well, I never seen it, but I *heard* it a couple times." Her mouth formed a tight line, and she rolled her eyes at the ceiling.

"What do you mean you '*heard* it'?"

"One time about a month ago, I was going out to the trailer to get Sonny to sign some checks. I hated to have to do that, but sometimes it was the only way to keep the place running. I was about to knock on the door, and I heard voices and noises inside. Didn't sound like they wanted company, so I left." She looked at the floor and shook her head.

"Tell the jury what you heard."

"I object, Your Honor," Ravenel blurted. "There's no way this can be anything but hearsay and inadmissible."

"Your Honor, we are not offering this testimony for its truth but merely to establish the atmosphere surrounding this couple."

"I'll allow it. Go on, Mr. Lawson."

"Again, Ms. Dorner, tell us what you heard."

"I heard Mrs. Pettyjohn saying something like 'No, Sonny, don't hit me again.' And then I heard a sound like a fist hitting something or a slap and then a groan. And I heard a man's voice say, 'Git up, bitch or I'll do it again' and I left. Didn't want no part of that."

Lawson turned the witness over to Ravenel, who had been sitting flushed during her testimony with his head in his hands, but Ravenel said he had no questions for her. There was a pause as Lawson sat at the defense table and whispered with Lucinda. The pause lasted until rustling began in the room, and the judge prompted Lawson to call his next witness.

He stood and, looking dramatically around the courtroom, said, "Your Honor, at this time, I call the defendant, Lucinda Pettyjohn, to the stand."

This caused a general murmuring and shuffling, and Porcher rapped his gavel for quiet. He asked Lucinda to stand. "Mrs. Pettyjohn, your attorney has indicated that you wish to testify in this proceeding. Is that correct?"

"Yes, Your Honor, it is," Lucinda replied in a low voice.

"And you understand that you do not have to so testify and that it is your right to remain silent and not take the stand? In other words, it is the State's burden to convict you without any testimony from you, and I will instruct the jury to take no inference from not testifying if you should decide not to."

"Yes, I understand that, Your Honor."

"Mr. Lawson, you may now proceed."

Lucinda made her way to the witness box. When asked by the clerk, she raised one hand, put the other on the Bible, and swore to tell the truth. In her dark blue suit, in the low light of the room, and against the dark paneling of the courtroom, she looked tiny. She had a tissue in one hand, which she took to her eyes from time to time.

Lawson sat at the defense table and took her through the background of her life. She had been born in North Carolina and had lived for most of her life in Maple Grove, home of the largest manufacturer of towels and sheets in the world. She and her family had always worked in the mill. She had done everything from weaving to doffing to hemming sheets and towels.

He stopped her. "For the edification of the jury, since some of them might not know what a term like 'doffing' means, please tell them."

She gathered her thoughts for a moment. "Well, a doffer takes full spindles of yarn from a spinning machine and replaces the full ones with empty ones. It all happens very fast."

He thanked her.

She had been married, but her husband had left her many years ago. They had two children, both boys, one of whom was in the courtroom today. The other lived with her mother and father in Maple Grove. Her mother was here today sitting in the courtroom.

"And tell us how you came to be down here."

She looked down and twisted her hands. "My life seemed to be going nowhere in Maple Grove. My father was abusive, accusing me of not working hard enough, of being tired of keeping my boys. I felt like I had to do something, so I left and came down here to look for a job and maybe get the youngest boy away from there."

"You have two boys, is that right?"

"Yes."

"And where is the older boy?"

"He works in Maple Grove, but he's here right now sitting over there."

Lawson turned toward where Tony was sitting and asked him to stand up. He flushed and slowly stood as he felt all eyes boring in on him again. The couple he had noticed earlier had swiveled around to get a good view. The woman glared at him with a tightly clinched mouth. The man seemed uninterested and continued to look forward.

"And were you successful in getting the younger boy down here?"

"No."

"Why is that?"

Here she looked down at her lap, twisting her hands before she finally looked up to answer. "I never found a proper job that would have let me bring him here."

"What job did you find?"

"I looked for a couple weeks and didn't find anything. Then one night, I went to the Fish Hook with a friend, and I met Sonny Murphy."

"What happened then?"

"He found out I was looking for work, so he told me to come to his trailer the next afternoon and maybe he could find me a job as a waitress. I told him I didn't think I could make enough as a waitress to support me and my boy. He said—"

Ravenel objected that this was all hearsay. The objection was sustained. "Well, Your Honor, I don't think it's hearsay, but we can get to it another way." So Lawson began a workaround to get the story told.

"So you had a conversation with the deceased. Is that right?"

"Yes."

"And a result of that conversation, what did you do?"

"I moved into the trailer behind the bar."

"Was the deceased still living there?"

"He wasn't supposed to, but the first night I was there, he came to the trailer and wouldn't leave."

"Besides not leaving, what else did he do?"

She began to cry slowly and wiped at her face with the tissues several times. When the pause lengthened, Porcher asked if she would like to take a recess so that she could compose herself, but she shook her head no.

"He was drunk. He hit me several times. When I tried to leave, he wouldn't let me go. Said I had to stay."

When Ravenel stood to object to the hearsay, Lawson told her not to tell the court and jury what had been said between her and the deceased. She nodded her head.

"And what else did he do?" She didn't answer.

"Mrs. Pettyjohn, did the deceased force you to have sex with him?"

There was a low murmur from the onlookers.

The woman who had stared and muttered at Tony said in an audible voice rising in her seat, "It ain't true. Sonny Murphy was my son, and he was a good man."

The judge rapped his gavel, "Mrs. Murphy you can sit down right now and be quiet for the rest of these proceedings or I'll have you removed from the courtroom. Do you understand?" Mrs. Murphy muttered to herself and slumped back into her seat.

Ravenel who had been standing during this exchange, said in a tight voice, "Your Honor, this is outrageous. They are trying the deceased. Plus, they did not offer a plea of self-defense. Their whole case has been that she wasn't there. I object."

Lawson only smiled and shook his head from side to side. "Your Honor, this is only to show why the accused would be interested in escaping and getting as far away from that trailer as possible at any time that she could. It is not offered as a defense."

Porcher gazed up at the ceiling for a few moments before overruling the objection.

"I'll allow it for purposes stated."

"Mrs. Pettyjohn, I ask you again if the deceased forced you to have sex with him."

Lucinda nodded her head in the affirmative, and Lawson reminded her that she had to answer so the court reporter could hear.

"Yes. Yes, he did." And she began to cry uncontrollably.

Porcher instructed the bailiff to hand her a box of tissues and told her to compose herself.

Lawson began again. "How long were you forced to live with the deceased in the trailer?"

"Three months, four months. I don't remember. It's all just a blur now. I tried to leave a couple times, but he caught me and brought me back. I didn't have enough money to even buy a bus ticket."

"Did you ever get out of the trailer?"

"When he wasn't there, he kept the door padlocked on the outside so I couldn't get out. He took me shopping every two weeks maybe to get things I needed. I got to go in the bar as long as he was around. He told me he wanted me to attract customers. But if I did and they hung around me too long, he'd come and get me. Told me I had a phone call in the back or something. He was very jealous."

"I call your attention to the afternoon of May 15th. Do you remember anything that happened on that day?"

She looked puzzled and shook her head slowly from side to side. "I don't know about that date. When you live almost all the time in a cramped place like the trailer, you lose track of dates and time."

"Well, let me ask you this. Do you recall anything unusual happening on the day you left the trailer?"

Here she raised her head and said clearly, "Sometimes Sonny would come to the trailer in the afternoon when things were slow in the bar, and he'd force me to do things. That happened the day I left. He had just come in, and there was a knock on the door. He had his pants off, but he went to the door anyway and went out. I heard talking in loud voices, but I couldn't understand what they said. Then there were two loud bangs, and I didn't hear anything after that. Sonny didn't come back in. At first, I was scared to go to the door, but a long time passed, so I went out and looked and didn't see anybody." She began to cry softly and dabbed at her eyes with the tissue.

Lawson gave her a few moments and then prompted her. "So what did you do then?"

"There was some money on the dresser that Sonny had left when he started undressing. I counted it. There was over two hundred dollars there. It was still quiet, so I grabbed some clothes and stuff and left. I went around the alley so no one from the bar would see me leave. I walked along the highway until I got near town, and then a man gave me a ride to near the bus station. I got as far away as Florida before I was arrested. I didn't even know Sonny was dead until they arrested me."

"Mrs. Pettyjohn, I ask you now, and you are under oath, and I want you to tell this jury—did you kill Sonny Murphy?"

She turned and looked at the jurors and said, "No. I did not. No, I did not."

Lawson thanked her. "The defense rests, Your Honor."

Judge Porcher looked around. "At this time, we'll take a one-hour recess. I have to hear some other motions in other cases. When we come back, Mr. DA, you can begin your cross-examination of Mrs. Pettyjohn. We will resume at 1:30 p.m."

The bailiff called for everyone to rise, and everyone filed out, murmuring among themselves about the morning's testimony. Outside, Lawson assembled Lucinda, Tony, Trish, and Grandma around him. The Murphys were in their own group on the other side of the sidewalk, whispering hotly and shooting hostile glances at Lucinda and Lawson.

"All right," Lawson began, "we did pretty good this morning. Now, Lucinda, he's going to come down hard on you this afternoon, so you have to be strong. Can you do that?"

She nodded that she could.

"Then let's go get something to drink, come back, and get this over. There's not much Ravenel can chew on, so I'm hopeful."

As they were going back to the courthouse, Tony pulled Lucinda aside. "I need to talk to you, Mom." He hesitated.

"What is it, honey?"

He thought for a moment. An impulse like standing up in the middle of a sermon in church tugged at him.

"Hurry. We have to go."

"I'm going to tell them the truth."

"No. No. She grabbed his arm and got up close to his face. "Lawson says that we've got more than a good chance of getting at least a hung jury, so you don't do anything. You hear me? Your whole life is in front of you. You got that girl who came all the way down here for you. What are you thinking about?"

Beside him were Trish and his future, but then there was Lucinda in jail for a long time.

"I don't trust Lawson at all." Tony said finally. "He loves all the attention he's getting from this. He don't really care how it turns out or about you really."

"Trust ain't got anything to do with it," she hissed. "You promise me. You hear?"

The others had reached the steps, and Lawson was looking back and motioning for them to hurry.

"Promise me." Her nails dug into his arm.

"OK," he muttered.

At one-thirty, all had reassembled in the courtroom, waiting expectantly for the judge to return. He swept into the room, the bailiff announced the resumption of court, and Lucinda was directed to take the stand again. The crowd listened alertly for Ravenel to begin his assault.

He looked penetratingly at the witness, and then in a measured voice, he said, "You have testified that you lived in Maple Grove, North Carolina, for how many years before coming here, Mrs. Pettyjohn?"

"I lived there on and off all my life until I came here."

"And you had never lived here before?"

"No. I visited here a lot. I have an aunt and uncle who live here."

"Then that must explain how you were arrested here not once but twice for drug possession and use two and three years ago. Isn't that true?"

Now it was Lawson's turn to get on his feet and bluster about the admissibility of this question.

"It goes to character and truthfulness, Your Honor," Ravenel said. The objection was overruled.

"Yes," she said in a low voice, "I was here on those weekends. The police came to a party where I was."

"Are you an addict, Mrs. Pettyjohn?"

"No."

"Isn't it true that you are an addict and that Sonny Murphy felt sorry for you and was letting you stay in his trailer until you could get clean?"

She shook her head and wiped at her eyes. "No. That's not true. He kept me there. I couldn't leave. He hit me if I tried to leave."

Ravenel headed in another direction. "You say that he locked you in so you couldn't leave. What about the phone? Did you ever attempt to call anyone and tell them that you were being held prisoner and needed help? Did you call the police?"

"He would unplug the phone and take it with him."

Ravenel walked to the state's table, and one of his assistants handed him a set of papers. He studied them for a moment then handed a copy to the clerk and asked that it be marked as a State's exhibit, then gave a copy to the judge and Lawson. He asked for permission to approach the witness then ambled slowly toward her, still looking intently at the paper in his hand.

"So it's your testimony that you never had an opportunity to use the phone?"

"That's right."

"Now, Mrs. Pettyjohn, I'll hand you this paper. It's a copy of the phone records for the last six months for the phone number listed to the one in Mr. Murphy's trailer."

She looked dumbly at the paper as though it were written in a language she didn't understand.

"These phone records go back three months from the date of the murder." He bent near her and pointed with his finger. "This column here is for outgoing calls. You see this number here? We've traced it to a boarding house in Maple Grove, North Carolina, where your son lived. He's sitting right over there." He pointed at Tony.

Lawson stood. "Your Honor, Mr. Ravenel is testifying now. Could you please instruct him to make his case by asking questions of the witness? And furthermore, we did not see these records in advance, had no chance to verify them on our own, so I object to their use."

Porcher sustained the objection as to the testimony but overruled the objection as to use of the records.

"Your Honor, I could call the employees of the phone company to testify to these matters, but I won't." He turned again to Lucinda. "Mrs. Pettyjohn, do you recognize the number I've pointed to?"

"No."

Ravenel went back to the defense table and whispered with his associates. They seemed to come to some agreement.

Ravenel looked up at the judge. "Your Honor, at this time, the State calls Tony Pettyjohn as an adverse witness for the purpose of identifying this telephone number, and I wish to reserve the right to continue my cross-examination of Mrs. Pettyjohn afterward."

"Completely outrageous. We had no advance warning of this. Mr. Pettyjohn was not named on the list of witnesses the State intended to call. I object." Lawson howled.

Porcher looked up at the ceiling and considered the objection.

"What say you, Mr. DA?" he asked.

"Your Honor, the State is calling this witness to verify the telephone number listed as an outgoing call on State's exhibit number one and for no other purpose at this time."

Again, Porcher gazed up at the ceiling trying to make a decision. Finally, he said, "I'll allow it for that purpose only."

Lawson stamped his foot.

"Mr. Lawson, you'd do well to have a seat and be quiet. I don't mind holding lawyers in contempt." He looked over the gaggle of spectators to where Tony was sitting. "Mrs. Pettyjohn, you can step down and have a seat for a moment while Mr. Ravenel gets this out of the way, and, Mr. Pettyjohn, you can take a seat and be sworn."

Lucinda was pale, her mouth a thin line. She rose slowly and moved to a chair beside Lawson.

THE LOOM FIXER

Tony remained seated.

"Mr. Pettyjohn," Porcher said in a louder voice. "You need to come forward."

Tony rose and slowly made his way through the low gates of the bar and moved to take a seat in the witness chair. Porcher stopped him before he could sit and told him to be sworn. "Turn toward the clerk and put your left hand on the Bible and raise your right hand."

When Tony had sworn to tell the truth, Porcher told him to take a seat. Tony sat, leaning slightly forward, trying to be invisible. Ravenel looked at him for a long time before he began his questioning, seeming to sense a vulnerability, an opening in a case that had not gone well for him.

"Mr. Pettyjohn, what is your relation to the defendant?" he finally began.

"She's my mother," Tony said in a voice so low that the judge prompted him to speak louder.

"And where do you live?"

"Maple Grove."

"That's North Carolina, right? And what do you do there?"

"I'm a loom fixer in the mill."

"And where do you live exactly in Maple Grove? What's your address?"

"I live at Mrs. Overcash's on Ridge Avenue."

"Is that a relative?"

"It's a boarding house."

"And do you have a phone there?"

"No."

"No phone?"

"There's a phone in the hall that we can use."

"And what's the number of that phone?"

He shrugged his shoulders. "I don't know."

"You don't *know*?" Ravenel said with mock incredulity. "How can you not know the number of your own phone?"

"I ain't ever had to *call* the number. I just talk on it if somebody answers it and says I have a call."

The crowd snickered, and Ravenel flushed and walked to the witness stand. He showed a paper to Tony and pointed to something on it.

"You're telling me you do not recognize that number?"

"No."

"I'll ask you if is this not a number assigned to the boarding house where you live?"

"No, no, no," Lawson said. "I object. He's testifying. Witness has already said he didn't recognize it. This is so prejudicial. I move for a mistrial." Lawson stomped at the defense table and waved papers in the air.

"Mr. Ravenel," the judge began in an exasperated voice, "I'm going to sustain his objection, and I direct the jury to disregard what you said with respect to the number, and I'll remind you that I can also hold *you* in contempt." He leaned back in his chair. "Now, let's get on with this trial so we can all go home before Labor Day."

"I have no further questions, Your Honor." Defeated, Ravenel sat down.

THE LOOM FIXER

"Mr. Lawson, he's your witness," Porcher said.

Lawson stood and thought for a moment. "So, Mr. Pettyjohn, for all you know, that number that the DA showed you might be to a taxi stand or something?"

"I object to the speculation, Your Honor."

"Mr. Lawson, if he doesn't know the number, he doesn't know. Now, move on," Porcher said in an exasperated voice.

"I have no further questions of this witness, Your Honor."

"Then you may step down, Mr. Pettyjohn."

"I recall Mrs. Pettyjohn at this time," Ravenel said.

But before Lucinda could go to the stand, Tony swiveled in his seat toward the judge and said in a tight voice, "Your Honor, there's somethin' I'd like to say."

All shuffling, coughing, and murmuring in the courtroom stopped. Attention was completely on Tony. The judge looked down expectantly. Lucinda, who had risen from her chair to go to the stand, stopped, face frozen, a "no" etched on her lips, hands slowly going to her face. The word became audible, scarcely at first, but then loud enough for all to hear: "No."

The judge banged his gavel and glared at Lucinda. "What is it, Mr. Pettyjohn?" Porcher asked.

There was silence.

Tony stared at his mother and slumped in his seat. "I don't guess anything, Your Honor. Nothin'."

"Your honor, I want to hear this," Ravenel said.

Tony looked down at his hands.

"He must have rethought it, Mr. Ravenel, so let's move on. Come down, Mr. Pettyjohn, and you retake the stand, Mrs. Pettyjohn."

And so Ravenel continued, but there was little more he could ask or say that hadn't already been covered in prior testimony. Finally, he asked, "Why did you run from here, Mrs. Pettyjohn?"

"I saw a chance to get away from him."

Ravenel winced, regretting the question. "Isn't the real reason that you had murdered Sonny Murphy and you knew you had to get away?"

Lawson objected. It was sustained. Ravenel resignedly admitted that he had no more questions. Neither did Lawson.

"The defense rests, Your Honor," Lawson said. "And at this time, I wish to renew my motion to dismiss this case for lack of evidence."

"Your motion is denied, Mr. Lawson."

The judge announced that they would recess for the day and begin closing arguments the next day. Lawson insisted that they all go to the Tick-Tock again to discuss the next day's plan. They went to the back room. Except for tea and soft drinks, they waved away the waitress. Lawson spoke quietly about what he thought Lucinda's chances were and what they would do if things didn't turn out like they hoped. There was a soft knock on the door while he was speaking, and the waitress stuck her head just inside and told Lawson someone was out front asking to see him and said it was very important.

"I'll be right back," Lawson said.

Trish gripped Tony's arm. Grandma sniffled through a tissue, and Lucinda played with her silverware. There was silence as they waited for Lawson to return. When he did, they all looked expectantly at him.

He sat and paused, letting the tension build even more. "OK. The DA knows he has a very weak case here. Shouldn't even have brought it. The reason the judge denied my motion to dismiss, I think, is because he thinks the jury is not going to convict you anyway, and he denied it as a political favor to Ravenel. What that was about just a minute ago was that Ravenel sent one of his assistants over here to make us an offer."

"What kind of offer?" Tony asked.

"I'm coming to that." He looked at Lucinda. "If you agree to plead to manslaughter, he'll recommend a sentence of two to three years and no probation. You'd be out of jail in no more than one year, more or less. Sounds like a long time, but really it's not."

The table was silent except for Grandma's quiet crying.

"What do you think I should do?" Lucinda asked.

Lawson folded his hands. "I think we have more than a good chance of either a not guilty or at least a hung jury, but you never know what can happen with a jury. You could be looking at life, but . . ."

"I don't know what to do. Tony? What do you think?" But he only shook his head.

"He said if we didn't let him know in an hour, then the offer was off the table," Lawson said.

Lucinda said, "I'm going to take my chances with a verdict."

"What happens if there's a hung jury?" Tony asked.

"I don't think Ravenel would try this case again. Too weak. Eventually it would just go away." He took a sip of his tea. "We need to go now. So you want me to turn it down."

She nodded her head yes.

"OK, then this is how it will go. Because we put on evidence, I have to make my argument to the jury first, and Ravenel gets to go last. Don't make much difference in this case. He doesn't have much to argue. I'm not going to go on for a long time. Just gonna point out how weak their case is. After that, the judge will charge the jury. Means he's going to tell them how to apply the law and what law to apply. Most jurors don't listen to it anyway. It's only important if we have to appeal. After that, the jury goes back into their room to decide. I hope it won't take long, but you never know. Any questions?"

All looked down at the table.

"OK, then let's go."

Tony remembered a movie from the theater in Maple Grove about some paratroopers on D-Day about to jump out of a plane. *This must be like that feeling*, he thought. *Not knowing how it will end but knowing whatever happens it will be forever.*

• • •

True to his word, Lawson didn't talk long. His voice was folksy, not condescending but every day-like, a little different from his usual overbearing tone. He went over the weak parts of the State's case. There was no gun, no evidence of the accused having fired a gun, not even a test to determine it. The accused had defended herself on the stand and had the courage to face her accusers and their questions. In fact, there was nothing to tie the accused to the death of Murphy except the fact that she had been there at some time and left as soon as she could after he disappeared. And why wouldn't she have left then? She was a captive in the trailer and had testified that she was never allowed to leave. Others testified that they had heard her being abused inside. So, of course, when she got the chance, she would leave. Not leave—*escape*. It was a normal behavior to run from circumstances like that. He reminded the jury that they shouldn't convict the accused unless they thought she was guilty beyond a reasonable doubt and the judge would explain to them what a reasonable doubt was. He thanked them and sat down.

It was then Ravenel's turn. Of *course*, there was no evidence of gunpowder on the accused. They hadn't found her for so long after the event that any trace would be gone. He urged the jury not to be fooled by this fakery by the defense. There were many places nearby where someone could get rid of a gun, so even though there was no weapon, it meant little. The main thing was that the accused, instead of calling for help or looking for the deceased, had immediately run. What better evidence of guilt other than trying to put as much distance between herself and the dead body? He, too, admonished the jury to listen to the charge of the judge and take their guidance from him. When he sat down, he had a look on his face of relief, perhaps hopeful that this trial was over and off his hands.

The judge charged the jury, looking down at a big black-ringed notebook and turning its pages as he did. He talked for a long time. When he was done, he told the bailiff to escort the jury to the jury room, and everyone else sat back to wait. Sonny's relatives clumped together, speaking in whispers occasionally but generally sitting with their heads down. Lawson went back to his office to check his mail and phone calls, telling the bailiff to call him if they came back before he did. Tony and Trish went outside to get out of the tension and stale smell of the courtroom, which now was full of speculative murmuring, slowly rising as time went by so that it was hard to hear.

They sat at the base of the Confederate statue. She leaned against his shoulder. "So I'm curious. What are the bad things you've done and haven't told me about? Everybody knows about the training school thing. Is that all?"

He squirmed and tore a blade of grass from the lawn and chewed on it.

"You remember Willis?"

She nodded.

"Well, he did some things when I was with him. Reckon since I was there means I was just as guilty as him."

"Like what?"

"We held up a store once on the way down here. It was a long time ago, and I really didn't want to do any of it but I was there, so . . ." He didn't tell her about that there were two holdups.

"That was a long time ago, wasn't it?"

"I guess."

"Well, it's been so long nothin' will ever come of it. You're not the same as you were then, so let's forget it." She took his arm and moved closer to him.

"There *is* another thing." He paused, and she lifted her head from his shoulder, but he hesitated.

"OK. What?"

"When Mama moved down here. I knew she was in some kind of trouble. Knew I had to help her anyway I could. . . ." But he resisted the impulse to tell her more about Sonny's death, at least for now.

At that moment, the bailiff came out on the porch of the courthouse and announced that the jury was back. Tony was ashen, wondering what it could mean that they were back so quickly. They stood and absently brushed dried grass from their clothes. He wanted to go in and yet was afraid to; he felt nauseated. Trish pulled his arm until he took the first steps toward the door and they joined the slow entrance of the crowd. Lucinda led Grandma by the arm. There was no fear in Lucinda's expression. It was as though she had been through things like this a lot in her life, and she would take whatever came. Lawson came hurrying back from his office. He pushed his way impatiently through the crowd and took his place at the defense table, Lucinda beside him, her hands primly in her lap. The crowd settled and became quiet as the bailiff announced the entry of Porcher. He sat in his chair and instructed the bailiff to bring the jury in. When they were seated, Porcher asked if they had reached a verdict. The foreman, an insurance salesman, rose and said that they had. Porcher instructed Lucinda to stand. Lawson stood with her, his arm around her shoulder.

"And what is your verdict?" Porcher asked.

"We find the defendant not guilty."

There was loud talking in the courtroom. Lucinda, aside from appearing to relax a little, showed no emotion. Lawson made to embrace her, but she seemed not to notice until finally she turned to him and smiled slightly. Tony stood and cried in relief with Trish hugging him.

Sonny's mother was on her feet. "This ain't right! This ain't right," she yelled at Porcher and turned to Lucinda, pointing. "That slut killed my boy, and now she's gonna get away with it."

Porcher banged his gavel and rose from his chair.

"Mr. Bailiff, remove that woman from the courtroom. I want quiet here." He paused and glared at the crowd. "These proceedings are over. Mrs. Pettyjohn, you are free to go."

"Ravenel began to gather up his papers. Sonny's mother had eluded the bailiff and was trying to get to Ravenel when a deputy finally caught her. Her husband made as if to slug the deputy and was restrained by another deputy before both were taken roughly out the door. Porcher thanked the jury for their service. They made their way out in a group. Tony watched for Sonny's mother, but there was no one outside but a few newspaper reporters who wanted to talk to Lawson and a television crew who wanted an interview. Lawson brushed off the print reporters and but allowed an interview with the TV reporter. Lucinda discreetly left before they asked to talk to her, and they headed for Lawson's office. When they were all in his office gathered around his desk, he leaned back in his chair—feet on the desktop, hands behind his head—and looked up at the ceiling. "Well, I pulled that one off pretty good. Not often you get a not guilty in a murder case." He swiveled his head toward Lucinda. "You did pretty good too, little lady." The room was silent for a moment.

"What do we do now?" Tony asked.

"Go back to living your life, son, like none of this ever happened."

"I mean, how much do we owe you? Do we get any money back from the bail guy?"

"Well," Lawson began and looked at Lucinda with the slightest smile curling his mouth, "you let me and your mom work all that out."

Tony looked at Lucinda. "Then I guess we need to leave here and go back home," Tony said. For a moment, Lucinda looked at her hands.

"I think I'll stay here for a while," she said.

Lawson had returned to staring at the ceiling.

"Why? What will you do? Where will you stay?" Tony asked.

"I just need time to think and rest. If I go back to Maple Grove, I'll have to answer questions from all the talkers about what happened. I don't want to put up with all that right now. Just don't worry. I'll be all right. I can take care of myself."

Grandma quietly shook her head from side to side. "You ought to come on home with us right now, Lucinda. Ain't nothing ever happened down here that was good for you," she said.

Lucinda walked over behind Grandma's chair and put her hands on her shoulders. "I'll be OK, and I'll be home before too long. So y'all go. Right now."

. . .

They went to Uncle Stan and Aunt Bertie's so Grandma could say goodbye to her brother. She sat on the screened-in porch and talked about what had happened as well as about all their relatives and where they were and what they were doing. Tony and Trish excused themselves and walked the two blocks down the road to the beach. There was a path between two of the front-row houses that led to the sand. They took their shoes off and walked in the surf. Tony felt relieved but not completely. It bothered him that Lucinda was staying. He didn't want to know how Lawson figured into it. Trish leaned her head on his shoulder and put her arm around his waist. He then put his arm around her waist, and they walked toward the far-off pavilion which they could barely see, but they turned before they got to it and headed back. They needed to get home, he told her.

Aunt Bertie came out to the car and stood by the driver's side door as they were getting ready to go. She put her hand on Tony's arm before he got in. "I hope everything works out good. I mean, with your mom and all. Let me know if I can help."

He thanked her, and they started back to Maple Grove.

. . .

Trish pressed him for a date for the marriage, at least to make some plans, but first he said he wanted to get everything straight with Mr. Striker and his job. Having seen his feelings wax and wane before, she was suspicious, but he assured her that he just wanted to think things through, and besides, he wanted to know what her folks were going to say about the marriage. What would they say about what had just happened in Myrtle Beach? There would be a lot of talk in town. She was insistent that she would take care of any objections they had.

She had circled her arms around his neck. "You leave that to me," she said.

When Tony went back to work the first day a little early, Mr. Striker saw him as he came in the door. His face split into a grin, and he put his arm around Tony's shoulder and said, "Am I glad to see you!" It was the first time he could ever remember someone saying that to him.

Tony was put back on the first shift with an older loom fixer so he could get back into the flow of the work in the weave room. The high ceilings, the chattering of the machines, the mist in the air, weavers hovering over the looms watching the cloth come out as evidence of their earnings—all of it was comforting to Tony after the nightmare of Myrtle Beach and the trial. He pushed thoughts of the killing as far out of his consciousness as he could, and slowly the events began to have their own narrative, one that he preferred, and the results of the trial helped to further them along. If asked about his mother, he said that her friend had been murdered, that she had been accused of it for some reason—maybe an incompetent police force—that she hadn't done it, and that a jury confirmed that by letting her go. When he told that story enough times, it became more and more plausible and true in his mind since it *was* true for the most part, and he was able to forget what had actually happened. It was easier to do because he knew what happened was justified. Murphy was a bad person who had done unspeakable things to his mother, who had been unable to help herself. So eventually his role became nothing more than having been a spectator in something that came out as it should have.

But it wasn't good enough for Trish's parents. They said he was too much of a chance to take. He had a long history of trouble. It was attracted to him. Just look at his mother, they said. She was a little more than a whore. Talk around town was that she had shacked up with the dead guy in Myrtle Beach and had something to do with the killing. They said a person didn't get arrested for nothing, but it didn't put Trish off. She wanted Tony, and she was going to have him. She was afraid her parents' attitude would make him go back to the quiet reticence he had shown her for most of the time they had been together. So she suggested going to Rock Hill again, and this time he didn't reject it out of hand.

In the late spring of the next year when things were greening up and there was a fresh smell in the air, they left early one morning, went there, and got a marriage license at the courthouse. After that, they went to see a justice of the peace, a thin, wrinkled man, almost bald with hair combed straight back over his head. He had a Bible in his hand when they entered his office. He charged them ten dollars for the ceremony, which lasted five minutes from start to finish. Tony wore a sport coat, and Trish wore a white dress. Afterward, they drove up to Charlotte and got a room in the finest motel they could afford, a Howard Johnson's. They had dinner in a place they had both been to before on jaunts from Maple Grove. It was a pizza place called the Open Kitchen, very exotic to them with red-checkered table cloths and empty Chianti bottles with candles in them in the center of the tables.

They wanted to order a bottle of wine to celebrate. When the waitress asked what kind he wanted, Tony, not knowing anything about wine, just pointed to the bottle wrapped in wicker in the center of the table, so they drank Chianti on their wedding night. Trish was too happy and excited to eat much, so he ate most of the pizza, but he didn't like the wine, and they left most of the bottle. They got back to the hotel early. While he got undressed, she cut the light off and went into the bathroom. Minutes later, she came out, leaving the door to the bathroom cracked so there was some light in the room. She was wearing a short nightgown that tied in the front with two lace ties. It was sheer, and for the first time, he was able to look at her without worrying about her parents coming in or being smashed down in the front or back seat of a cramped car. She was beautiful, ample. He had never seen the dark *v* of her crotch before or beheld the roundness of her breasts. She untied the gown and slipped it off, leaving it in a crumpled pile on the floor; then she climbed onto the bed and ran her hands over his face, his chest, and took him in her hand. He reached up and pulled her down.

• • •

They didn't tell her parents for a week. They were furious at first, but she gradually calmed them down to the point that Tony was able to come to the house without her father shouting at them or sitting in stony silence. After the second month, they began to accept it, realizing there was nothing they could do to change it, and one evening, they invited Tony and Trish to have dinner with them in the kitchen. At first, the conversation was spare, Tony not being garrulous to begin with, but her father, who also worked in the mill like the rest of the town, asked how things were going in Number Three. Tony—who, after murmuring greetings to them, had said perhaps two thank-yous as things were passed to him—looked up as though having an electric shock.

"They're fine. Just fine," he stuttered.

"Hear we're going on short time next month," Trish's father said. "Damn Japs. Flooding the world with cheap stuff. Government ought to do something about it. We won the war, not them."

Tony nodded his agreement. And then they talked more about work and the mill, and Trish nodded and smiled and hoped that they had accepted him and maybe even would come to like him.

Tony continued to rent the room at Mrs. Oakley's boarding house as he and Trish looked for a place of their own to rent. The mill had built most all the houses in Maple Grove and named the streets as well. One section of houses was located in Tree Town because all the streets were named after trees: Oak Street, Maple Street, Elm Street, and a forest of others. Another section was known as Car Town. There was a Dodge Street, Ford Street, and Plymouth Street, and there was GI Town. The houses were tiny, no more than a thousand square feet, and Tony and Trish put their name in at the mill rental office to get one. The lady at the desk said maybe in six months or a year something would come open, but Grandma called her brother, the mill vice president, and suddenly one came open for them.

It was white clapboard and square and looked like a Monopoly house. There was a living room–kitchen combination on one side of a central hall and two small bedrooms separated by a bath on the other. An oil floor furnace was in the center of the living room floor. It provided heat to the entire house. Trish loved it. Before they moved in, she spent a week cleaning it. Tony and her father, using a pickup truck borrowed from her uncle, moved their meager furniture into it. Her parents had bought them a small dining room suite and gave them a chair and a sofa that had been stored in their attic for the living room. Tony had saved enough money to buy a mattress and frame for the bedroom and a small television set. To Tony's surprise, the rent charged by the mill was only fifteen dollars a month, about what he paid each month for the room in the boarding house. The water and electricity, also supplied by the mill, were equally cheap. It explained how the people who rented these modest places could afford the big new cars that were in a lot of driveways.

Tony and Trish moved in and began a life together. At her insistence, they even joined a church. Trish got a new job in the mill office mail room. She also took classes at the local business school to become a secretary. The extra money helped. Tony looked at a new Ford Fairlane but couldn't bring himself to spend that much money yet.

GI Town was within walking distance of No. Three Weave Room, so their lives meshed with the rhythm of the mill, waking up in the dark when the first whistle blew in time to be at work when the second whistle blew. Tony became used to walking in every morning in the low light beside all the other first shift workers going in carrying lunch pails or brown bags. He knew all the weavers and liked them. One of the women made it clear to him that she liked him a lot. She was a little older and not unattractive, but he was not interested and tried to let her know without making her mad. Mr. Striker had confidence in him. Tony enjoyed the tedious puzzle of re-threading hundreds of broken strands through their proper eyes to get a loom running again and feeling good about the thanks a weaver gave him when he got it running quickly. He worked without supervision now and even was asked to help train a new loom fixer.

One afternoon, months after he had come back to work, he saw Willis standing by the dope wagon, eating a candy bar. He had changed much since the last they had met—heavier looking and older. Tony nudged him on the shoulder.

"Willis?" he asked.

"*Tony*! What are you doing, man? I haven't seen you in a while."

"I still work here. Just haven't run across you lately. What about you?"

"After I saw you last time I got a job at Piedmont Airlines in Charlotte, but they started laying off, almost as soon as I got hired, and I got the can, so here I am in the lint factory again. Say, didn't I hear you were in some trouble at the beach or something?"

"Not me. It was Mom."

"Right, right. What happened?"

"Guy she knew got killed. They didn't have anybody else to blame it on, so they blamed it on her. Jury let her go."

"That's good. It didn't have anything to do with that fight or whatever you got into and got blood all over my seat covers, did it?"

"No."

"Boy, your mom was always a looker."

"What do you mean by that?"

"Easy, man. I was just sayin'. Hey, remember when we used to take off and go to the beach? Those were good times. We ought to do it again, even if we're not teenagers and we're a little old to hang around the pavilion or the Pad. How old are you?"

"Twenty-one and I'm married now. Life's different."

"*Tony, Tony*. You're going to be a middle-aged man before you know it, and you're going to be stuck here doing the same thing for the rest of your life. Looking at the same people, the same job. Let's do it. I got a new car since I last saw you. A '54 Mercury. Black with fender skirts and lowered about six inches. It can burn rubber, and it's a chick magnet."

Tony shook his head. "No. I been through a lot. Took a lot of chances, and I came out all right. Not taking any more chances now."

"You married Trish Smith, right?"

Tony nodded.

"She was always a nice, juicy-looking little thing. Tell her I said hello. And think about taking a little trip ever now and then. You may be married, but you ain't dead. I gotta go before the foreman comes looking. Need to keep this job for a while. One thing you can count on is that you can always come back to here." He tapped Tony on the shoulder, and he was gone.

• • •

On a Sunday, several weeks before Christmas, Tony and Trish were decorating a tree in the living area when he saw a long black car pull up to the curb in front of their house, not the kind of car seen often in GI Town. Then he recognized the driver as Lawson. The man leveraged his bulk out of the seat and stood by the curb waiting for Lucinda to get out. It was the first Tony had seen her since the trial, and he had only talked briefly with her once. She had not given much information then, only that she had a good job and that she thought she would be staying there for good. She had not mentioned Lawson, and he had not asked. Now he realized that Lawson hadn't disappeared from their lives as he had thought and hoped. Tony opened the door as they came up the walk, Lucinda in front.

She hugged him at the door and kissed him on the cheek. "Oh, sweetie, you look so good, and it's so good to see you." She was wearing a black dress, a strand of pearls, some kind of fur piece with foxes that were biting each other as they circled her neck, and a black hat. She was more dressed than he had ever seen her. She was well made up, her hair blond with no streaks of gray, her skin smooth and silky.

"What's he doing here?" Tony asked.

Lawson offered his hand, but Tony only looked at Lucinda for an answer.

"Let's go inside, and I'll explain everything."

There was only room for three of them to sit, so Trish went to the kitchen to get something for them to drink. Lucinda told the men she was going to help Trish and followed her into the kitchen. She stood behind her at the sink. "I just want you to know that I'm glad you and Tony got married. I'm happy for you. Please make sure you're always good to him." Trish said nothing, just continued what she had been doing. Lucinda turned and walked back to where the men were sitting in stony silence.

"Then you haven't talked to Aunt Bertie?" Lucinda said as she sat down again.

Tony shook his head no.

"Well, Sidney and I have decided to get married."

There was silence.

"After his divorce is final, of course. I guess this comes as a surprise to you."

Tony's throat was dry, but there was a bitter bile taste in the back of his mouth. He had not thought about what he had done and all that followed in a long time. This day had brought it all back like it was yesterday.

"I was hoping you'd be happy, honey."

"You ain't ever had a lotta luck picking men," he said.

"Now, wait a minute, son," Lawson said. It was the first sound he had made since being there.

Trish came in with four unmatched glasses of colas and handed them to everyone. No one made a move to take a drink. They stared at one another in silence, and Trish went back to the kitchen.

"Maybe we'd better go and talk later," Lucinda said. "I'm going to see Ma."

"Probably a good idea," Tony said.

Lucinda and Lawson stood, and she took a step to hug Tony goodbye, but he was rigid and made no move toward her.

"OK. I'll call you," Lucinda said.

Tony could see them talking as they drove away. Trish came to him and touched his arm, but he pushed her away.

"Tony, you can't let her ruin what we've started here. This is no different from how she's acted her whole life, is it? And she keeps dragging you into her messes. Don't let her do it this time."

THE LOOM FIXER

He walked away and went into the bedroom and lay down on the bed, and she finished trimming the tree alone. *Just another mistake that won't work out and maybe will affect us all. Is she even divorced from Dad?*

• • •

Grandpa died in January, and even though he had mistreated Grandma and the rest of his family for much of his life, she still grieved for him, most likely because it was a reminder that her own death might not be far away. The funeral was in the church that Tony and Mitch had attended as boys. They made their way past the casket, each stopping for a brief moment to look at the waxy face. The hair was parted and combed perfectly, but since almost no one had ever seen Grandpa without his ragged hat, the hair came as a surprise. The undertakers had done a good job. He looked like he was just ready to sit up and deliver a tirade at one of them for eating too much or making too much noise.

The mourners were few: Grandma, Tony, Trish, Mitch, and a handful of the people Grandpa had worked with most of his life. Aunt Bertie had called to say that they couldn't come because Uncle Stan was not feeling well.

The organ was playing a low hymn when Lucinda made an entrance. She was dressed just as she had been when Tony saw her last: black dress, pearls, the fur stole of foxes chewing their way around her neck, and the black hat. She stood out in this small group. She was alone. She made her way to their pew, and all slid down so that she could take a seat beside Grandma. She put her arm around the woman's thin shoulders and clutched her to her side, prompting tears and quiet sniffling from Grandma. Tony stared straight ahead and gave no greeting.

The minister stood and began the service. "I am the resurrection and the life, saith the Lord: he that believeth in me though he were dead, yet shall he live: and whosoever liveth and believeth in me, shall never die," he intoned with his arms outstretched.

Sunlight streamed through the stained-glass windows behind him just as Tony remembered from his childhood.

"Purnell Pettyjohn worked hard all his life," the preacher continued.

Tony was startled by Grandpa's given name. He didn't remember having ever heard it before.

"He provided for his family all those years and lived a hardworking but quiet life. He will be missed and mourned by Gaynelle, his wife of sixty-two years, and by his daughter and his grandchildren."

The preacher went on for a few more minutes seeming to talk about a man Tony had never met. Then it was over, and the attendants from the funeral home wheeled the casket out to the waiting hearse, and they drove in a short procession to the cemetery to put Grandpa in the ground for good. Tony overheard Lucinda whisper to Grandma that she would help pay for the funeral expenses. He thought he could see a bruise under her left eye underneath the makeup.

Grandpa's coworkers didn't go to the grave site, so there were just Tony, Trish, Lucinda, and Grandma with the preacher and the undertakers. It was a cold, raw day. When it was over, they stood beside the limousines provided by the funeral home to take them back to the church.

When they got back, Lucinda pulled him aside. "You haven't said two words to me. Is everything all right?" she asked.

"Yeah. Everything's OK."

"But why are you not talking to me? It's like you're mad about something. I never liked that girl, and now she's turning you against me. Why?"

"Got nothing to do with Trish," he said.

"Then what?"

"Where's Lawson? Wherever he is, I'm glad he didn't come."

"Why don't you like him?"

"He's an asshole. And why is there a bruise under your eye?"

"That's not a bruise."

"Then what is it?"

"*OK.* I slipped and hit my head on the corner of a table." She shook her head. "Whatever you might think of him, he did a lot for me. For us. By getting me off."

"You didn't have to do any of that. I would have told them that I did it."

"And where would you be now? You wouldn't be married to her and living in a house of your own and be working a good job, would you?"

He said nothing and just stared at the ground.

"Oh, baby, let's don't fight. You know you're more important to me than anything." She looked at her watch. "I've got to go. Are you not going to say anything at all?"

"Just don't call me if things get bad down there when he's tired of you."

She gasped and put her hand to her mouth then turned and went to her car.

• • •

The winter was over. The floor furnace in the little house, which glowed red when it ran for long periods, finally got a chance to relax. Even when it was at its reddest, it still didn't put out a lot of heat into the bedrooms, and Tony and Trish had spent the cold nights huddled up under the sheets. Tony slept peacefully and uninterrupted except for the moments he thought or dreamed about Lucinda and how she was or what she was doing. But as time went by, he thought of her less and less.

Mr. Striker had put him in charge of fixing all the looms in No. Three Weave Room. He only had help when multiple looms went out for some reason, and he tried hard to make certain that he didn't ask for help often. It was his weave room, and he wanted to take care of it himself. He got a raise, and they bought a new car, a Ford Fairlane. It was two-toned, black and white with long chrome strips down the sides. It had a radio with a device that could set stations so that with the punch of a button, it went to a station, and it wasn't necessary to search for it on the dial. It cost more than he thought he would ever spend on a car, but he got a loan from a credit company and made monthly payments, something he'd never considered doing. It was beautiful, and they spent some Saturday nights riding around a circular street that bisected the shopping area in Maple Grove with a tree-lined island. It was clogged with other cars making the same circle. Most of the other drivers were younger than them and unmarried, but Tony had never got to do this when he was in school, so Trish tolerated him doing it occasionally now. She snuggled over in the seat so that she was right next to him for all the world to see.

The mill stopped running only twice a year: on Christmas day and for the week of the Fourth of July. The week of the Fourth, all the workers went on vacation. They either stayed home or went to visit relatives that could tolerate them for that long, or if they had enough money, they went to the beach. Tony called Aunt Bertie and asked if they could rent the downstairs apartment for the week. They were lucky. It was unrented and they could have it for fifty dollars. Aunt Bertie didn't want to charge them, but things were tight. Tony had saved some money, so they took it.

He had not been back to Myrtle Beach since the trial, but the road and the towns were familiar: Cheraw, Loris, Marion, Conway, and then the beach. They passed a little liquor store outside of Chesterfield. He realized when they had gone by that it was the one he and Willis had robbed years ago. He pulled the car over to the side of the road, turned around, and headed back toward the store.

"What are you doing?" Trish asked.

"Thought I'd get some vodka for the week."

"*What*? You don't even drink."

"Maybe I'll start."

She shrugged, and he pulled into the sandy parking area in front of the store. Live oaks hung with Spanish moss surrounding the building that looked like it hadn't been painted since it was built. He entered through the screen door and peered around the dim interior until he spotted the lady with the thick glasses in a wheelchair behind the counter.

"Kin I help you?" she asked.

"Just looking for vodka."

"Over on the right," she said.

He picked up a pint bottle of the cheapest off the shelf and made his way to the counter.

"That'll be two dollars," the woman said as she put the bottle in a bag.

Tony handed her a twenty-dollar bill and turned to leave.

She brought the bill up to her eyes. "Wait a minute, mister. You got change coming."

"Keep it," he said and went out through the creaking screen door.

"I don't know what's got into you," Trish said when he got back in the car.

"Just thought it might add to a little fun while we're here," he said as he pulled off onto the blacktop. He reached over and pulled her to him, feeling good about himself, like he had made something right. "Let's have a good time." She leaned her head against his shoulder and sighed.

The beach was crowded. Traffic was heavy. They even had a hard time finding a parking place near Aunt Bertie and Uncle Stan's. Aunt Bertie met them at the door.

They could hear Uncle Stan coughing on the porch. "Who's that, Bertie?" he yelled then went into a coughing spasm.

"It's Tony, Gaynelle's grandson, and his new wife, Trish."

"Well, bring 'em out. I want to see 'em."

Uncle Stan was sitting in a rocker holding a fishing rod and peeling the line off the reel, cigarette hanging from the corner of his mouth. A glass of clear liquid and a pack of Chesterfield cigarettes sat on a table beside him. He smelled like stale smoke and gin. He peered at them through the thick glasses. "So you're Gaynelle's boy, are you? She still married to that turd? And is this your sister?"

"No, sir. I'm her grandson, Tony, Lucinda's boy, and this is my wife, Trish, and the turd died last year."

Stan peered more intently at Trish. "Sorry to hear about him dying, I reckon." Then he looked at Trish. "Do you like to fish, honey?"

"Yessir, I guess so," she replied.

"Good. Good. Cain't ever get anybody to go fishing anymore. How long you gonna be here?" He was struck with another coughing spasm, his face a deep red.

"Till next Saturday."

He recovered and gasped a little, took a pull on the cigarette. "Then we'll go fishing. How about Wednesday?"

"They need to unpack and get some lunch after their trip, Stan," Bertie interrupted. "They'll come back later, and you can make plans then."

He continued to strip line off the reel. It was piling up in a tangle at his feet. "OK, but I want her to come back. She's pretty. Want to teach her how to catch a spottail bass in the surf. You don't fish for 'em out past the breakers like ever'body thinks. You catch 'em right in . . ." His hands got tangled in the fine line, and he lost his train of thought.

"She'll come back. Let them get settled," Bertie said and pushed them into the house. She handed Trish some towels and sheets and asked her to take them down to the apartment. When she was gone, Bertie motioned for Tony to have a seat at the kitchen table. "When's the last time you saw your mother?" she asked.

"Grandpa's funeral. Why?"

"I'm sorry we didn't come, but you see how he is."

"I understand. It was OK."

"She look OK then? Your mother, I mean."

"Yeah. Was wearing a fur coat and pearls. Why?"

"You hear things. You know Lawson divorced his wife, but he still didn't marry your mom. Now I hear things aren't so good between them."

"Not my concern now," he said.

"Good. Time you started living your life without worrying about her. You two have a good time this week. Maybe even go fishing with Stan." She laughed.

That afternoon after they unpacked, Tony and Trish walked the two blocks down to the beach and spread a towel on the sand among all the other vacationers. Trish had bought a new bathing suit for the trip, a one-piece with cutouts near the waist. They sunbathed for a while and then walked a mile or so to the pavilion and the boardwalk. In the amusement park on the other side of the street from the pavilion, the Ferris wheel slowly turned in the air, and the sound of a hurdy-gurdy organ swept over the place. As they got nearer, they could smell popcorn and cotton candy, and they heard the ringing and thump of pinball machines. They bought two Cokes and shared a footlong hot dog and took in the delicious smell of onions, sausage, and peppers frying on a griddle. It was crowded for the week of the Fourth, working families everywhere being as far from home as most of them would ever be.

When Tony and Trish got back to their spot on the sand, he persuaded her to go in the water. She was afraid of crabs, jellyfish, and stingrays. She went anyway, but every time a piece of seaweed or shell bumped against her in the current, she jumped. It was low tide, and they went a long way out into the water before getting to the breakers. When they were in waist deep, Tony slowly immersed himself, getting used to the warm water, and then grabbed her by the waist and pulled her down with him despite her protests that she didn't want to get her hair wet. No one was near them that far out, and he kissed her, enjoying the salty taste of her mouth. They bobbed in the water for a long time, just their heads showing above the low waves, holding each other and floating slightly.

When they went in and dried off, she said she thought she'd had enough sun for the day, so they gathered up their clothes and towel and walked back to the apartment.

He took a shower and lay back on the bed, waiting for her to dry her hair and looking out the window at the gardenia leaves just visible in the fading light while smelling their sweet fragrance. She cut off the light in the bath as she came out, so there was only the faint light from the windows. In the gloom, he could see the dark outline of her suntan against the light color of her breasts and stomach. She came and lay down beside him, and he could smell the soap on her skin and the perfume of her damp hair. He touched her shoulder and drew his hand down her chest over the rise of her breast, marveling at the different textures of the flesh, skin, and nipple. She kissed him, breath hot and urgent, and he rolled over on top of her as she opened up to him.

They slept afterward then realized they were hungry, so they got dressed and drove north to Ocean Drive and ate at Hoskins Restaurant. He ordered shrimp, and she ordered flounder. The waitress brought them sweet tea and a basket of hush puppies before the food came out. The hush puppies were hot, just out of the deep fryer. They were golden brown and tasted of sweet cornmeal and onions. They slathered each one with butter, a half pat. He told her he had eaten there many times before when he had enough money, and it was always good. The waitress was a college girl, working for the summer. She wore a checkered uniform like all the waitresses and had a nurse-like cap on with the Hoskins logo, a shrimp. She brought their food together with French fries and a small bowl of coleslaw. He asked if they could have more hush puppies.

"Sure," she said and went off to get them.

Trish paused eating and looked intently at him. "Tony?"

He stopped and raised his eyebrows, looking at her.

"I've never been happier, and I hope you are. I *think* you are, but you never say much."

"I am," he said finally and started to say more but stuttered, blushing deeply. "I never thought my life could be like this. I mean . . ." He stopped.

Trish waited, but the rest never came. "It's OK. I think I know what you're trying to say." And she reached across the table and touched his arm.

They walked around the main street of the small town, arm in arm, until they came to a place with a faded wooden sign out front that said "El's Pad." It was a ramshackle clapboard building that seemed to shake from the volume of a jukebox and the gabble of voices coming from the inside. He steered her toward the door.

"What's this place?" she asked.

"Willis always liked to come here. Let's go in and look around for a few minutes."

Inside, there was a dance floor crowded with dancers turning, coming together, going apart, coming together again, and twirling. There was a long serving area, better lit than the rest, where several men were opening beer cans by putting them in a metal device and bringing an opener down on the top with a loud pop. Tony and Trish stood at the edge of the crowd and watched for a few minutes until a slower song came on and she enticed him out onto the sandy floor where they joined the others swaying and holding each other. When the song was over, she wanted to go, and they picked their way past all the bodies until they were on the sidewalk. Then they crossed the street and made their way to the open concrete pavilion. It also had a jukebox. There weren't as many dancers there, but it looked out on the surf, and in the moonlight, they could see the long white curl of the breakers coming slowly in and could hear their low crash and slap as they hit the shallow sand.

"Willis always said this place had the coldest beer in town. Want to split one?"

She nodded, and he went to the bar and ordered a draft. The bartender sat it down in front of him, and as Tony paid, the mug formed a coat of ice like magic. He took it back to her, and they sat on a bench sharing the beer and watching the surf come in under the moon. When they finished, they walked back to the car, her leaning on his shoulder with her arm around his waist.

On Wednesday, Uncle Stan insisted that they go fishing with him. He was up early, moving around the garage behind the house. Their bedroom window looked out on the garage, and he woke them up, rustling and clanking looking for his tackle box and fishing rods. It was the first they had seen him out of the chair on the porch. He had on a straw hat with a wide brim that sheltered his grizzled face and neck. A Chesterfield was tucked into the side of his mouth.

"What are you doing out there, Uncle Stan?" Tony asked sleepily.

"Need to get enough gear for all of us to go to the pier and catch us some spottail bass. Wake up that purty little wife of yours. Git some breakfast. Want to get there just as the tide starts to rise."

There was a soft knock on the apartment door. Tony slipped on his jeans and opened the door a crack. Aunt Bertie was there, hands on hips and irritated.

"He's been up since six talking about this and waiting for you two. I got breakfast for you upstairs, so get dressed and come on up. He ain't gonna be put off. He's going fishing, and you're going with him if it's the last thing he ever does." They could hear coughing coming from the garage. "And it might be," she said.

"You sure he can do this? Can he walk that much? I mean, out onto the pier and all?"

"You're gonna find out, I reckon. I'm sending his walker with you, and if he gets too tired and can't use it, call me. I'll bring the wheelchair."

Uncle Stan was waiting for them by their car, urging them to hurry because of the tide. They ate as fast as they could. Leaning against the trunk of the car, he had a tackle box that was dappled with paint spatters and only had one hinge. Rusty leaders and hooks were hanging out of it. There were three fishing rods with reels that were a mass of tangled, jumbled line.

"I got enough gear here for all of us. Let's go before we miss the tide."

They got him in the front seat between coughing spells. He waited, wheezing noisily while they put the tackle in the trunk. Tony remembered where the pier was, but Uncle Stan gave him detailed directions anyway while filling up the previously unused ashtray with ashes and Chesterfield butts. Trish helped him get out when they had found a parking place as close to the pier as possible. While Tony brought the gear, Trish and Uncle Stan stopped at the register to buy their tickets. The owner knew Uncle Stan and, smiling, came around from behind the counter to shake his hand and pat him on the back.

"Good to see you, Stanley. It's been a long time."

Uncle Stan bobbed his head and smiled, enjoying being recognized. "This is my nephew and his wife. We come to catch some spottail bass. Uncle Stan put his hand to his mouth to stifle a coughing spasm."

"Stanley, you need to give up those butts," the man said.

But Uncle Stan shook his head as he tried to catch his breath.

"Well, there aren't many people here yet, so you can get a good spot, and I wish you luck."

Uncle Stan bought a pound of bait shrimp and some bloodworms, and they made their way out onto the pier. Its gray wood planking and railing were covered with years of shrimp parts, worm blood, fish carcass, and gore. It was T shaped, about sixty yards long, the top of the T being at the far end where a small group were casting out as far as they could throw.

Stan stopped them just as they got to the point where the surf was breaking. "This is where the spottail bass are," he said, pointing down at the water. "Those folks further out don't know that. They won't catch nothing but spot, croaker, and pin fish out there. We'll get the bass right here."

They rigged their lines. Tony put a shrimp on each of Trish's hooks and showed her how to cast the line out and down into the water below. Uncle Stan had planted himself on one of the benches next to the railing. He put his Chesterfields and a thermos on the bench beside him. He busied himself untangling line on an ancient reel attached to a bamboo rod. When he had it like he wanted, he took out a pocket knife and cut a piece of flesh off a little bait fish that he had put on the railing in front of him. He carefully threaded the flesh on a hook, and then, cigarette affixed to the corner of his mouth, he leaned over the railing and cast into the area just behind the breaking waves, mumbling to himself the whole time.

Tony was leaning against the railing midway between Uncle Stan and Trish, who had edged further down the rail until she was standing next to a group of other people who were catching small fish and happily throwing them into a bucket, talking among themselves as they rebaited. Suddenly Trish shrieked and yelled for Tony. Her line had pulled taut and was jerking off the reel. When he got to her, she tried to give the rod to him, but he refused.

"You pull it in," he said. "Don't be afraid. It ain't gonna pull you in the water."

She took hold of the crank on the reel and, turning it, began to slowly gain some of the line back. The people who had been near her all gathered around at a respectful distance to see what she had.

They shouted encouragement. "Don't horse it. Let it git tired."

Uncle Stan, who had been absorbed in his fishing, smoking, and coughing, noticed the crowd around her and the commotion.

"What have you got?" he yelled. "It's a spottail bass for sure. Has to be. Pull it in. Don't let it break the line. It's gonna try to wrap you around one of the pilings."

Just then, something jerked at his line. He pulled back and began to reel. Trish's fish turned and ran down toward Uncle Stan. The lines crossed and soon were completely tangled, Stan tugging and coughing, Trish reeling and laughing. The crowd, now closer, surrounded both of them. Trish's fish was tiring, and slowly she was drawing it nearer and nearer. The tangle with Uncle Stan was making it slower, but soon her catch broke water. It was perhaps a little more than two feet long, glistening reddish gold with black fins and two visible black spots near its tail. Uncle Stan also reeled in, and his fish came out of the water. It was hard to see because of its small size, perhaps eight inches long; it was pan-shaped with a small spot near its gill opening.

"I got a spottail bass. I got a spottail bass. Look at that beauty," he said as they continued to reel the crossed lines out of the water and closer to the rail.

"Think she got the bass, old timer. You got the croaker," laughed a lady in the crowd.

Tony lifted the crossed lines over the railing. The big fish flopped and fought so much that Tony had to unhook it before the tangle was figured out. After a few minutes of unwinding the crossed line, he asked Uncle Stan to reel slowly. When he had reeled in all but four feet, the little fish wriggled at the end of his tackle and made a grunting, croaking sound.

"Thought I had a spottail. Glad she caught it anyway." Stan took a sip from the thermos cup at his side.

The crowd gathered around them, and a lady took out a boxy-looking camera and directed them to get closer together and hold up the fish. Trish wouldn't touch her fish, so Tony held it in front of her, and Uncle Stan leaned in with the little fish dangling from his line. The lady yelled for them to say cheese. After she snapped it, she waited a few minutes, and the picture came out of the camera and developed itself while they watched. It was the first time Tony or Trish had seen a Polaroid camera. They were amazed that they had the picture of the three of them and the two fish immediately.

"Here, hon," the woman said, "you keep this to remember the good time you had today and that big fish you caught."

Trish marveled at it, put it in her purse, and thanked the lady. They fished for another two hours, but when it got close to noon and the fish had stopped biting, they decided to go home for lunch.

Trish carried her fish home in a bucket they had brought. "You bring it home, you have to clean it," Tony said. She grimaced. "OK, I'll clean it for you." And he did with the supervision of Uncle Stan. Bertie cooked it for dinner, and they all agreed it was delicious.

• • •

On Thursday, Aunt Bertie and Trish went to one of the outlet malls that lined the highway running parallel to the beach. Tony tried to take a nap, but after tossing on the bed, he got out the local phone book and looked up Lawson. The home address was 1302 Crape Myrtle Drive. Not knowing where it was, he got in the car and drove downtown until he saw a taxi stand.

The dispatcher gave him directions and, looking him up and down, said, "Ritzy neighborhood. Gonna buy something there?"

"Probably not. Thanks."

It was south of town, on the beach side of the highway. The entryway was landscaped shrubs, palms, and yaupons; a sprinkler watered the manicured grass. The houses were set back off the road, most of them bigger than anything he had ever seen in Maple Grove except out in Miller Woods, where his vice president uncle lived. He drove until he came to the Crepe Myrtle Drive street sign. He went slowly, looking at the numbers on the houses until he came to 1302. He drove by once then turned around and came back. He parked across the street but did not get out of the car. He watched the house for an hour but saw nothing. He had no way of guessing how big it was, how many bedrooms or bathrooms. Several middle-aged walkers went by. One group came by twice and eyed him hard the second time. Knowing he had to do something, he walked up the long sidewalk at 1302 and rang the doorbell. When no one came, he rang it again, and then the knob began to turn. He felt a rush of emotion, expecting to see Lucinda, but instead there was a diminutive black woman in a uniform staring at him from behind the screen door.

Neither spoke for seconds, and then she said, "Kin I help you?"

He fumbled and stuttered, "I'm looking for Lucinda Pettyjohn."

"She don't live here no more," the woman said. "Left a couple months ago."

"Do you know where she went?"

The woman shook her head.

"Do you have a phone number?"

"Nope." And she closed the door.

Tony drove to Lawson's office. As usual, the anteroom was full of restless, bored, and scared people. The secretary was reading a magazine laid flat on the desk. She closed it as he walked to the desk. "Help you?" she asked.

"I need to see Mr. Lawson."

"And this is in reference to what?"

"It's personal."

"You'd have to see him after office hours." She looked around at the room. "He's real busy."

"I can wait."

"He don't see anybody but clients during office hours, like I told you."

"Tell him Tony Pettyjohn is out here."

She pushed a piece of paper across the desk toward him and handed him a pen.

"Write your name down on that paper."

She took it from him and went in the closed office door. When she came back, she sat down without looking at him. He took a seat and waited with the others dozing and fidgeting in their uncomfortable chairs. He waited two hours while the receptionist ushered clients into the office. Finally, the door opened, and Lawson appeared. He was heavier than Tony last remembered; otherwise he looked as before, dressed in a loud plaid sport coat, wearing a string tie, his hair slicked back from his long, sharp face. He eyed Tony with a hard gaze and motioned for him to come forward. When he reached the door, Lawson handed him a piece of paper. There was an address on it.

"As far as I know, you can find her there. Reckon that's what you want," Lawson said and quickly closed the door, leaving Tony staring down at an address written in pencil.

It was on Highway 17, south of town. He drove south on the four-lane, passing restaurants and cheap motels, used car lots and camp grounds until he was close to the address. Some of the places didn't have street numbers, but finally he had eliminated everything but a motel set back off the road in a grove of live oaks. It was white, one story, made of cinderblocks, and built so low to the ground that it didn't look tall enough for normal people to enter without ducking. Air-conditioning units hung from the windows in the front of each room. He pulled into the sand parking lot and stopped in front of the office. A vacancy sign was in the bug-specked window, and cicadas were rasping in the nearby live oaks.

The door leading in squeaked when he opened it to a dim interior. Along one wall was a table with yellowing brochures from restaurants and golf courses. Pictures of people playing on the beach and fishing were on the walls. He stood at the check-in counter for a moment before a woman came from within to help him. She was dark-skinned and short with straight black hair. *Some kind of Asian*, he thought.

"Need a room?" she asked, turning the registration book toward him.

"No, I'm looking for Lucinda Pettyjohn, and somebody told me she was living here."

There was a pause while the woman appeared to be considering this. "Sorry, but we don't give out the names or room numbers of our guests."

"She's my mother, and I'm just trying to find her. Haven't seen her in a long time."

Again, there was a pause. She took a square of paper from a pad on the counter and wrote something on it. "Ask for her at this place," she said. "I can't tell you anything else."

Outside, he looked at the address. Somewhere north on Highway 17. Everything was on Highway 17.

It was a restaurant called The Nautilus. A spiral shell logo was on a sign out front. The parking lot was paved and surrounded by palmettos and hibiscus plants. It was early, and there were few cars in the lot. Inside, he waited by a reception stand with a sign saying "Please wait to be seated" at the entrance to a long dining room spread with cloth-covered tables. The sound system was playing soft elevator music. Lucinda came toward him from the dim light. She wore a dark dress with a flower pinned to the bodice. Her blond hair was short and tightly curled, her lips a soft pink. As she got closer, she got older. He could see lines around her mouth and eyes. In times past, aging had been very good to her, giving her a delicious ripeness that glowed, but now there was gravity, a slight shifting, faltering thickening. She carried menus in her arm, but when she saw him, she paused and put the menus on a table and came to him.

She took his face in her hands. "What are you *doing* here?"

"We're down here on vacation. You know. The mill stands this week. Staying at Bertie's. Thought I'd look you up."

She hugged him, drawing him into the aura of her warm scent. "I'm glad you did. How did you find me?"

"Wasn't easy. I went to Lawson's, and he gave me the address of the motel. They told me to come here."

She looked around. "It's early so we won't get many people. Let's sit down over here." She led him to a table. "You want something to eat or drink? Tea?"

He shook his head.

"So I'm not with Lawson anymore, as you can see." She paused as though she expected a reply, but he said nothing. "I guess you had him figured out right from the start, but I always seem to not see what I should. I realized after a few months that after he got a divorce he wasn't going to marry me. After the divorce he moved me into that big house he lives in, but she hired the meanest asshole lawyer in South Carolina, a real nobody-gets-out-of-here-alive type, so he got tired of fighting it and spending money, so he kicked me out, and she moved back in even though they haven't remarried. She likes the high life better than self-respect, I guess." Tony sighed disgustedly and shook his head. She went on, "So he said he would give me ten thousand dollars to make it right if I would go away, which was OK by me. I was tired of him pawing me all the time anyway. So I moved out and eventually got this job, but I haven't seen that money yet, and he won't take my calls anymore either. But I swear, I'm going to get it." She leaned back in the chair. "Go ahead. Tell me you warned me."

"I'm just glad you're away from him. I think I'd stay away from him and forget the money. You ain't ever had much luck picking men, so just let well enough alone."

"Yeah, but I could invest the money, keep it for my old age, which is fast coming on." She said this as though she expected him to say otherwise, but he was silent. She seemed to cast around for something to say. "This job is not much, but it's lot better than working in that cotton mill in Maple Grove."

"Maybe that was one of your problems. Thinking that you was too good to work in the cotton mill. It's been pretty good to me. I dodged around trying to avoid it a couple times and between that and trying to help you I almost fell out of the world. You're still in it right now, and you ought to be grateful. We both got a lot to be thankful for considering what could have happened."

"I didn't mean for it to sound like that, baby. I know you've done well. I've always loved you and helped you. Don't forget that and think ill of me. I just couldn't stand thinking about working there all my life and then turning out like Ma. Marrying another redneck like Pa, and spending the rest of my life standing over a stove and cooking greens and having to listen to him snore. Going to work every day hemming sheets or washcloths. I liked to party and spend money."

"Well, the one you married didn't hang around long enough for any of that to happen. I don't remember ever seeing him."

She looked down at her hands.

He glanced at his watch. "So you're going to stay down here and live in that roach trap and work this job for how long?"

She was crying softly. "Yes," she whispered.

"It's getting late. I need to go," he said.

"Please come to see me again, or at least call me once in a while."

He nodded his head.

She pushed a piece of paper across the table to him. "This is my number."

He took it and left before she could get up to say goodbye.

Trish and Bertie were back from shopping when he returned. Trish was going through bags of purchases. She showed him some blouses and sweaters, telling him about how much she had saved at the outlet. They talked for a moment, and he said he was tired and wanted to take a nap. She came to him after he lay down.

"You went to see your mother, didn't you?"

His arm was across his face.

"Didn't you?"

"Yes."

"I'm going down to the beach," she said.

He heard the front door close. He tried to sleep, but there was a constant roaring in his head. Finally, he got up and went to go find her. He walked toward the pavilion and boardwalk with his bare feet in the surf, dodging the fishermen and children running in and out of the water. He saw her walking toward him. When they reached each other, he put his arms around her and pulled her close.

"People are watching us," she said.

"I don't care. Let 'em watch."

They walked arm in arm toward the pavilion, in the edge of the surf, making a sinuous pattern of footprints as they dodged people. It was getting toward the end of the big vacation week for most everyone, a sad time and one that they all tried to fill with as many things as they could before returning to their lives, many of which were in cotton mill towns all over the Carolinas.

At the pavilion, they played pinball, and Trish shot a BB gun at targets, trying to win a teddy bear.

She nestled next to him. "Let's go back to the room," she said, and she put her hand inside his thigh. "And after, we can go eat a big seafood meal at Hoskins."

He smiled and they made their way back down to the surf and walked home.

• • •

The next day, they said their goodbyes to Bertie and Stan. Stan was insistent that they come again soon so they could go fishing. "Spottail bass run as thick as fleas in the surf in the fall. This little lady knows how to catch 'em too," he said as he hugged Trish to his chest. Bertie smiled.

"It was more fun than he's had in a long time," she said in an aside to them. They assured them that they'd come back and left for home.

They drove in silence for a while, and then she turned to him and said, "Think we could get a bigger house? You know, maybe one of those houses on Ridge Avenue across the railroad tracks from No. Three Weave Room and the mill office?"

"Why do you want a bigger house? We've only been in GI Town for a couple years. I like it there."

"Ridge Avenue is closer to where you work. You could walk." She moved closer to him. "And we might need an extra room for a crib."

He turned to her. "What? Are you gonna have a baby?"

"I don't know for sure, but my boobs are sore and getting bigger. Or didn't you notice? And I've missed my period."

He was silent.

"Well, are you mad about it if I am?"

"No. No. I just hadn't thought about it, I guess."

She moved away from him and leaned her head against the window and began to cry.

"Wait. Don't do that. I just need to think about it. Like, will you work or what? It's gonna mean more expense."

"Well, maybe you'll get a big raise. Mr. Striker likes you, and they're short-handed."

"Can't count on that."

Tony went back to work the next week, back to the routine of the chattering looms in the huge bay of the weave room. He moved among others with slight tufts of lint on their clothes and in their hair, back to the work of coaxing hundreds of broken threads in stopped looms into their proper places. Trish had her suspicion and wish fulfilled when the doctor confirmed she was pregnant. They celebrated, but sometimes Tony had to ask himself how he got to this point from where he was years before when he had robbed a liquor store, killed a man, and had no vision of what his future was except working indifferent jobs and living in a boarding house. Where was he? He remembered Lucinda's disdain for mill life, but he was satisfied with it.

One afternoon near the end of his shift, he got a message from the mill office that Mr. Thurman Huffstetler wanted to see him right after his shift. It took a few seconds for him to remember the name. He brushed the wisps of lint off his clothes as best he could and made his way to the mill office. He had not seen Uncle Thurman since the Sunday gatherings at Grannie's. He remembered those times. The extended family would drift in throughout the afternoon. The men sat by rank with the vice president closest to Grannie, and then the order descended from superintendent, to foreman, to Grandpa, a mill hand who had no status at all and rarely spoke. They discussed the mill and work and complained about the cheap textiles being imported and made by Japs and why they had to keep the unions out or the whole thing would go to hell in a handbasket. Most of them smoked cigars, and Tony remembered the huge stand-alone ashtrays they used and the smoke so thick it was hard to breathe or see.

Tony had never been in the mill office before. There was a receptionist seated at a desk, an island in the room with a high ceiling and marble floors that broadcast every step taken on them, echoing loudly in the huge hollow space. The receptionist was a prim little woman with the firm but curt attitude of a keeper of the gate. She asked him if she could help him, and he handed her the note that had summoned him. She asked him to have a seat in one of the wooden chairs along the wall and spoke quietly into one of the several phones on the desk. After a moment, she beckoned to Tony and told him to take the winding staircase on one side of the room and someone upstairs would show him where to go from there. At the top of the stairs, he was met by a smiling young woman who extended her hand to him.

As he took it in bewilderment, she said, "I'm Becky Lewis, Mr. Huffstetler's secretary. Please follow me. I think I was in the class ahead of you in high school, but I remember you."

They went down a walkway, which divided several rows of women at typewriters and adding machines clicking and humming, until she stopped at a door labeled "Thurman Huffstetler, Vice President, Sales." She opened the door and announced him to a man seated behind an enormous desk across another long expanse of floor. The desk was flanked on one side by an American flag. On the other was a Confederate battle flag. The room smelled like cigar smoke, and the man who stood to greet him was smoking a cigar as he came around the desk with his hand extended.

"So, you're Tony, my sister Gaynelle's grandson."

Tony shook his hand. "Yessir."

"I haven't seen you since you were a little shaver. Have a seat." He pointed to one of the wooden chairs in front of the desk.

"Yessir. I guess that's right."

Uncle Thurman sat back in his swivel chair and took a puff from the cigar, blowing smoke at the far-off ceiling. He had brown hair, graying at the temples, wore horn-rimmed glasses, and had a very pronounced hawklike nose just like his sister and all of her relatives that Tony had ever met.

"I guess you're wondering why you're here?"

"Yessir."

"Well, I saw your grandmother the other week, and she told me you were working in Number Three. I didn't know that—really didn't know anything about you. Didn't have much contact with her while Purnell was alive, so I decided to go see her, and she told me about you. She's very proud of you. I looked up your file. You seem to be doing well. Curt Striker thinks a lot of you, and he's a good man. I called you here to tell you that there's a house over on Ridge Avenue that's going to come open pretty soon, and you can have it if you want it. That sound all right?"

"Yessir, but I'm not sure we can afford it. My wife is going to have a baby, so she won't be working anymore, so . . ."

"Gaynelle told me about the baby. Don't you worry about the rent. I think it will be affordable." He studied his cigar and looked at the ceiling. "Now, if you continue to do as well as you're doing now, good things might happen to you." He exhaled more smoke. "Our family has always been in textiles, and some of us have done pretty good. When I started here, you know what I was doing?"

Tony shook his head.

"I was a sweeper. I swept the floors on the third shift. I worked hard and slowly moved up to where I am now." He blew smoke at the ceiling. "In those days, you didn't make much. If I made a quarter a day, I tried to save a nickel of it. And it paid off. I haven't done bad. Nowadays, you got the union and all the blacks trying to get in here with that crazy school up in Chapel Hill beating the drums for communists and crazy people. Don't guess that means much to you."

"No, sir."

"Good. You stay away from those unions. Get a union in here and between them and the Japs, we'll be out of business. They flood the place with that cheap stuff. I used to think we won the war." He blew more smoke at the ceiling. "Well, I just wanted to meet you. See what you looked like after you grew up. You go see your grandmother more often. She's lonely."

"Yessir."

As if by magic the door opened behind Tony.

"Becky will show you out." He extended his hand across the desk and shook hands again. Tony followed Becky Lewis out the door and to the top of the stairs.

"Good to see you again," she said. "You should visit us more often."

Then he was on the street, headed for home, trying to understand what had happened.

• • •

So they moved into the house on Ridge Avenue. It was only a block down the street from where his great grandmother had lived and the scene of the Christmas gatherings. It was across the street from the Southern Railway tracks, and beyond the tracks was the mill. Number Three Weave Room was easily visible and behind it the mill office and on its roof the logo with the name of the mill. At night, it glowed, and even at this distance, they could hear the low throb of the machinery, looms, spinning machines, and carders.

The house was white clapboard like all the other houses on the street and those nearby, but the ones on Ridge Avenue were a little larger than those behind them. There was no floor furnace. It had radiators and a furnace in the basement that Tony had to supply with coal from a bin to keep the heat coming. Trish said it was a prediction by his uncle of something to come. He thought it was simply luck, a favor to his grandmother from her brother. He was amazed to learn that the rent was no more than on the house in GI Town; he guessed that was thanks to his uncle.

The routine of their lives was the same as before except that now Tony walked to work across the tracks to Number Three Weave Room every morning. Mr. Striker put him in charge of all the loom fixers in No. Three ahead of several of the older workers, but it seemed to work out. Striker even began to send him to the other weave rooms to help with problems they couldn't figure out. The man joked, only half-heartedly, that he was afraid Tony might get promoted out of the weave room, but Tony wasn't interested in leaving.

Trish had the baby in April, a little girl. At first, Tony felt awed by this new life and overwhelmed by the obligations it would mean long into the future. Mr. Striker gave him an hourly raise the day after he returned to work. He was happy, happier than he'd ever been. He had almost pushed memories of things he'd done out of his mind. It was as though those things had happened to someone else, not him, and he wasn't that person anymore. Then one evening after supper, as they were sitting down to watch television, the phone in the hall rang.

Trish stood in the doorway. "It's for you. It's your mother."

Lucinda was crying, saying she needed him to come and help her. Lawson still hadn't given her the money he had promised her a year ago. She had lost her job; she was broke and on the verge of being kicked out of her apartment.

"What can I do about it?"

"You can talk to him."

"Why would he listen to me?"

"I don't want to cause you problems. I know you have a good life now, the baby and all. I sent a baby gift. I think . . . I have until the first of the month to pay my rent or I'm homeless. I think I have another job lined up, but I won't know until after the first." She sniffed and blew her nose. "If you won't talk to him, can you lend me $200 until I get the new job?"

He thought for a moment. He had the money, and it was certainly a better option than going there or having her come back to Maple Grove.

"What's your address?" He wrote it down. "I'll think about it. I have to find the money. If I do, I'll send it to you. I'll do it but just this one time. Don't think you can call me for money again. I got other things to think about now."

"Oh, honey, I wouldn't think of doing it again. I've met this nice guy who runs this high-class restaurant and bar. He's going to give me a job, and this will be the last time I call you about it. I know it seems like I'm always bothering you, and I hate to do it. But, you know, I've helped you out too." She let him think about that for a moment. "I still want that money that Lawson owes me. And I'm gonna get it too." There was another pause. "I'd really like to come and see my granddaughter. Her name is Ellen, right?"

"Sure, you can do that sometime," he said. "I've got to go now."

"Thanks, honey. Bye now."

He put the phone down and went back to the living room. Trish looked up at him from the TV. She went over and turned it off.

"She's in some kind of trouble, right? And she wants you to help, doesn't she? Tony, she's bad news. She's never been good for you. Let her work it out for herself."

"Sounds easy to you, but you don't know everything."

"What do you mean?"

He looked at the floor and shook his head from side to side.

"Nothing." He slumped onto the sofa beside her. "Don't worry about it. I ain't gonna get involved with her again."

She rested her head on his shoulder and he put his arm around her, but later that night, after she had gone to bed, he took money out of an envelope he kept in the top drawer of his dresser. He had saved almost five hundred dollars, which he intended to put toward the purchase of a used boat, but that would have to wait. The next day, he bought a money order at Western Union and mailed two hundred dollars to Lucinda.

Several months went by, and he heard no more from her. Things were busy in No. Three. Mr. Striker called him into his cramped office one afternoon before his shift was over. He was looking at some brochures on his desk. He told Tony to have a seat and passed one of the brochures to him. He studied the picture for a few minutes, trying to fathom what the sleek green machine was. "The Newest Loom by Loewenstein" was written at the top of the brochure.

"Ever heard of this company?" Mr. Striker asked.

Tony shook his head.

"Well, they make looms, and we buy a lot of them. If you go out and wipe the lint and grease from off the top of the machines we're using now, you'll find that name on most of them. Good company. Stuff lasts a long time. We're going to take a look at a few of their new ones. Have them installed over on the far end near the wall. The weavers we assign to them won't like it. Means they have to learn something new and reduce their production for a while, but in the end, if it works out like I think, they'll be glad we got 'em. You will too. Maybe they won't break down as much." He paused and looked up at Tony. "What do you think?"

He shrugged. "Well, it's something new to learn. What weaver you gonna put on 'em?"

"I was thinking about Old Mary. Would that work?"

"For you or me? Probably would work for *you* 'cause you won't have to listen to her bitch all the time like I will. Plus, don't forget she smokes, so she spends a lot of time in the smoke shack. What about somebody younger, like maybe Betty? She's worked long enough to be good at it. She's not half as mean as Mary. I'd rather try her."

"Good. I think that's a good choice. That's the reason I called you in here. The machines will be here next week. They'll send a man to show us how to run them. I want you and Betty *and* Mary to get checked out on them. And one more thing. You've come a long way here about knowing how looms work, so I'm making you a foreman. One thing I want you to work on. You're a good loom fixer but now you have to be able to manage these folks. So I want you to be a little more outgoing. You can do it. Underneath that 'quiet, tough guy' layer there's something else. OK? You'll be helping with the installation of the new machines. After they're in, you'll be running the day-to-day on this shift under me. Think you can do it?"

For once, he didn't hesitate or stammer. "Sure," he said.

"Hey, you get to wear a tie to work like me," Mr. Striker said, extending his arms to show his short-sleeved white shirt and clip-on tie. "Go home and break the good news to that sweet wife."

Tony made his way toward the gate among the other first shifters going home and carrying empty lunch pails. He passed the lake where years ago he had watched the man in the car drown, and then threaded his way across the railroad tracks toward Ridge Avenue and home, rolling over in his mind what had happened to him and how the trajectory of his life had changed from a few years ago, how he had become someone he had only looked at from a distance before, someone he never imagined he could be, or, for that matter, would want to be. How incredibly lucky he was. When he got home, Trish was in the kitchen stirring something on the stove. She greeted him with a kiss blown over her shoulder as he settled into one of the chairs around the breakfast table.

"Where's Ellen?" he asked.

"Playing in her room, I hope. Go check on her."

"They made me a foreman today."

"*Tony*," she said as she turned to him with the spoon still in her hand. "That's wonderful!" She put the spoon down and came to him, sitting in his lap and putting her arms around his neck. "I'm so proud of you and so glad I married you or got you to marry me." She hugged him and kissed him on the lips, holding it a long time.

"I even have to wear a tie to work," he laughed when she finally backed away.

"I love you," she said. "We'll celebrate proper later tonight." They could hear Ellen talking to herself in her room.

• • •

The new looms were installed. Tony and the two weavers followed the Loewenstein man for a week to learn how they worked. Old Mary complained constantly about having to do something different, and Tony acknowledged that it was difficult. The looms had fewer moving parts and were less prone to self-destruct. Mr. Striker and the men who were higher up in the mill hierarchy came and watched the installation. One of them pulled Tony aside as the Loewenstein man was explaining some feature of the machine.

"Son, you want to make sure these things are what they're cracked up to be 'cause they sure cost a hell of a lot of money. We're relying on folks like you to tell us. We're gonna have two weeks after the sales guy here leaves to run them ourselves and make sure we want 'em. A lot will depend on what you and Striker and your weavers say about them. If we buy 'em, it means we spend a half million dollars." He punched Tony playfully on the shoulder. "Don't let us down."

After the instructor left, Tony and Mr. Striker set up a trial to see what the difference in production would be with one of the new looms compared to the old. At the end of two days, the new ones had produced much more than the old with almost no downtime. The weavers were happy. The company purchased the looms. Three months later, Mr. Striker told Tony that management had been impressed with the help he had provided in their purchase. Nothing but good things were ahead.

Then, Lucinda called, hysterical. He couldn't understand her until she had calmed enough to speak without sniveling. "He fired me. He fired me," she said over and over.

"Who fired you?"

"I told you last time we talked that I had met a guy who owned this fancy motel and restaurant. He gave me a job as the evening hostess in the restaurant. Everything was going fine. Business was good. I even got a percentage of the wait staff's tips."

"Well, what happened?"

She sobbed some more. "He hired this young waitress named Gloria for my shift, blond, good-looking. And I could tell right off she wanted my job. Oh, Tony, I was ready to move out of that roach trap I've been living in. Things were going so good. Then one night we checked up short at the register by over fifty dollars. I couldn't figure it out until I remembered that she had asked me if she could get change for a fifty out of the register for a customer to leave a tip. We were busy. I was trying to seat two groups of customers, so I told her to open it and get the change. Then it happened again two nights later. The first time, the boss wasn't too upset, but the second time, he was. Then that night after the place closed, I saw him walking to the parking lot with her, the waitress. Then it started to make sense." She paused and cried for a few seconds. "Then when I came to work the next day, he met me at the door, gave me two weeks' pay in an envelope, and fired me. Wouldn't tell me why. Just said it wasn't working out. Then I found out that Gloria was working as the evening hostess in my place. I'm sure he's screwing the little bitch."

He sighed. "So what have you done since? Have you looked for another job?"

"Yes. But I haven't found anything. I'm going to lose my car and get kicked out of this place too." She paused. "That asshole Lawson still hasn't paid me the money he promised me either."

"Mom, forget that money. Forget the beach. You can come home and live with Grandma and get a job in the mill. Times are good. We need hands."

He could almost see the disdain on her face. "I don't want to do that," she said.

"What else can you do? Sleep in your car if it doesn't get repossessed? I can't run your life for you from here. I've got a family now. I can't do it no more." He could feel the anger radiating from her.

"All right," she hissed. "I'm gonna try one more week to find another job. If I can't, then I'll come up there."

"That makes sense. I hope you find a job, but if you don't, then you have a place to come to." He hung up.

Trish was watching him from the doorway, holding Ellen in her arms. "Is she coming back here?"

"Probably."

• • •

The next week, the phone rang while they were watching TV. Trish answered, then stood in the hall doorway with the phone in her hand. He knew it would be Lucinda from the look on her face. When he took the phone, he could already hear her crying.

"OK. What's happened?"

"They repossessed my car," she whispered, "and I don't have a job. I got no way to get back up there with my things."

He said nothing.

"Can you come get me?"

"Have you talked to Grandma? Does she know you're coming?"

"No. I'll call her after we hang up here. Will you come?"

"Yeah. I guess so." He thought about the timing. It was Thursday. "I'll come on Saturday. I'll be there right after noon. Can you be ready then?"

"Yeah. I guess."

"Then I'll see you then. You be sure and call Grandma." He hung up and went into the den to tell Trish.

• • •

THE LOOM FIXER

Tony took the old route, passing through the familiar small towns like Red Cross and Locust Level and through the peach orchards in the upper sand hills. He slowed as he came to the familiar scene that had run through his mind so often—the robbery of the liquor store outside of Chesterfield. He slowed and pulled into the parking lot. The rusty screen door still sagged on its hinges, and the place was as dark as it had been on the first two times he had been there. He looked for the nearly blind woman behind the counter, but there was a middle-aged man there instead. He was short, wearing bib overalls and a baseball cap. He was sitting in a cane chair, leaning back against the wall when Tony walked in. Tony wandered the aisles until he found a pint of cheap vodka and took it to the counter to pay. The man eased his chair up and took a bag from beside the cash register to put the bottle in.

"Where's the lady that used to run this place?" Tony asked.

"My aunt. She died a couple months ago. You know her?"

"Nah. But I used to stop in here on the way to the beach. I saw her a couple times. Sorry." He handed the man a twenty and turned to walk out.

"Hey, you got some change comin'," the man said.

"It's OK. You keep it."

He got in the car and didn't know whether he felt good or bad. That all happened in another life. He was not like that now, but he wasn't like that then, not completely. It was Willis who caused that to happen. He had just been riding in the car. It was like Sonny Murphy. He didn't want that to happen. Every time he had crossed over the line, it had been mostly because of someone else, even the time he stole the blouse, but that was a small thing compared to the others. Murphy deserved what he got. It was either Murphy or his mother, and that was an easy choice. At least it was then.

He rolled along the blacktop, getting closer to the coast as water and swamps and moss-covered cypress trees began to appear on either side of the road. Then he came to the intersection with the long ribbon of Highway 17. The hundreds of small stores selling beach gear and exotic plants that lined each side of it stretched away and shimmered in the afternoon heat. It took him a few moments to remember on which part of the highway the squalid little motel Lucinda had been living in was located. It was getting close to dusk, and the place looked like a black-and-white photograph sandwiched among the shade of the trees. The concrete block walls were a dingey white-gray. The roof was black and covered with old pine needles. There were maybe twenty rooms but only two cars in the sand parking lot. He parked in front of her room. There was a piece of paper taped to the wooden frame of the screen door: *I'm at Lawson's office. Pick me up there.*

Why is she there on a Saturday? he thought as he drove back up Highway 17 toward the business area of town.

There was little traffic around Lawson's office. He parked in the lot and walked up the sidewalk, listening to the cicadas singing in the surrounding trees. The front door of the office was slightly ajar. The waiting room, always full all the other times he'd been there, was dark and empty.

"Hello," he called from the waiting room.

When he got no response, he tentatively moved to the door to Lawson's office and pushed it open. The room was dimly lit by a light on the desk. He waited for his eyes to adjust to the light. He started when Lucinda called to him from a chair in the corner.

"Thanks for coming, honey."

Tony struggled to make her out in the gloom. She appeared to be holding a black object in her lap. There was a pungent smell in the room. He turned to Lawson's desk. The lawyer was slumped in his swivel chair. He was wearing a bright Hawaiian shirt with a red-and-yellow flower pattern. His glasses were down on his nose, and there was a round hole almost in the center of his forehead. His belt was unbuckled, and his pants were gaping open. A stream of blood ran from the wound under his glasses and disappeared under his chin and down his shirt. His eyes were open and staring slightly down.

In that instant, Tony knew that everything was about to change. He saw his wife, child, job, the life he had made in the last few years disappear. It was as though he had just come down the road with Willis, escaping whatever scrapes happened, living from day to day, waiting for something to happen like any of the other inconsequential people in the world. But he had a choice: turn and walk out of the office and leave her to her own ends or try to help with the risks he knew it would mean. He turned to look at his mother again.

"I had no choice. He wouldn't give me the money even after I'd let him treat me like shit again and do the awful things he wanted me to do to him and him do to me. So . . ."

Tony still said nothing, wavering, almost walking out the door.

"I helped you once, don't forget. Took an awful chance for you," she said.

"I sort of looked on it like I was helping *you* then. You was sort of a prisoner there. Or at least, we helped each other."

"You're all I've got. Nobody else to help. Please."

"What can I do? What can anybody do? What's your plan? I came here to help you move back and damn." He shook his head.

She looked up at the dark ceiling. "I don't have any plan."

"Then what do you want from me?"

"Just get rid of this." She held up a revolver. "Do something with it. I think I've got time to get out of town before they find him. Haven't had any connection with him in months. Nobody saw me come here. If I wipe everything and get rid of the prints, I've got a chance. Will you do that for me? The pistol, I mean?"

He knew instantly how dangerous this was, but he weighed what she was asking against what she could have asked. If he could get rid of it, go home, and be rid of her, it would be worth it, much less than he could have risked. He weighed it for a second, thinking that he could toss it in one of the canal ditches outside of Conway and be home by midnight to his real life.

"Give it to me. And make sure you wipe down everything."

She rose from the chair and handed the pistol to him. Then she hugged him. "Thanks. Thanks," she whispered. "I'll call you when I can." She took a handkerchief from her purse and wiped the surface of the desk, the wood on the chairs, and the door knobs. Then she left.

Tony looked at the black gun in his hand and tried to decide what would be best, but there was nothing to do but get in the car, get rid of the gun, and go home. He tried to remember what he had touched, then Lawson's office phone began to ring. It rang so many times he couldn't count them, and then it stopped. He put the gun in his back pocket and walked through the dim, silent waiting room. He drew the building door closed gently, wiping the knob clean, and walked to the parking lot.

As he was getting in the Ford, a man walking a small dog along the sidewalk passed the parking lot and nodded at him. He turned his head away so the man couldn't see his face, and then he eased out of the lot and headed for Highway 17. It was getting dark. By the time he had wended his way through town traffic and gotten to the highway, it was fully dark. Conway was about twenty miles north from the beach. He would have his first opportunity to toss the pistol there. It was cutting into his back, so he stashed it under the seat and drove carefully—but not too carefully, nothing to attract attention.

Just before he got to Conway, he looked in the rearview mirror and saw a small blue light behind him. It got close quickly, and soon he could hear the wail of a siren and see the lights flashing on the grill. He slowed and pulled over to let it pass, but it slowed rapidly and pulled up next to his rear bumper. There was little room on the side of the road before it fell away to a low swampy area that paralleled the road. Part of his car and the cop car were still out in the highway. Two cops got out with weapons drawn and approached him but stopped before they got all the way to the car.

One, hatless and wearing a white short-sleeved shirt, motioned for him to roll down his window. He was burly with ham-like arms and hands. "Roll down your window and keep your hands where we can see them," he yelled above the roar of the passing traffic.

Tony rolled the window down slowly.

"Step out of the car, sir, with your hands up." One of them directed a strong flashlight beam at his face so that he couldn't see.

"What's this about? I wasn't speeding, and I ain't been drinking."

"Not about drinking, buddy. Step out of the car. Turn around and put your hands on the hood." Cars were flashing by, slowing and swerving to look and avoid them. One of the cops took Tony's billfold out of his back pocket. "Mr. Pettyjohn, can we search your car?"

He hesitated but then said, "Sure."

They looked on the seats, in the glove box, and then under the seats. It took only a moment for them to find the pistol. One of them smelled the barrel. "Since there ain't anyone else in the car, I reckon this would belong to you. Right, Mr. Pettyjohn?"

Tony was handcuffed and shoved into the back of the police car. When they turned around and headed back from where he had come, he said through the barrier, "That ain't my gun. I never saw it before."

"You can tell that to the detectives in Myrtle Beach, bud. Save your breath for them." Tony, with his hands fastened behind his back, swayed back and forth uncomfortably as they sped down the road.

"What's this all about? Why did you stop me? I ain't done nothing."

The cop on the passenger side turned toward him. "Somebody saw your car coming away from a murder scene. Got your license and saw it was a North Carolina tag."

The cop driving punched the other. "Shut up. Let the detectives do this," he said.

• • •

Tony was roughly ushered through an entryway and office area where cops were typing, looking at files, or reading newspapers. They all paused what they were doing and looked up at him as he was led by. He was put in a small, brightly lit room furnished with a green metal table and a metal chair in place on each side. They put him in the chair facing the entry door and handcuffed his right arm to the chair. Then he was left alone for what seemed like an hour when finally a man in a wrinkled black suit and a food-stained black tie came in. He was swarthy, his hair short in a crew cut that was lumpy and uneven. He had a sharp nose and a small downturned mouth. His face looked like it had been slightly compressed, pushing the nose down close to the mouth and giving him the overall look of a small hawk. He took a seat in the chair opposite Tony, put a file folder on the table, and rested his palms down next to the file. His fingernails had little halfmoons of dirt under them, and he smelled like cigarettes.

"I'm Detective Caldwell, Mr. Pettyjohn. You know why you're here?"

"No." He shook his head.

"You knew Attorney Lawson?"

"Yeah. Why?"

"He was murdered this afternoon in his office. A man walking by saw a car like yours and someone who would fit your description driving away."

"Wasn't me. I don't know what you're talking about. I haven't seen Lawson in a couple years."

"How'd you know him?"

"He represented my mother a couple years ago."

"What was her name?"

"Lucinda Pettyjohn."

The detective looked at the wall over Tony's head for a second, and then he got up. He returned after a few minutes. He was smiling slightly.

"I remember that case. Your mom shot Sonny Murphy. Right? Got off scot-free too."

"She didn't do it."

"Well, nobody else was ever charged. 'Course that might have been cause Murphy was a rat drug dealer and ever'body was better off with him dead. Curious that with your past history that this has happened. *Coincidence*. What about the gun we found under the seat of your car that we are having checked now for a match with the one that killed Lawson?"

"I ain't sayin' nothing else. I want a lawyer."

The detective frowned and looked down at the file and shook his head. "You can make this a tough as you want, Pettyjohn. I'm just trying to give you a break. Wouldn't give anybody heartburn in this department for Snake Lawson to get what he had comin'. If you know what I mean. He never did any of us a lot of favors except for his cheap yearly Christmas party."

Tony looked down at the table. "I want a lawyer."

The detective grimaced and slapped the table lightly with his hands. "OK. We'll get you a lawyer."

They put him in a cell in the bowels of the police building. A dirty bunk hung from the wall on a couple chains, and there was a metal commode, stinking and smeared with brown smudges. A small swarm of gnats hovered over it. A lavatory was on one wall. He sat on the bunk, thinking of what to do. He needed to call Trish. She needed to know where he was. When a jailer walked by, he went to the bars.

"Don't I get to make a telephone call or something?" he yelled as the man passed by.

He returned in a few minutes. "OK, Mac, you get your call."

He put a key in the lock, but before he could turn it, Tony stopped him. He hadn't made up his mind about what to say, how to explain it, what his plan was. She would be furious, and he wasn't ready for it. "Wait a minute. I don't want to make it right now."

"Make your damn mind up, bud. I ain't got time to waste with you."

Tony sat down on the dirty mattress. He wouldn't have known what to say. He didn't know how to explain it. He would wait until he talked to the lawyer.

. . .

One morning, a few days later, after he had eaten a plate of rubbery eggs and a piece of untoasted white bread for breakfast, the jailer came to the door and unlocked it. They hooked him up to a string of other prisoners all dressed in orange jumpsuits and wearing rubber shower shoes, then herded them shuffling down a dim corridor up some steps and out into the bright sunlight.

When he passed a guard, he asked, "Where are we going?"

"Courtroom," the man grunted.

The prisoners entered a side door on a building Tony could vaguely remember from Lucinda's trial. When they came to a door with a sign over the top that said "Courtroom," they were stopped. They stood for long minutes outside. The bailiff came to get each of them as their cases were called. When finally he came for Tony and the door opened, he was led into a familiar courtroom. He also recognized the man standing at the prosecution table. It was Ravenel, who had turned to watch him enter. He stared at Tony and raised his hand in recognition, smiling slightly.

The bailiff turned Tony toward the judge, who was reading a paper before him.

"What matter is this, Mr. DA?"

"Your Honor, this is case 67-10084, *State vs. Tony Pettyjohn*. Mr. Pettyjohn is charged with the murder of Gilbert Sidney Lawson on or about the seventeenth day of July of this year."

The judge looked curiously at Tony. "Mr. Pettyjohn, do you understand the charge against you?"

"Yes, Your Honor."

"Do you have an attorney and do you have the ability to afford one? If you do not, then the court will appoint one to represent you and the state will pay for it."

Tony said nothing.

"Well, Mr. Pettyjohn?"

"I don't understand, judge. I had fifty dollars in my billfold when I came down here. They took it from me, but I reckon it's still there."

"Fifty dollars won't get you far with our high-priced lawyers around here, Mr. Pettyjohn."

There was snickering from the bystanders.

"The clerk will give you a form to fill out, which will list all your assets. Meantime, I'm going to appoint one of these fine counselors to represent you."

The judge looked toward a bench behind the prosecution table where five or six men were sitting. One, an older man, was dozing with his chin on his chest and gripping a briefcase with both hands on his stomach. At the other end of the group sat a man much younger than the others, and unlike them, he was listening intently to the conversation between the judge and Tony.

"Mr. McCoy?"

The younger lawyer jumped to his feet.

"Yes, Your Honor."

"Have you represented anyone in a murder trial yet?"

"No, Your Honor."

"Well, you're going to now."

The expression on McCoy's face, which had gone from red to ashen, was a mixture of panic and enthusiasm.

"Mr. Pettyjohn, Mr. McCoy will be representing you at your arraignment, which will be in just a few days. At that time, you will enter a plea to your charges. Mr. DA, call your next case."

• • •

A jailer appeared at Tony's cell door. "Your lawyer wants to see you. Come on and bring that tray with you so I won't have to come get it again. If you're finished, that is."

Tony was handcuffed and led to the same small room from the night of his arrest. McCoy was standing at the table. He was perhaps thirty, Tony thought. He wore a dark blue suit and had longish blond hair combed back on each side of his head. He had a large nose and a downturned mouth as well as the beginnings of a sparse moustache. An open briefcase was on the table with a yellow pad and pen beside it.

After Tony had been handcuffed to the chair, the deputy said, "You got thirty minutes, Counselor." The word "counselor" was drenched in sarcasm. And he left.

They looked at each other for a moment. McCoy spoke first. "My name is Thomas McCoy, and I've been appointed to represent you, Mr. Pettyjohn." He pulled out the chair across from Tony, sat down, and picked up the pen. "Let's start by you giving me a little information about yourself, like where you live, what you do for a living, any family information, that sort of thing, and then I would like for you to tell me your story about what happened and how you come to be here."

"Can I get bail or something? How do I get out of here?"

"Bail will be set at the hearing tomorrow morning. Look, I don't know if you'll get bail. Charge is going to be murder, and you aren't a resident. I'll do what I can, but don't be disappointed if they keep you in jail until the trial."

"When will that be?"

"I don't know. We'll get a little better idea of that tomorrow."

"There's a bondsman here. My momma used him once. Stowe, something. Gabe Stowe. You know him?"

"Yes, and how is it your mother used him?"

"She was tried down here a couple years ago."

"For what?"

"Murder." He paused. "Lawson represented her."

There was silence while McCoy considered this. "*Damn*. I remember it now. She shot a guy. What was his name? Yes,

Sonny Murphy. Over behind the Fish Hook. Or she was charged with it. It was my last year in law school. Didn't Lawson represent her?"

"Yeah. I just told you."

McCoy put his hands over his eyes again and slowly shook his head. "Now, how did this coincidence come about? Just tell me that. You get arrested for the murder of the lawyer who walked your mother on a murder charge back when." He looked at the ceiling. "Seems like maybe fate doesn't like you in Horry County, Mr. Pettyjohn."

"If I can't get bail, or if I can't make it, when will they try this case?"

"Depends on how fast the DA wants to do it. I would say a couple months at the earliest. Besides, I was just finishing law school when your mother was tried and the DA caught a lot of flak for her walking. He's gonna want to make the most of this. He might let it cure for a while."

Tony's head sank, chin resting on chest. "I got a job, a wife, and a kid. I can't wait that long."

"I'll do what I can. I can make a motion for a speedy trial. Means they have to try you six months after the arraignment. Now, let's talk about what happened."

He had been so confused and his thoughts so jumbled since the arrest that he had not considered a story that would be plausible. He was silent.

"C'mon, Mr. Pettyjohn, I'm your lawyer. Just tell me what happened." His pen was poised on the clean yellow pad.

"My mom lives down here. She lost her job and was getting kicked out of her place. I came down here to help her move. I went to her place, but she wasn't there. I waited for an hour for her to come back, but she never did, so I turned around and started home, figuring she got somebody else to help her. I was just outside of Conway when they stopped me." He was silent.

"That's *it*? That's what happened?"

"Yeah."

"What about the gun?"

"It's not my gun. I don't know where it came from. Maybe they planted it."

McCoy looked down at the pad, put his hand over his eyes again, and shook his head.

"Shit," he said. "You have any witnesses that can put you anywhere last Saturday afternoon except at Lawson's office? I haven't talked to the DA except just briefly, but they have a man who says he saw you or someone who looked like you in a Ford same make, model, and color as yours coming out of Lawson's parking lot late the day of the murder. Says the car had North Carolina plates with your number, he thinks. *Thinks* is the only thing we've got to work on. We're gonna need something to put you somewhere else." He looked at Tony. "Well?"

"I need to think."

"You better think of some better explanation for the gun while you're at it."

But he knew there was no explanation except the unbelievable one that it was planted.

• • •

Tony had left home four days ago. Trish would be frantic. He knew he had to call but still didn't know what to say. He was embarrassed to admit that Lucinda had again got him into the most serious trouble he had ever been in. He was torn between telling her the truth of what happened and making up a story, but he couldn't think of a story that wasn't laughable or so implausible that it would be ludicrous. But he called.

"Trish," he said when she answered.

"Where are you? Why haven't you called sooner?" Her voice was near a scream.

"Something's happened," he said. They were both silent.

"She's got you in trouble again, hasn't she?"

"I'm in jail in Horry County." He could hear her slumping onto the stool near the phone table.

"What? For what?"

"I was driving back Saturday night and got stopped outside of Conway. They found a pistol under the seat of the car."

"What pistol? Whose?"

He was silent until she prompted him again.

"Whose pistol?"

He had to decide if he would tell her the story, or make up a story.

"Tell me what happened."

He knew nothing else to do but tell the truth. He was too tired and too guileless to concoct a story, and so he told her just as it happened. She sobbed quietly while he talked.

"She's ruined our lives. Ruined it all finally," she hissed, and then she demanded, "Are you going to let her do this to us?"

He leaned against the dirty green wall the phone was on. He started to reply, but before he could, she screamed, "You have to tell the cops what happened. Think of *us* for a change. Think of yourself instead of always her. Don't you think she's sucked enough out of your life?"

"It ain't like she never did anything for me." He could hear her cursing. "There's things you don't know about what happened down there that last time. Things I never told you."

"What things?"

He said nothing.

"What things?"

"I shot that guy down there a couple years ago. Sonny Murphy. And she took the heat for it."

She was silent while she considered this. "I don't believe you, and even if it's true, I don't care. What's done is done. If you don't tell them what happened, I will. I'll come down there and go to the cops myself."

"Don't. I've got a lawyer. Let me just see how this looks like it's going to play out, and then I'll decide what to do."

"You're crazy. She killed one of the most famous people in the county. She was involved with him a couple years ago. This is going to be a big story. You aren't going to beat this or get off with some plea bargain."

"I gotta at least try. She helped me once before. I got to help her now."

"Yeah. She's always been a big help to you."

. . .

Tony's bail was set at five hundred thousand dollars. He didn't even try to contact the bondsman. There was no way he could make that under any circumstances, so he had to wait in the county jail until Ravenel was ready to try the case. McCoy attempted to work a plea deal, but Ravenel wasn't remotely interested.

"Not on your life, Mr. McCoy, or I guess I should say not on your client's life." He smiled at his joke. "He and his mama gave me a black eye a couple years ago. Almost cost me an election. Not gonna happen again."

So that his client wouldn't have to stay in jail any longer than he had to, McCoy made a motion for a speedy trial, requiring the DA to try him within six months. Ravenel accommodated him. He calendared the case to be tried in sixty days.

• • •

Tony met with Trish in the ugly interrogation room the day before the trial.

"I'm going to the DA," she said, "and I'm gonna tell him that she did it and you're taking the fall for her," she said.

"No, don't do it. First off, he won't believe you. It will just make things worse."

"So you're gonna give up me, Ellen, your whole life for her?"

He was silent, head down considering it all. He knew she was right. His life would be gone, but he also knew that no one would believe that he had not killed Lawson. Everything pointed to him—the car, the gun—and nothing pointed to her. His mother had amazing luck; she seemed untouchable. He didn't answer her question.

"Then, go ahead. Throw it all away for that woman." And she left.

• • •

It didn't go so well this time. The players were still the same: Judge Porcher and DA Ravenel. The sheriff had changed. Rowdy had lost the last election. But no one was more competent than before. Lucinda was not suspected, and she had disappeared, probably to Florida. McCoy did the best job he could do with what he had. He worked hard to discredit the witness who had seen Tony leaving the parking lot, hammering his recollection about what he had seen in the failing light of dusk, but the man didn't waiver as to the color, make, approximate year of the car, the license tag, and that the driver was a white male who looked like Tony.

Trish and Grandma sat in the gallery, both of them crying audibly throughout the two days of testimony and arguments. McCoy argued that there was nothing to tie Tony to the murder except the shaky eyewitness testimony of the dogwalker and the pistol.

And it was the pistol that sealed his fate. No matter what McCoy tried, he couldn't lessen the damage it did. It had Tony's fingerprints all over it, it had been recently fired, and an expert from the State Law Enforcement Division testified that it was the weapon that killed Lawson, that the bullet found in his chair, which had passed through his head on its way into the chair, had come from that pistol. McCoy argued that no test had been done on Tony to see if there was powder residue from a recently fired pistol. The State responded that it was not necessary. It was never completely accurate at any rate.

Tony would not testify. McCoy warned him that it would be the only way to get his slim story before the jury, no matter how weak it was, but Tony didn't want to sit in that chair with all those eyes on him—Porcher, Ravenel, the jury, Grandma, Trish, and all the spectators—and fumble through a lie and look like a fool. It left his entire fate resting on what little had been gained from McCoy's cross-examination of the eyewitness, and on that, the defense rested.

Since the defense had offered no evidence, the prosecution had to address the jury first, and McCoy would get the final argument. Ravenel was brief. There was really no reason to wax eloquent over as clear a case as he had: a witness saw a car like the defendant's leaving the parking lot at the deceased's office at or near the time of death determined by the coroner. The driver generally fit the description of the defendant. The defendant was arrested later on the road headed toward his home in North Carolina with a pistol under the seat of his car. The gun had recently been fired, had his fingerprints on it, and was determined to be the weapon that had killed Lawson.

The weak point in his case was motive. Ravenel argued that the defendant and the deceased knew each other from the prior trial of the former's mother and that his mother had maintained a long relationship with the deceased until some months before his death, so there was a connection. And where was the mother? Why wasn't she seated behind her son during this ordeal? But what did any of that matter when there was eyewitness testimony and the possession of the murder weapon? Ravenel asked for the maximum sentence: death in the electric chair, "Old Sparky," in Columbia. It was deserved for such a brutal crime. He finished his argument at the rail in front of the jurors. They looked back at him grimly.

And then it was McCoy's turn. He was pale as he stood, clasped his hands, and turned to face the jury box. When he first spoke, it was almost inaudible. His tongue seemed to stick to the roof of his mouth, but he paused and recovered. He talked about the enormous power of the state when it was turned on a simple citizen like Tony, how difficult it was to counter all the weapons it could turn against someone of little means. He went through the testimony of the eyewitness and how unreliable eyewitness testimony was. But what about the pistol? He related how the arresting officer had asked Tony about the pistol, and he had replied that it wasn't his and he didn't know how it got in his car. So was it planted by someone? The police? The real murderer?

Ravenel objected at this point, saying there was no evidence to support it and that McCoy was testifying. The objection unsettled McCoy, but he was almost finished anyway, so it didn't make much difference. He ended by pointing to Grandma and Trish. He made reference to their loyalty and the fact that Tony was a father with a small child. Why would he have come south to kill a man he hadn't seen in years? It made no sense. He asked the jury to consider all these matters and rested.

Tony waved to Trish and Grandma before the bailiff took him back to the holding pen to wait for the verdict. It was not a long wait. After one hour, he was led back into the courtroom. Porcher asked the foreman if they had reached a verdict.

"Guilty of first-degree murder," he said, and it was unanimous.

McCoy, not knowing what else to do, asked that the jury be polled. They all confirmed the verdict. Porcher asked Tony to stand. McCoy stood with him, looking even more stricken than Tony. Porcher asked Tony if he had anything to say before he was sentenced.

He looked up at Porcher, turned, and with his head slightly bent, scanned the jury, then looking at the judge, he said in a low voice, "I want ever'body to know that"—and he paused—"that I ain't a bad person. I mean, when I was younger, I did some things I ain't proud of, but they were little things, kinda things you do when you're not old enough to know better. I stole some stuff, but it was to help my mom." He looked down at his feet. "I reckon most of the things that have got me into trouble have to do with my mom, but she's not a bad person either."

His voice began to rise so that the jurors who at first had been leaning forward to hear him better now moved back into their seats.

"I mean, I know about Jesus and Cain and Abel. I heard those things in Sunday School when my grandma took me to church. We just never had much money. I was always on the edge of my grandpa kicking me out of the house until finally I just left. What I mean is, sometimes something seems right to you, and you've looked at it from all sides and feel it oughta be done, but maybe it don't look that way to somebody else, or even to the law, I guess." He stared at the jurors. "But no matter what's happened, I ain't a bad person. I'm a loom fixer. A *loom fixer*. That's an important job in a cotton mill. It's more than I ever thought I could do back in the day when my grandpa kicked me out, and I'm good at it and proud of it. And not only that, I got a wife and a little girl."

He turned and pointed at Trish, who had covered her face with her hands. The courtroom was still except for a few shuffling feet and muffled coughs.

"I didn't do this. I know it looks like I did, but I swear I didn't. I swear I didn't." He looked up at Porcher, who was leaning back with his eyes closed. "I reckon that's all."

Porcher opened his eyes, leaning forward in his chair. "I'm going to recess this proceeding until tomorrow at ten o'clock, at which time I will sentence the defendant. Mr. McCoy, you will have an opportunity to present mitigating evidence with regard to sentencing at that time." He banged his gavel.

"All rise," intoned the bailiff, and Porcher swept out, and the rest began to mill about. The bailiffs came to take Tony, but as they were taking him away, a heavy woman followed by a withered little man made her way to the railing. She clutched a pocketbook with both hands in front of her. Her mouth was a tight line.

"*Well*," she said in a voice loud enough for surrounding people to hear. "You finally got some of what you deserve. You and that slut mother of yours and that sleazy lawyer. You don't remember me, do you? I'm Sonny Murphy's mother, the man your mother shot down like a dog and then got away with it. So maybe she won't ever get what *she* deserves, but you'll have to do, you and that filthy lawyer. I'm glad he's dead, and I hope they sentence you to the electric chair."

One of the bailiffs had gone to the railing and told the couple to move on. She waddled away among the other spectators, looking back sneeringly over her shoulder with the little old man following behind. The other bailiffs led Tony away.

McCoy arranged for him to meet with Trish that evening. It was in the same dingy, stale-smelling interview room where everything seemed to happen. She looked beaten down, hopeless, but at the same time angry. When they brought her in, he almost flinched at her expression, but she came around the table and stooped to put her arms around him and cried softly into his shoulder. He was chained to the table and unable to rise, but he twisted and put his hand on her shoulder.

"I'm so sorry. I'm so sorry," he said.

"Nothing left to say now." She moved around the table and sat down. "She could come back and tell people what happened. But she won't do that, I guess. I could go to your lawyer and tell him that you told me what happened and testify if he wanted me to."

"And do you think anybody would believe you?" He shrugged. "Ain't it kind of evened out, I guess? I mean, she took the heat for me on one killing, and I took the heat for her on another." He looked down at his hands. "Just didn't work out the same way."

"No, and it has a lot of different results. You weren't married then. You didn't have a child. What am I supposed to do now? Daddy's so mad at me. If it weren't for Ellen, I don't think he'd let us live with them. Which is what we're gonna have to do. You realize that, don't you? And have you thought about that before you ever get a chance to get out, if they don't send you to the chair, Ellen will be grown and we'll be old people? And it was all because of her."

She was crying now, and he sat with his head down, staring at his fingers. There was a knock on the door, and a bailiff appeared.

"That's all the time you got, folks." He held the door open for Trish.

She turned to Tony as she walked out. "Bye, Tony. I love you." Her back had turned to him before she had finished speaking, and she was gone.

The bailiff took him to his holding cell. There was an envelope on the bunk. He looked at the outside, but there was no return address. He didn't recognize the writing, almost didn't know what to do with it, but finally he gingerly tore it open and unfolded it. *Dear Tony*, it began. *I'm so sorry I left you with that mess, but I didn't have any choice.*

He dropped it into his lap without finishing it and swiveled onto the dirty mattress, staring at the ceiling spattered with motes of grime and cobwebs. He couldn't imagine being old, Ellen being grown. It would be a different life. He couldn't imagine being dead either.

On short notice, McCoy had only been able to get Grandma and Mr. Striker to come and offer evidence as to his Tony's character. Grandma haltingly, and with prompts from McCoy, recited how Tony had grown up from an early age, that he had always worked and paid for his own room and board, that she had taken him to church when he was small, and that he had never been in trouble for her even though he had made one mistake and taken a blouse from a department store. He had spent a year in a training school for that mistake. It had done him much good, and he had turned out a good man, was respected in the town, and had a good job. She finished by crying into her already wet handkerchief.

Then Mr. Striker took the stand. He gave a brief history of Tony's work in the mill, how he had become one of the best loom fixers he'd ever seen, how he was never late, and how he had a young family. He was sure there was some mistake in this. He just didn't see how Tony could have killed anyone. And then it was over. The DA offered nothing and didn't rebut any of the testimony. Porcher took another fifteen-minute recess before pronouncing sentence.

The spectators had mostly kept their seats during the interval, waiting to find out what justice would finally be delivered. The bailiff commanded all to rise as Porcher returned, robes streaming behind him. He sat, put his glasses toward the end of his nose, looked at some papers on the desk before he gazed at Tony—or maybe some point above his head—and said, "Stand up, Mr. Pettyjohn."

Tony rose, and McCoy rose beside him.

"For the murder of Robert Lawson, I sentence you to not more than sixty years and not less than twenty years in the state penitentiary in Columbia." He rapped his gavel. "That ends these proceedings."

Sixty years is so long, I can't imagine it. Maybe the death penalty would have been better, Tony thought.

It was hard to tell whether the crowd was satisfied or outraged at the sentence. There was murmuring that got louder with each minute as they filed out the door.

"He'd 'a got Old Sparky if it had been anybody but a lawyer that he killed," one man said loud enough for all to hear, which prompted snickering from some of the crowd.

Tony turned to see Trish standing alone in one of the bench rows. She waved at him, and then she was gone. The bailiff took him by the arm to lead him away.

"We can appeal," McCoy said to him before he was gone, but Tony scarcely heard him.

Tony stumbled through the door, being jerked along by the bailiff, the rustlings and murmurings behind him being the last he would hear of unchained humans for a long time.

. . .

The guards had to wait to assemble enough prisoners going to the penitentiary in Columbia before making the trip, so it was several days of nothingness in the rancid holding pens for Tony and several others, all of whom insisted that they were innocent, had got a bad deal, a bad lawyer, or bad luck. Tony would be fifty-two if he served his minimum sentence. Ellen would be grown.

When they had accumulated enough people to justify a trip, they herded them all onto a bare-bones bus with hard bench seats. The bus had made other stops on the way, and there were already a number of prisoners on it when it picked up the group from Conway. They all looked like they had been on it for days, haggard, some slumped in the corners of the hard seats trying to sleep up against the metal walls and dirty windows. A greasy food smell permeated the tight space, and the floor was littered with cardboard boxes and wrapping paper from box meals eaten days ago. Tony and the man shackled to him were shoved toward an empty bench near the back.

Tony punched the shoulder of a man on the seat in front of him. "How long you been on this bus?" he asked.

"Three days. State don't have but one, and it goes through a bunch of counties after big court days to make pickups for

Columbia. I think we got at least two more stops before we git there."

At least Tony had the seat next to the window. He tried to rest his head against it, but the chain attached to the person next to him didn't give him much slack, and every time the bus swayed, it pulled him away from the window. His companion, a slightly built boy who didn't look older than sixteen, cried quietly for hours and mumbled to himself, maybe praying or talking to his mother, apologizing for what he had done.

At noon, they pulled into a small town in the midlands and stopped at a courthouse complex surrounded by live oaks. All courthouses and grounds seemed to look alike. Another string of prisoners stumbled up the steps and found seats in the back. Then a guard came down the aisle handing out paper bags. Inside there was a sandwich, two pieces of bread with a green-gray slab of meat between them, and an apple. The guard stopped before he got to the new arrivals and turned to go. "

"What about us?" a new prisoner asked.

"You just come from the jail. You should have already ate," the guard answered.

"Shit. Screwed again. Always this way."

"Shut up. Or you won't get supper either."

"Here, buddy, you can have this miserable crap," a prisoner in front of the complainer said and tossed his crumpled bag over the seat. "I can't eat it."

The bus wound through Lake City and Florence, where it picked up more prisoners. It crossed a big river, and then they could see the outlines of the city and a drab gray building, walls punctuated by towers at long intervals. As they got closer, they could see a high chain-link fence with razor wire at the top and with steel towers at intervals like the ones used as fire lookouts that Tony had seen in the long stretches of woods on the way to the beach. Uniformed guards manned the towers, each carrying a shotgun.

It had been raining, and the ugly building was wreathed in mist. The windows, what few there were, had been painted over and made useless for seeing in or out. The bus stopped at a gate and waited while a guard opened the fence and raised a bar that ran across the drive. They lurched forward, closer to a building. To Tony, it looked a lot like the mill, but it wasn't throbbing, humming, and clacking like the mill. It was silent and oppressive, almost as though it were observing its new occupants, ready to gobble them up.

The bus stopped at a concrete ramp. Two guards sat at a table at the foot of the ramp. A guard came on the bus and told the prisoners to get up, which prompted a lot of shuffling and clanking of chains and cursing as the manacles caused them to trip. When they were all standing, the guard told them to move to the door, step off the bus, and form a line at the table. They stumbled off and were roughly shoved into a crooked formation by other guards.

"Get closer to the table," a guard yelled and grabbed the closest prisoner and pulled him toward it, causing stumbling and lurching through the ranks.

THE LOOM FIXER

The boy who had been crying next to Tony fell. Tony reached as best he could to help him up. A guard behind him hit him in the small of his back with a wooden baton.

"Don't touch nobody else, rat. We'll take care of him." He yanked the boy to his feet by his chained hands. The boy was sobbing loudly. "Shut up or we'll give you something to cry about, faggot."

Each man was questioned at the table, and when the interview was over, the manacles were removed and each was led off in various directions to whatever fate awaited him. When Tony's turn came, the guard seated at the table asked his name. He then ran his finger down a list of names on a clipboard.

He looked up at Tony. "Murder, huh? We got a special place for you. What did you do on the outside?"

"I was a loom fixer in a cotton mill."

"Too bad we ain't got any looms here, but I think I know where to put you. How'd you like to make flags all day?"

Tony shrugged.

"It could be worse, rat. I could put you in the laundry."

"Guess it'll be all right."

"Good. How far did you get in school?"

"I finished high school."

"More educated than most of these rats. OK." He looked at a guard standing behind Tony. "Take him to Block K. See if they can find room for him."

Tony was unshackled from the man behind him, but the manacles were left on his arms and legs. The guard motioned for him to walk toward the nearest building, and he shuffled along as best he could, prodded in the back by the guard. When they reached a gray metal door, the guard pushed a button on the outside. There was a buzz, and then the sound of a bolt opening as the door swung open. Bulbs on the ceiling of a long corridor provided a pale yellow light. The air had a musty smell mixed with the faint odor of disinfectant. The door slammed shut behind them. They eventually came to an empty cell. His guard removed the manacles and pushed him into the cell and then closed the iron bars behind him. A bolt slid shut.

"Guess you could say welcome to your new home," the guard said.

The block was a special area only for murderers, and he had no cellmate. Murderers were kept to themselves for the safety of the other prisoners, although the longer he was there, the more he came to think that the killers were more rational and predictable than the rest of the population. Thieves and dopeheads were the worst. The thieves had mostly been liars all their lives. The dopers would do anything or say anything to get what they wanted.

He was put to work all day, every day except Sunday, making flags in a room the size of a small gymnasium. They made the American flag, the Confederate battle flag, and the South Carolina state flag. They made more of the battle flags than the other two. The various jobs were rotated among them so that he wasn't on one task but a month and then he moved to another, all of them simple and numbingly the same. From bolts of cloth that were imprinted with the design, they cut out squares that were then hemmed on a machine. Then grommets were punched into one side. After that, the finished flags were pressed, folded, and packed into boxes for shipment. No hand tools were used or allowed for any of the work. Where something had to be cut or a hole punched, a machine was used under supervision by a guard. As years went by, he could do all the functions in his sleep. He knew how many stars were on all the flags, how many stitches went into every seam. Every day was the same; he got up at the same time; ate the same breakfast; made flags; ate the same lunch; made flags; ate dinner at the same table with the same men until some were released or died; went back to his cell and went to sleep only to get up and do it over again the next day. Day after day, month after month, year after year.

But it could have been worse. Some of the prisoners worked only outside in all kinds of weather, helping to repair roads or cleaning highways. Occasionally, if the orders were caught up, the flag makers were put on a road cleaning detail. He was glad for it. He got to get outside, even if it was cold, and stand in the sun under whatever sky there was, blue or gray or even rain. Cars sped by, their passengers peering out at the men stooping to pick up trash, being herded and watched over by a guard with a shotgun on his shoulder.

For the first few years, Trish wrote to him and sent him pictures of Ellen. Then the letters got further and further apart until finally they stopped. Lucinda wrote to him too. She said she wanted to visit him but was afraid to come to

South Carolina because she didn't know what might await her there. He felt no sense of loss when the letters from Lucinda got further and further apart. It was the same with Trish. The good part of his life, his marriage, his child, his job, all seemed like a dream. He had enjoyed them for such a short period before they all descended into nothingness and loss. It was like his other life, as brief as it was, had never happened, but he had no feeling of injustice. He reasoned that he had not had to pay for the first killing. Lucinda had shielded him from that, so he paid his debt to her by taking the heat for the second. He just wasn't as lucky as she was. She had all the luck even if, in the end, it didn't seem so. McCoy, not long out of law school, was not Lawson.

The last letter he got from Lucinda was to tell him that Grandma had died. He had never felt loss much; he had just accepted it as something bad that happened like other bad things, but to the extent he ever grieved, he grieved for Grandma. She had loved all of them relentlessly, no matter what had happened. She lived with Grandpa's grinding, slovenly irascibility, lived with the constant disappointment of feckless Lucinda, and then Tony's failing. There were no details in the letter, only that she had died and the time and place for the funeral. He applied for compassionate leave to attend, but it meant the system would have to provide a guard to go with him, which they explained was expensive, so it was denied.

One day, years into his sentence, a guard appeared outside his cell. He unbolted the door and motioned for Tony to come out, then handcuffed him.

"What's this all about?" Tony asked.

The guard prodded him in the back. "Going to see the chaplain," he said.

"Why? I never asked to see a chaplain."

"Ever prisoner, unless he's a Hindu or a Mohammedan or somethin', has to have a talk with the chaplain if the chaplain wants it."

"Why? Why now after I've been here this long?"

"It's the rules. Don't you know by now that this place is all about rules?"

"Shit. I reckon so."

They went out of the cell blocks into an area of dingy gray offices and stopped in front of a door with a sign that said, "Milford Smith, Protestant Chaplain." The guard knocked gently.

"OK. Come in," came a voice through the door.

The guard cracked the door and stuck his head in. "Pettyjohn is here, Padre." Then he swung the door open and motioned for Tony to enter.

Chaplain Smith was sitting behind the usual metal desk with two metal chairs in front of it. A bookcase full of volumes loosely arranged, some on their sides, some straight up, was behind him on a wall that had a small, dirty rectangular window near the top. He was perhaps fifty with a pudgy, pale face that was slightly unshaven. He had a broad, rubbery-looking nose, very short, stubbly gray hair, and eyes that were red rimmed with whites more yellow interspersed with red. He was wearing a black corduroy jacket with a shirt that was either gray or just dirty and a gray tie heavily spotted with food droppings.

"Thank you, Wilson," the chaplain said as the door was closing. "Have a seat, Mr. Pettyjohn," he said, indicating one of the chairs in front of the desk. He coughed, a phlegmy, grating cough that sounded unfinished, leaving something still clotted within, then he turned his head and spat into a tissue he took from a box on the desk.

Tony thought he smelled a faint odor of whiskey. The man coughed again, but before he could speak, Tony asked why he was there. The chaplain looked down at an open manila folder on his desk. He coughed again. "When every prisoner comes into the system, we try to determine what denomination they are, if they're religious, and then we set up an interview with all of them to see what help we can give them in a spiritual way." He paused. "I see you fell through the cracks somewhere. We're way late getting to you, years as a matter of fact, but that happens a lot around here. Of course, it's just if you want to talk. We don't force anything on anyone. Least as far as religion is concerned." He looked down at the folder again. "I see when you came in, you indicated that you were a nondenominational Protestant. I guess you haven't changed in the years you've been here. Is that right?"

"Not sure I understand what that means. What's 'nondenomi . . .' whatever?" he asked.

"You said you had gone to church at some time, but it wasn't the Catholic church, so someone just checked the 'nondenominational' box. Was it a Methodist or a Baptist church?"

"I don't know. I don't remember."

"Well, it's not important anyway. You know you aren't Catholic, right? I mean, you didn't go to confession, or pray to the Virgin Mary, anything like that?"

"No. We went to Sunday School and to preaching after. I went with my grandmother. We learned a lot of Bible stories, Adam and Eve, Cain and Abel. That stuff."

"Then I think we had it right. *So*"—he leaned back in his chair—"let's have a little talk about you."

Tony slumped in his chair. Though he wasn't sure what this could be about, it was better than working.

"The file also indicates you're in here for murder." He looked at Tony as though he was expecting a response, but Tony was silent. "Do you know what the Ten Commandments are?"

"Sure."

"Can you tell me what they are?"

Tony squirmed in the chair, started to speak, stopped, and then said: "You're not supposed to murder." He paused. "Uh, you're not supposed to steal or lie." He stopped and flushed. "I can't remember the rest.'

"Well, that's OK. Most people, even the ones that profess to be really pious and know the Bible, can't recite most of them. So it's OK if you don't know them. I'm going to give you a Bible before you leave, so you can read them. Or do you already have a Bible?"

Tony shook his head no.

Smith turned his head and coughed again. "You can find the commandments in Exodus and in Deuteronomy when you look for them." He was silent for a moment and looked down at his hands, which were small, uncalloused. "Let's talk about the first one you mentioned, murder. Since you knew that one right off, how do you square it with what you're here for?"

"What do you mean?" Tony shrugged.

"Well, you knew the commandments said not to kill, and yet you did it."

Tony closed his eyes for a moment as though thinking about this. "I didn't kill the guy I got convicted for."

The chaplain smiled faintly. "I guess you know that most folks say the same thing when asked about it."

"But I really *didn't*. It's a long story. I reckon it's OK because I *did* kill somebody else that I didn't get caught for, so maybe it evens out." The chaplain narrowed his eyes and leaned forward, putting his elbows on the desk.

"I don't understand. You didn't kill the person you're in for, but you did kill someone else?" There was silence while he peered expectantly at Tony.

"I don't really want to talk about it, but, yeah, that's right," he said finally.

"You know that anything you tell me is totally privileged. I cannot testify about it."

"What's that mean?"

"Means you can tell me anything you want and I can't and won't reveal it and can't be forced to tell it, even in court."

"I ain't ever talked about it before, and I ain't gonna now." He looked straight at Smith and said: "Both of the people that got shot deserved it. They were bad people, did bad things to other people. Didn't nobody miss 'em but their mommas."

"I don't think it works like that either with man's law or in the eyes of God. It's not up to us to decide whether or not someone deserves to die."

"Well, if He sees ever'thing, then He knows what kind of bastards they were. I don't want to talk about this anymore."

Smith sensed that there was no point in going any further. "Sometimes it makes a person feel better to get all of it off their chest."

"No, it ain't gonna make me feel better."

The chaplain opened a drawer and took out a Bible. He handed it across the desk to Tony. "Did you ever have a Bible?"

"Yeah. They gave us one when we moved up a grade in Sunday School a long time ago. And I almost forgot. They gave me one when I left the training school. Seems like somebody was always handing one out somewhere." He paused. "Don't know where any of them are now, though."

"Here, you take this one."

They took him back to his cell. He tossed the Bible on the bunk and lay down in the gloom. Then he picked up the book and leafed through it. It had been a long time since he had held a book. He couldn't remember the last time—maybe in high school or with a loom manual at work. It fell open to Genesis, and he scanned a page and saw Cain and Abel, Adam and Eve. He turned back and began the story of the first murder. Sometimes after that, instead of solitaire or listening to a small radio, he read the Bible in his spare time. Some of the stories were vaguely familiar; some he had never heard before. Some of the words were funny and hard to understand. He remembered the story of Moses, the leaving of Egypt, parting of the waters, and manna. But he was puzzled by God's reaction to Pharaoh. He never realized that Pharaoh had agreed to let the Israelites go, but then had his mind changed by God himself so that he was punished even though it seemed he had decided to do the right thing. Then, too, there were places where God seemed too bloodthirsty to be believed. When he ordered the Israelites to destroy a city or a people and they let a few of them go, he was angry and punished them. It was as hard to understand as to why he refused Cain's offering but accepted Abel's. He remembered that he had been confused about it before, back those many years ago when he and Mitch went to church with Grandma. He remembered that talk he'd had with the guidance counselor in the projection room at the high school. He remembered her fumbling answer to his question.

After the first visit, Tony saw Chaplain Smith almost once a week, not because he requested it but because Smith sent for him, and it was always better than working. They had rambling conversations about anything that Smith wanted to talk about, but he constantly steered them toward what Tony had done and what had happened, and Tony was just as insistent as he had been at first that he was not going to talk about it. But he had many questions about the book, ones that took a lot of time and made Smith struggle to answer. Tony came back again and again to God's rejection of Cain. The best Smith could do was to say that he thought the reason was that God wanted to show that sin was a choice and that even though it was lying at the door, it was Cain's choice to overcome it, and Tony had to remember that this was the God of the Old Testament, a different God than the one in the New Testament.

But Tony hadn't read much of the New Testament. When he tried, he couldn't understand how they were connected. Smith explained that Jesus had been prophesied in Isaiah, but that was too remote for Tony. He read the passages Smith gave him but couldn't see what the chaplain was talking about.

"You know, you're going to be in here a long time still, even if you get a lot of credit for good behavior, which I'm sure you will. I've talked to the warden about it. He knows you. So wouldn't you like to get this off your chest and tell somebody about it? What you did, I mean."

Tony looked at him for a minute, then said, "I never asked you this before, but why are *you* in here?"

Smith's face colored slightly, more color than Tony had ever seen in it. It accented the haggard eye sockets and the pale eyes themselves. He slumped and looked down at his hands. Tony shifted in the chair, beginning to wish he had never asked the question.

"I was a pastor in a small church near the coast. It was a very small town, less than five hundred people. There was a young woman, the daughter of one of the most important members of the congregation." Here he paused and looked up at the grimy ceiling. He coughed and turned his head to wipe his mouth with the handkerchief he always kept in his pocket. "After I'd been there for about six months, she came to me after services one Sunday morning and asked if she could talk to me. She told me she wanted to leave the town and go to work in another place, a larger town, but her father refused to let her go. She implied that she was being abused. She needed someone to talk to. She was very coy. In retrospect, I think she was just bored. It was a small place, like I said. I was lonely. Seems like I've always been lonely. I began to see her every week and then every other day. And one thing led to another. I fell in love with her, and I thought she cared for me. We never"—he paused, searching for the right words—"we never were . . . uh . . . intimate. Do you know what I mean?"

"You mean you never screwed her?" Tony said.

Small tears trickled down Wilson's cheeks. He nodded his head. "Yes, that's what I mean." He gathered his thoughts before he went on. "But this was a very small town, and it only took weeks, really days, before people noticed her coming to the church often. So rumors started. They said we were fornicating in the church, doing the devil's work right there in front of the whole town." He blew his nose noisily into the yellowed handkerchief and smiled slightly. "We might as well have been, as you put it, 'screwing' every time we met because that's what the town thought. Her father was furious. I was called before the bishop and relieved of my job immediately. They didn't give me anything else to do right away. I thought they would kick me out of the denomination, but instead they let me stew for a while, called me in for a conference, and gave me the choice of either leaving the pastorship or coming here. By that time, I had convinced myself that I was guilty of a terrible sin. I was confused to the point I thought we might have done it even though we didn't. I dreamed about what it would have been like. She may even have told people that we did, I don't know." He threw up his hands. "So that's it. That's how I come to be here."

"What happened to her?" Tony asked.

"Nothing. I never saw her again, but I tried to keep up with her for a long time. At one point, I even rode down there and looked around the town. Went by her house. I found out later that she had married the son of the local undertaker. Had a couple children. It's been a long time. I only think of it once or twice a day now. I used to think about it constantly. I drank a lot. Did it alone, thinking about what could have been. Guess I still do. Drink a lot, I mean." He sighed, shrugged, and seemed to get paler, faded, more diminished. "Guess I got what I deserved." He stared a moment at Tony then said, "So I've told you my story. Now you tell me yours."

"Why do you think you got what you deserved? What's *deserved* got to do with it? You didn't do nothing. Why would you be punished? What commandment did you break? You didn't even screw her."

"It was the way it looked. I might as well have done it. I did it in my heart, and people thought we did. So . . ."

"But if God knows everything, he knows you weren't guilty of anything, so why did He allow this to happen to you?" Tony leaned forward with his elbows on his knees. "You just let this happen because you didn't stand up for yourself. Did you tell who you worked for that nothing happened between you and the girl? No. You just took what they handed out."

"It didn't look right. I should have known better. I embarrassed the church."

"Sometimes it don't matter how something *looks*. It might not be the truth about how it looks." There was silence for minutes, then Tony said, "OK. You want to know what happened to me? I'll tell you." His eyes went flat. "But you swear on that Bible there that you'll never tell anybody."

"I told you. Anything you tell me is totally confidential. They can't make me tell them, and it can't be used in any legal proceeding."

"Yeah, but you're the kind of person that caves pretty easy, ain't you? Look where you've let yourself be put."

The chaplain lowered his head and only nodded. He put his hand on the Bible on his desk and said, "I swear."

"OK," Tony said, "here's what happened." He unraveled the long story—how he had shot Murphy; how an incompetent sheriff had bungled the case, charging Lucinda without enough evidence to convict her; the incredible luck he had in not even being suspected; his good fortune at the mill being a loom fixer; his marriage to Trish and how fortune had suddenly shined on him; and then the entanglement with

Lucinda again. He left out how Lucinda had lured and entrapped Lawson with her looks and sex as he had tried to ignore it all his life. She had got them all—Murphy, Lawson, and always him.

The chaplain said nothing for a few minutes after Tony finished. He shook his head and muttered, "My goodness, my goodness."

"I woulda never done this, gone down to Myrtle Beach again for her, I mean. But I felt like I had to cause of her gettin' tried for what I did."

"Ever occur to you that you did something for her in committing murder before she did anything for you by standing trial?" He looked intently at Tony for seconds. "I bet you've done things for her all your life. Am I right?"

"Yeah, I guess so."

"Did you know your father?"

"Never met him. He was gone before I was old enough to remember him. I looked for him but never found him. Always like chasing a deer through the woods in the dark. You could see its white tail but never got close enough to see the whole thing."

"She see other men?"

"Yeah. She was beautiful. More than pretty, some scent or something she put out. Men came to her like flies to honey. That's what my grandma always said. But somehow it never worked out for her. She always got the mean ones or the losers."

"And you loved her very much?"

"Yeah. I did."

"Is she still alive?"

"Far as I know. I ain't heard from her in three or four years. Maybe longer." His voice had become rough, husky. "She'd be old now. I been here almost twenty years. She'd be sixty-five, something like that."

There was a soft knock on the door and a guard stuck his head in. "Sorry, Padre, but they need him down in flags."

"So, OK, Tony. We'll talk again."

The visits with Smith became a routine over the years. The chaplain was particularly interested in mill life and what the town was like. He had come from a farm family in the Low Country away from the textiles of the urban south. He was fascinated by the shift culture. He couldn't understand how someone could go to work at three in the afternoon every day and get off work at 11:00 p.m. and lead a normal life or how someone could go to work at 11:00 p.m., get off at 7:00 a.m., and live like everyone else.

"They get used to it," Tony said, "and they wouldn't have it any other way."

Smith was amazed at how cheap the mill housing was and the utilities. No one ever maintained a sharecropper's miserable shack where he came from. He was baffled by Tony's description of a loom fixer's job, the tedious rethreading of the strands in the broken loom that took hours with an anxious weaver who made no money with the loom stopped looking over his shoulder.

"And so you liked it?"

"What?"

"Working in the cotton mill?"

"I liked my life, yes. I remember once maybe when I didn't like it. Really never thought about it. I mean, it was just work. Something you had to do all your life. And I remember how a lot of people I worked around talked bad about the mill, their job, all the time. But it was good to me. I was the number one loom fixer. I was making good money. I was wearing a tie to work at the end. I was a foreman. Had a pretty wife, a pretty child." He paused. "I'd give anything to go back to it now. I sometimes wonder why I did what I did. Probably didn't do much for my mother. She's probably hooked up with some guy right now who treats her bad." His voice trailed off. He threw up his hands in a small gesture.

"Maybe if you pray to God for things to get better, they will."

"I'm sure you've prayed about your situation. Don't look like it's done much for you."

• • •

The meetings with the chaplain became a part of the long continuum of days just like making flags. At one point Tony kept up daily with how long he had been there, but after a while he quit. It was useless and depressing. He got up, ate breakfast, made flags, ate lunch, made flags, ate dinner, slept, and then did it all over again the next day. Somewhere in the years Trish served him with divorce papers. He had expected it, and it made little difference in the dull routine of his life.

The warden called him to his office one Monday morning and told him they had reviewed his case and, since he had been a model prisoner, and they needed room because the prison was overcrowded, he was going to be paroled. They asked if he had somewhere to go. Where was home? He could think of no other place, so he told them his home was in Maple Grove, North Carolina. It would have to be arranged for his parole to be supervised by authorities up there, but it could be done. What would his address be? He didn't know. If he had no address, he would have to stay in South Carolina. There was a boarding house in Columbia that took prisoners like him. Did he want to go there and use that address? Good, they would make the arrangements. It would be much easier for all that way. He would have to check in weekly with a parole officer whose office wasn't far from the boarding house.

Tony stopped by to see Chaplain Smith once before he left.

"I'll miss our talks, Tony, but I'm sure you won't."

"Reckon not," he said. "Would rather be out, I think."

"Where will you go?"

"I'll stay here in Columbia for a while. Don't know anyone at home—I mean, Maple Grove—anymore. Grandma died. My wife got a divorce from me years ago. I don't know where she is. I had an aunt and uncle in Myrtle Beach, but they were old when I came in. Sure they're dead by now. So it's just me."

"What will you do? I mean, can you get a job?"

"They say there's a little mill still running somewhere in town. They told me to go talk to them. They might need somebody to fix looms. Don't much see how that's possible, but I'll try."

"Well, I guess God answered your prayers."

"Did He? How? After I've spent the allowance they'll give me when I leave, what am I gonna do after that?"

They gave him a shirt, a pair of khaki pants, socks, shoes, a light coat, a plastic overnight bag, and two hundred dollars. It was an early spring morning. He hadn't been outside the walls in years except to pick up trash on the highway. The sky and clouds and open space were overwhelming. There were birds flying by, and he could see houses nearby. He was loaded onto a small, drab bus with two other former prisoners. All other buses he had ridden had been clearly marked with "Dept. of S.C. Prisons." This one was unmarked. He thought, *No doubt to keep from alarming citizens who might see it stop near their houses to deposit a criminal.* After wending its way through the city, passing people walking on sidewalks, dogs in yards, shops and stores, the bus pulled up in front of a two-story gray clapboard house that looked like it had been built at the turn of the century. It had a sign out front that said "Rooms for Rent." And they left Tony there.

He stood at the top of the cement sidewalk leading up to the door for minutes trying to think what to do next. There was no one to tell him where to go or what to do. But after a moment, he made the trip down the walkway and up the stairs. There was no doorbell, and he was uncertain whether he should knock or just walk in. While he stood there, undecided, the door opened.

A grizzled little man wearing a button-up sweater of an indeterminate color looked at him and said, "C'mon in. I reckon you're from Central. Right? I can tell 'cause you don't quite know what to do yet. Been a long time since you knocked on a door or just walked in one. Right?"

"Yeah. That's right."

"Well, c'mon in and let's get you registered. Or would you rather just go back now?"

Tony stared at the man without speaking.

"That was a joke. Guess you didn't think it was funny. I'm Gilbert. I run this place. What's your name?"

"Pettyjohn. Tony Pettyjohn."

Gilbert thought for a minute. "Right. I got a notice about you two days ago. C'mon in."

Gilbert stopped at a scarred desk near the door and made an entry in a ledger. Then he shuffled down a dim hallway with Tony following. The entire place had a gray color, a gray texture. It was a lot like Central. They came to a battered door with "12" over the sill.

"This is yours. It'll be five dollars a week. The bathroom is down the hall on the right. You get a room to yourself. Don't happen to all our guests, just the ones that were in for homicide. Putting those with roommates makes the roommates nervous." He snickered. "You understand, don't cha?"

When he got no response, Gilbert started to leave, stopping at the door. "Don't serve food here and don't want you to bring it in. Crumbs makes the roaches worse. No drinking, no women. There's a cafeteria and a diner a block down the street. Price of the room includes towels and sheets changed ever two weeks." He paused and looked at Tony. "You ain't got much to say. It'll probably get better in a week or so. If it don't, you can always find a way to go back. Any questions?"

He shook his head, and Gilbert left.

The room was bigger than his cell. It had an iron single bed, a small dresser, a wooden chair, and a small table that had initials and names carved into its surface. There was a window that looked out onto a fenced backyard with what looked like a separate garage near the back line. The yard was strewn with scrap paper, empty cans, and weeds. The room was gray, the yard was gray, and the towel draped over the end of the bed was gray. It was all very much like where he had come from. He sat on the bed, feeling the springs through the thin mattress; then he put his few belongings in the dresser and sat again, not sure what to do next but slowly realizing he could get up, open the door, and go where he pleased. And so he opened the door tentatively, walked down the dim corridor, opened the heavy front door, and walked out onto the sidewalk and the street for the first time in many years without wearing manacles and someone walking behind him with a gun. The sun had come out; there were people walking on the sidewalk, so he walked for an hour, stopping to look at displays in store windows.

He went into a small grocery called Delight. There was a smell of cigarette smoke, some lung-filtered and stale and some fresh. It was a small labyrinth all to itself. Shelves were piled high with everything from aspirin to fishing tackle.

There were three rows full of food items like canned beans, Spam, loaves of bread, canned soup, crackers, and chips. There was a row with nothing but candy bars and chewing gum. At the rear, there were two coolers with soft drinks and beer. There was a standup cooler with milk and eggs.

The man behind the counter was skinny with a dark complexion, wiry black hair, a beard that was a little more than a badly needed shave. He was leaning up against shelves behind the counter that were lined with rows of cigarettes, cigars, chewing tobacco, and snuff. There were packages of Lucky Strike, Chesterfield, Pall Mall, Domino, and Camel cigarettes; El-Rees-So, Swisher, and White Owl cigars; squares of chewing tobacco called Brown's Mule, Days O Work, Apple; and cans of snuff, like Tube Rose and others Tony had never heard of. The man asked if he could help him find something, his voice strong and strangely accented. He was wearing a name tag with a funny name: "Mustafa." Tony looked at him for seconds, long enough for the man to repeat his question. He silently picked up a pack of chewing gum and handed it to Mustafa.

"OK, very good. Be twenty-five cents."

Tony handed Mustafa a dollar bill and got the gum and the change back. It was more than he had ever paid for gum before. He made to leave.

"You come back soon," Mustafa said as he left, the voice lilting up in that strange accent.

Tony stayed in his room for a few days. Inactivity was something he was accustomed to. It took time to realize he could get up when he pleased, eat when he pleased, and go out into the street without permission or being watched. For a week, he didn't eat except for snacks he bought at the Delight from Mustafa, then he found a cafeteria. He knew how to go through a line, so he began to eat a meal a day there.

He took a bus to the mill the warden had suggested to him. In the mill office, he sat and waited for the supervisor to talk to him. While there were many desks in the office, there was only one person working, a secretary who looked as though she had been there forever.

A phone on her desk buzzed. She motioned with her head for him to walk down a hall. "Last door on the right."

"Supervisor" was written on the etched glass of the door. He knocked and heard a grunt from within. Hoping it was an invitation to enter, he carefully opened the door.

"C'mon in," said a short man standing behind a desk cluttered with spools, spindles, yarn, and thread of all sorts. A tag on his beat-up sweater said his name was Ralph. His hair was thin and standing up on top of his head like he had just taken off a clinging cap. "What's your name?"

"Tony Pettyjohn. They said you might be hiring. So I came by to ask if you needed a loom fixer."

"Sit down." He motioned to a battered chair. "Who is 'they'?" the man asked.

"The warden, Mr. Jeffries, over at Central."

"I see." He looked down at the top of the desk. "And what were you in for?"

"Murder."

There was a long silence.

"And what experience do you have in textiles?"

"I was a loom fixer at Maple Grove Mills." Tony stirred in the chair. "It was a long time ago. Maybe you don't even need loom fixers no more."

"Not so much. To be honest with you, we're about to shut down. The owners ain't announced it, but I can feel it. Almost all cotton mills are leaving. Everything's being made in Japan or someplace like that. They make stuff for a lot less than we do, so owners go over there and pay less to make it, bring it back here, and sell it to the few people who have jobs and money."

He rubbed his eyes tiredly. "You know, years ago when I was in the service, I'd come home and drive through towns in New England, pass a lot of mills that were closed. Window lights broken out, weeds in the empty parking lots. Those plants closed 'cause they moved down here, where we worked for less. There were unions up there and none here. Now it's happened to us, only the jobs are going to the slopes someplace in Asia. Cars are made in Japan. You see all those little tin bastards all over the place? And they won't let us sell cars in their country. What the hell? We won the war. We ought to keep all those tinny little cars out. Keep out the cheap textiles too. And now we're starting to see Mexicans coming up here too, taking all the construction jobs. Living twenty to an apartment." He picked up a wooden spindle and turned it over in his hand. "Mr. Pettyjohn, you'd be better off finding work somewhere else, not in textiles. It'd probably be steadier."

Tony thanked Ralph and made his way out to the bus stop on the street and waited for an hour until it came. Two more transfers and he could walk to the boarding house. He stopped in and bought a candy bar from Mustafa.

"You find job yet?" the man asked with smoke from his cigarette wreathing his face.

Tony shook his head.

"Lot of these guys go down to place where they come in morning and pick up people to work. You know that place?"

Tony shook his head no.

"You ask man who runs house where you live. He tell you where it is. You try that before you run out money, and thanks for your business," he said as Tony left.

He found the place. Every morning, men—white, black, and Mexican—gathered at a corner in a part of town full of warehouses and dilapidated factories and waited for trucks and buses to come by to hire them to do labor, almost always the hardest, toughest jobs in construction. It paid a minimum wage. Since he was younger than a lot of the others, didn't smell like booze and wine, and looked like he could work, he got picked almost every day. He was paid in cash when the work ended. It was enough to eat two meals a day and pay for the room.

After he had been picked by the same company for successive days, the man who did the hiring asked him if he'd like to work for them full-time. It was a construction firm, building houses. Tony had done cleanup work at its construction sites. He had worked steadily, didn't stop to smoke, and ate lunch quickly if he ate at all. They liked him, the foreman said, so Tony began work for them. They arranged to pick him up at the boarding house and dropped him off every evening. After he had worked for them for three months, he realized that often he was the only worker doing cleanup when before there had been several assigned to pick up all the scraps and junk that were discarded at the sites. They liked him for a reason. He did as much work as three of the day laborers they had hired before. But he didn't see that he had much choice. It was better than waiting in the cold at the corner and then perhaps not being hired, so he stayed on and even got a small raise after six months. He was trying to save enough to buy a used car.

He stopped at the Delight often—often enough that he learned that Mustafa was called "Moose" by regular customers, and he was always smoking. They became friends. Moose was nearly the only person he talked to. One Friday after they had dropped him off after work, he stopped in to buy some chips and a soft drink. Moose always wanted to talk, wanted to know where Tony was born, and in turn, Tony asked where he was from. He had been born in Palestine.

"Where's that?" Tony asked.

"Very far. Across Atlantic Ocean." He thought for a moment. "You know about Jesus? It is where Jesus lived."

"No shit?"

"Yes. Near Jerusalem, Sea of Galilee."

"The Garden of Eden too?"

Moose looked puzzled. "I don't know that."

"It was where Adam and Eve lived. I remember that from Bible School."

Moose smiled and shook his head. "Anyway, it's a long way from here." He lit another cigarette from the one he was smoking and frowned. He was silent for a moment, then said, "How much they pay you where you work?"

"Two-fifty an hour. But they take out for picking me up and bringing me back."

"So how much you have every week?"

"'Bout sixty-five dollars. That's taxes and all that stuff."

"What you in prison for?"

"Murder," Tony answered after a long pause.

Moose took a deep drag on his cigarette. "You ever steal anything?" he asked, blowing smoke at the ceiling.

"Not really. I mean, I did once when I was a kid." He ignored the times with Willis. His voice trailed off. "Why do you want to know this? I mean what difference does it make? I pay you for ever'thing I get here."

Moose smiled and lowered his head. "I got no family old enough to help with Delight. No brothers or sisters. Children too young. I was jus' thinking."

Tony looked puzzled. "Thinkin' what?"

Moose leaned against the tobacco wall behind the counter. "You nice guy. Different from most who live at boarding house. I was thinking . . ." He stopped and lit another cigarette. "Aww, never mind."

"What?"

"Maybe you like to work here. Just to try. I pay you what they pay you, and you don't work in cold and rain."

He stopped. "But maybe you don't want to work for no 'rag head.' That what they call people like me. From Palestine? Sand nigger?"

"You mean work behind the counter, sell stuff, and all?"

"Yeah. You could try maybe for weekend. See how you like. I be with you."

The possibility of this was so startling that he could think of nothing to say. He felt good, flattered, that Moose would trust him, that he would think him capable enough. "Well, I guess I could try it."

Moose smiled broadly. He reached across the counter and held out his hand. Tony, for a moment, didn't realize what this meant. No one had asked to shake his hand in years.

"You come to work tomorrow at eight o'clock? That OK?"

Tony just nodded.

• • •

Tony started work full-time at the Delight a month later. The first month, he struggled to learn where everything was, which customers to trust, how to make change, but he came to like it, better than working in the cold and rain and not working when the weather was too bad.

He had saved enough to buy an old used Ford, and in the spring, he asked Moose if he could take a few days to go to Maple Grove and see the place one more time, maybe find some news about where Trish and Ellen had gone, and maybe ask about Lucinda. It was only a three-hour trip through

Charlotte, which had grown so much it was unrecognizable with buildings taller than any he had seen and traffic that moved at a crawl, but Maple Grove was a bigger shock.

The mill and all its buildings were gone. Plant Number One had occupied six blocks, and nothing was left. Number Three Weave Room was no more. The YMCA, the lake—all were gone, and in their stead, there were three red brick buildings with white columns that looked like they had come from a Southern plantation. He was told they were part of a research project started by all the major universities in the state.

"Researchin' what?" he asked an old man sitting on one of the benches in the little park near the center of the old business district.

"I don't know. Heard one of the things was how to make food out of banana peels. Some crazy shit like that. Guy that runs it is a Yankee that bought all the mill. Some crazy Yankee idea, if ya ask me. Sold all the houses that folks used to rent from the mill to the people who lived in them or to somebody else if they couldn't afford 'em. Times was hard for a while. Still *are* hard. The old days when you could buy a new car ever three years is gone. Now, people work in Charlotte. No mill work left. All those Chinks are making sheets and towels now. We just buy 'em at K-Mart if we can afford 'em."

Tony drove through the town, the old neighborhoods, Tree Town, Car Town, and GI Town. Some of the old places were gone. Grandma and Grandpa's house had been torn down, as had most of the houses around them. Houses were no longer all white. There were pastels and grays, yellows, and even some pinks. Some looked like they hadn't been painted in years. Whereas before there was a neat, orderly appearance, and all the yards were kept up, now that the mill no longer controlled everything, things were random and mixed. There were even some junk cars in a few front yards, something that would have caused a tenant to be thrown out in the old days. What used to be the bustling commercial district was almost deserted. Only a few shops were open, mostly selling consignment clothes or bric-a-brac, but the old theater was still operating, even if it looked unkempt with trash littering the entryway. He remembered all the John Wayne movies he had seen there.

He looked for Willis's name in a phone book. It gave his address as 503 C Street. Tony remembered where that was—near the high school. He pulled up to the curb in front of the house. It was a Sunday, so he thought Willis must be home. A late model Ford truck was in the driveway. It had oversized tires that showed the suspension and shock absorbers, which had been painted orange. It had dual exhaust and a Confederate flag decal on the rear window. The house was painted a light tan. Overturned tricycles and plastic toys were scattered over the yard, which looked like it hadn't been mowed or raked in a long time.

Tony made his way over toys on the cement walkway to the front door and rang the bell. He could hear sounds from a television. After a few minutes, a hand pushed up the curtain over the glass panes on the door, and a woman looked out at him. The curtain dropped back, and he heard her call to someone and a muffled answer in reply. Minutes passed, and then Willis opened the door. He looked as though he had just got out of bed, his thin hair tousled. He was wearing a T-shirt with a picture of a stock car driver in a racing suit. The shirt didn't cover the ample stomach that stuck over his pants. He had an irritated expression, but when he looked hard at Tony, it faded into a smile of dim recognition.

"Tony?" he said. "What the hell? Is that *you*?"

"I reckon so."

"Come in, come in," he said as he moved aside. The room was warm, cloying, and smelled like bacon. There were toys scattered over the floor and on the couch and chair in front of the television now playing a commercial. A little girl peeked shyly around the doorjamb from an adjoining room.

"Where you living now? Heard you were in trouble in South Carolina and got sent away, but nobody knew nothing about the details. Sit down, sit down," Willis said as he cleared a space on the sofa, knocking a blanket and a doll onto the floor.

"Yeah. Had a little trouble. Spent the last twenty or so in prison in Columbia."

"Man, that sucks!" He sank heavily into the chair and muted the television. "But at least you're out and looking fit like always. What are you doing? How you making a living?"

"I just started a new job working in a little grocery. See how it works out. I only been out for four months. What about you?"

Willis winced a little. "I'm between jobs right now. I was working in Charlotte at an auto parts store, but I got laid off last month. Things have been tough around here since the mill closed. You know, I worked on and off there for almost thirty years. I used to bitch and complain about it all the time. Ever'body did. Then when it was gone . . ." His voice trailed off. "Damn, you remember how it was when the mill was here, and you rented from them, and they kept the place up. Got your electricity and water from them for nothing." He shook his head. "Man, those were the days. We've lived in this house for fifteen years. When I rented it from the mill, it cost me forty-five dollars a month. Utilities were maybe fifteen dollars a month. I had to buy the house when the mill finally closed. Now my mortgage payment is a hundred and fifty-two dollars a month. Utilities are sometimes close to seventy. Shit, we just didn't know how good we had it." He shook his head again. "Wish those times were back."

While Willis was talking, Tony was looking at his face, its lines and wrinkles, how Willis's hair had become thin, left with just a little in front, the middle bare, and a motley fringe around the sides. He could remember when he had long sideburns that reached to the middle of his ears. Then he thought that *he* must look the same to Willis, that Willis must be looking and thinking that here was the kid who looked so much like Elvis, and now whose hair was thinning and sprinkled with gray, whose skin was now pale with wrinkles around his eyes and mouth. Tony always carried a picture of himself in his mind that was how he looked when he was young, but he knew that it wasn't how he looked now, but still he held onto the picture.

"You ever think about the good times we used to have going to the beach? You remember that little likker store we stuck up? Where was it? Cheraw, Chesterfield? I can't remember. Was after I screwed up the car racin' with that asshole. Damn, that was a good car. Couldn't beat that Ford. Getting it repaired almost took all my money, but we more than made up for it. You remember that?"

"Yeah. I remember, but I seem to remember that it was you who held the place up. I just sat in the car."

"Yeah, but I also remember that you didn't have no objections to takin' part of the money. Right? *And* we did it again."

Tony lowered his head and nodded with a slight smile. "You know, I been to that other place twice since then and bought stuff. I always left whatever change I had comin'. I'm sure it didn't make up for what we took, but it made me feel a little better. I ain't ever done that since. It was a mean thing to do."

"Me neither. We was lucky we didn't get caught. Just luck." He leaned back in the chair. "Speaking of mean things, seems like you quit that stuff, and I heard you started killin' people."

Tony didn't smile and didn't answer.

"Guess that wasn't too funny."

The little girl, followed shyly by a smaller boy, peered around the doorjamb again, both dressed in dirty pajamas. The boy was sucking on his thumb.

"Willis, you a little old for kids this young, ain't you?"

"Those ain't mine. They're my daughter's. She lives here with us. Lost her job at the mill she worked at for five years. Now she can't find anything steady but waitressing, and that don't make enough money to pay rent and babysittin' and food. And gas. So she lives here."

"Husband?"

"Shit. Last we heard, the son of a bitch was in Florida somewhere. Worthless anyway. You want something to drink? Coffee, Coke, beer?"

"No. Say, do you know where Trish is? Ever hear anything about her?" He had not wanted to ask. He was afraid of what the answer might be.

"Years ago, and I mean a *long* time, maybe five or ten years after you went in, she married a guy who sold cars over at Randolph Motors. Lived here for three or four more years, then he took a job sellin' cars over in Tennessee, I think. Last I ever heard of them. When the mill shut down, folks sort of scattered all over."

"I guess she took Ellen with her?"

"I don't know. Don't recall how old Ellen was then, but I expect so."

"What about Mom—Lucinda?"

"How old would she be now? You're same age as me, fifty. Right? That would make her about seventy or seventy-five." He shook his head, bemused. "She was always a looker. Bet she hasn't changed much."

"You know where she might be?"

"Somebody told me, and I think it was that guy that used to run the car repair and body shop she used to hang around with. Can't recall his name now. Died of cancer couple year ago."

"I know who you're talkin' about, but go ahead."

"Anyway, he said he ran into her in Augusta, Georgia. She was tending bar. If I had to guess, I'd bet she's at Myrtle Beach somewhere. Seems like that's always where she wound up, and she always seemed to land on her feet."

"Yeah, I know," he said, looking up at the ceiling with a rueful grin.

Willis leaned forward in the chair and patted Tony's knee. "So how long you here for? Maybe we could get together. Have a few beers. Go to some of the old places."

A woman called from the back of the house, "Willis."

He shook his head.

The voice came again. "Willis, I need you back here for a minute."

"All right. I'll be there in a second," he yelled back. Looking at Tony, he shrugged his shoulders. He lowered his voice. "Whattaya say? We could have a few at the Oasis. I think it's still there. Huh?"

"Not this time. Maybe when I get back up here." He rose and turned toward the door, pausing again as he opened it.

Willis stood, slumped a little, and rubbed the stubble on his face. "OK, then. Don't wait forever to get up here. We ain't so old we can't have a little fun."

The woman's voice came again, louder and more irritated.

"Sure. See ya." Tony hugged Willis awkwardly and left.

He drove through town in the bleakness of the early spring afternoon. The sky was off and on cloudy and clear with the sun blinding in its low place in the sky when the clouds cleared. Leaves blew around the streets, mixed with paper cups and bits of newspaper. The huge brick buildings that had replaced the mills reflected the strong sunlight and looked like things dropped on the planet by aliens, completely different from the forever pulsating buildings that had been the mills. They looked deserted on this Sunday, no evidence of life around them, unlike the throbbing mills where people were going in and out all the time, even on Sundays.

Tony headed south past Charlotte, and when he got to the highway junction with one road going southeast toward the beach and the other just south toward Columbia and the Delight, he slowed, making a decision. Then he turned left and headed toward the beach to look for Lucinda, maybe one last time.

The road was familiar with small, sleepy towns; several that he remembered were bypassed now. The liquor store they held up was gone. The rights of way closer to Myrtle turned into the brown canals he remembered from before, finally widening into tree-clogged swamps. But when he neared the intersection with Highway 17, the main beach road, everything began to change. There were continuous strip malls; signs touted factory outlets for pottery, clothing, and furniture. He also noticed that the license plates on the cars were not from South or North Carolina. Cars from Ohio,

Pennsylvania, New York, Indiana, and Canada crowded the roads and parking lots.

When he got to Highway 17, the ocean was mostly hidden by high-rise hotels. It was late, and even though he didn't have much money, he decided to stay at least for the night, so he went north toward Ocean Drive, thinking he would find a cheap place to stay and get something to eat at Hoskins, where he and Trish used to eat. Since it was early spring, he was able to find a room at a good rate. He asked the clerk if Hoskins was still there. He was told it was and that it hadn't changed much.

But it had changed a lot. It was much bigger and much more expensive. After looking at the menu in the window, he walked to a diner a block away and had a hamburger. While he was eating, he thought about the old dance place but couldn't think of its name. He asked the waitress about it.

"You know, I haven't been here in a long time. Twenty years or more, but there used to be a place around the corner where you went to dance. Not much to it, just a concrete floor, a jukebox, and a beer bar. It had a funny name."

"You mean the Pad?"

"Right, right. Is it still there?"

"No. Been gone for years. The dancers all go to Big Lou's now. It's down the street. You ought to check it out. You'll probably be surprised, though. Most of the folks who do the old dances are gettin' old themselves, and not too many young people are interested in doing the shag. They do those boogie dances. You know, where really all they do is stand in one place and gyrate or something."

He thanked her and left.

Big Lou's wasn't hard to find. It was crowded even on a spring night. The deejay was playing songs from the late '50s and '60s. When Tony entered, he recognized the old song that was playing, "Sixty Minute Man." And just as the waitress had said, the dancers were old. Heads were gray, and faces were wrinkled. He watched for a while from the bar as the couples on the floor swirled, came together, then separated, their upper bodies scarcely moving while their feet and legs went through the intricacies of the shag. Tony was outside of the crowd, feeling like he were in some type of time warp. He left after one beer and went back to the hotel. He tried to think of where to look for Lucinda, deciding he would spend one day looking, but when he woke the next morning, he got in the car and headed back west toward Columbia.

Outside one of the little towns he saw a small grocery store surrounded by cultivated fields except for a grove of pines standing beside and behind it. There were gas pumps out front. He needed gas so he pulled in next to one of the pumps, but when he got out he could see that years had gone by since it had delivered any gas. He started to get back in the car, but then he noticed a man sitting on a bench next to double screen doors that led into the building. The man waved at him. "You can't get gas here no more." He said. Tony walked over and sat down next to him. He was wearing bib coveralls. His face was as brown and lined as an old baseball glove. A worn straw hat was pushed back on his head. "There's one of them new convenience stores a little ways up the road. You can get gas there and even a pizza pie if you want it," he said. "Where you comin' from?"

"Maple Grove. Up in North Carolina," Tony said.

"I know the place. Used to have a sister that worked in the mill up there for a long time 'til it all shut down. You from there?"

"Yeah. It sure shut down alright. No mill there now."

"Well, stuff like that is happenin' all over. See that field across the road?" He gestured toward a broad field several hundred yards deep running to pines trees at its further edge. "That's tobacco you see in those long, straight rows. It's just been planted. That's what you see, the little green plants, but they'll grow and get tall and brown by late summer when they're ready to be pulled and cured. The two Carolinas raised more flue-cured tobacco than any places on God's green earth. People made a good living at it too. Now, the do-gooders are shutting it down, them and greedy politicians who look at tobacco and tobacco farmers like they was piggy banks." He slapped his knee. "So it's goin' away just like textiles and furniture went away. And what will be left for us? It's globalization, the papers say. I say it's gobble-ization, and it's ruining us."

"Reckon you're right." Tony said. "Maybe I can help you out." He stood up. "You got a cold drink in there?"

"Sure. Let me go get it." Tony handed him some money.

"Tell you what. Give me a pack of cigarettes too," Tony said.

"What kind?"

"What kind's best?"

"Do you smoke?

"Nope."

"Then why do you want cigarettes?"

"Just trying to help you out." The man went inside and came back out with a Pepsi and a pack of Camels.

"These are what I smoke. You try em," he said to Tony. Tony thanked him and got back in his car.

Tony thought about what lay ahead—the Delight, Moose, an unknown future. He would rely on luck. At least it had favored him once. Maybe it would again.